GABRIEL'S RETURN

BOOK 2 OF THE EVAN GABRIEL TRILOGY

STEVE UMSTEAD

For more information on the author, visit
www.SteveUmstead.com

ISBN-13: 978-1468039283
ISBN-10: 1468039288

DEDICATION

To my boys, for actually realizing this writing thing is enjoyable and fulfilling for me, and to my wife, who is more supportive than she even realizes.

Thank you.

ACKNOWLEDGMENTS

I'd like to give a big thanks to some fantastic fellow authors who took time out of their busy lives to read Gabriel's Return after my edits and before publishing. The beta reader phase is invaluable; an author simply can't see that the leaves on the trees in their forest are out of place, or don't line up properly, or are the wrong color. Just having a complete forest is hard enough, so kudos and my undying gratitude to Helen Hanson, A.J. Aalto, Karen Smith, J.T. O'Connell, and Mike Pallante for their active plot problem sensors, and Jennifer Gracen for her laser-sighted copy editing pen.

And a special thanks to the incredibly talented graphic artist, game designer, and fellow author A.J. Powers. If the cover of any of the three Gabriel books caught your eye, it was his fault. And I'm sure he'd take that blame in stride.

PROLOGUE

October, 2171

The first thing Tomas Katoa saw when he opened one blurry eye was a front tooth. It was scorched and blackened, a corner chipped off, and he knew right away, in some distant corner of his brain, that it was his own.

His eyesight gradually cleared, and he focused his open eye in on the lone tooth, sitting on a dirty leaf. Another corner of his brain identified the leaf as being from a pricklefruit tree. Surrounding the leaf were dozens of tiny moorants chewing on bits and pieces of figmoss. Their moist yellow segmented bodies glistened in the sun.

Morning, Katoa thought. *It's morning, judging by the angle of Eden's sun. But the sky was...sideways. And the tooth on the leaf, surrounded by figmoss and moorants, strangely hung on the wall.*

He attempted to open his other eye, to no avail. *I'm lying on the ground.* His left eye refused to obey, stuck shut with some sticky substance. His mouth tasted of blood mixed with Eden's loamy soil and some kind of burned meat. His head reeled, and dizziness prevented his inner ear from determining which way was up. He felt a tickle in his mouth

1

and spat. A bloody gob of saliva-covered moorant hit the leaf, and more spittle dribbled from his torn lips. *There was no sound*, he thought to himself. Nothing made any sound, which was puzzling until he realized there was a low buzz in his head, drowning out any outside sounds. *Oh my God, I'm deaf*, he thought with a panic.

The smells came next. Jungle smells, fresh neopines and pricklefruit trees intertwined with a dead and decaying odor given off by the jungle floor, all overlaid on top of the distinct smell of burning metal.

He willed his body to roll onto his stomach and was rewarded with a face full of hungry moorants. His right arm scrabbled at the ground, trying to ward off the inch-long insects; his left arm didn't move. He pushed back away from the figmoss, from the biting pests, and used his functioning arm to pull himself several feet towards the sun. His legs responded slowly and he crawled a few more feet, and he found himself on the edge of a small hillock overlooking several burning buildings.

He wiped at his sticky eye, pain coursing through his system at every move. His hand came away smeared with black blood. A low thrum pulled his attention away from his injuries, and he felt a small relief at the slow return of his hearing. He tugged at his right ear with his bloody hand, then yawned, attempting to pop open what he assumed were clogged ears. Without any success, it dawned on him that the hearing damage was concussive: *an explosion.*

The thrum grew louder, and Katoa looked down the scorched slope towards the burning buildings. A shuttle sat a few dozen yards north of the largest building. Its quad pulsejet engines were spooling up as it prepared to take off, and the grass smoldered beneath the hot exhaust. From the side of the building came two combat-suited troopers with a stretcher carried between them. They hustled out, not looking back at the carnage, and quickly trotted to the open hatch of the shuttle with their cargo.

On the stretcher was another trooper, without a helmet, and with heavily damaged armor. Katoa's brain was missing pieces. He couldn't quite place the trooper, the face was familiar...but he had a difficult time even remembering what the building was. *School maybe?* he thought. He shook his head to clear it, more pain shooting through his body, and he squeezed his eyes shut against it.

When he opened them again, the hatch was closing on the shuttle. Some primal part of his brain realized he was being left behind, and he tried to yell out, but his voice only croaked out a few low syllables. *Wait!* his mind shouted silently as he raised his one good hand towards the shuttle. *Don't go, you forgot me!*

The pulsejet engines came to full power. The shuttle lifted off the charred ground and backed slowly away from the buildings. Katoa watched helplessly as the craft rose into the sky, knowing he was stranded on a far-off world, with no clue what to do next.

He lowered his hand as the shuttle shrank to a dot against the bright sun. His hand brushed against a nearby vine, and to Katoa's fuzzy-minded surprise, it responded by encircling his wrist. As he watched with his one eye widening, the vine extended small thorns along its length and began to constrict, wrapping itself around his arm. The thorns pierced his skin, and he grunted in pain.

As the razorvine tightened further, the thorns released a neurotoxin, numbing Katoa's arm and shutting out the pain. For a brief moment, he felt relieved and tried to pull his arm away from the strange plant. The plant pulled harder, and Katoa finally found his voice, even as his mind began to fog into unconsciousness. A blood-curdling scream escaped his lips as he was dragged further into the jungle, leaving the moorants alone in the clearing.

Katoa lurched up from his prone position, right arm stretching out, and gasped for breath. He was blind, just a dark gray haze in front of his face. It was quiet, but he wasn't sure if it was because he was still deafened. He remembered being pulled into the jungle. It didn't feel like moss and leaves under him now; more cool and crisp on the backs of his legs.

He leaned forward into more of a sitting position, and waved his right arm around in front of him. Nothing there. No sound, no sight, and maybe most alarmingly, no smells. He was no longer in the jungle.

"Hello?" he called out, his voice cracking from dryness. No response. He cleared his throat and tried again. "Hey!" he yelled as loudly as his pathetic voice would allow.

His senses slowly returned. A beep. Small, hollow, and repeating itself every few seconds. A shuffle, perhaps feet on a tile floor. Breathing. A faint whiff of body odor. Someone was there now. Waiting, watching him. Katoa tensed his body, preparing for his next move.

"Who are you?" he said, his voice returning with each syllable. "I know you're there. Answer me, or so help me God…"

"So help you God, what, Petty Officer?" came a reply with a slight Spanish accent.

Katoa was caught off guard; he hadn't expected an answer, or at least one so…friendly.

"Who are you?" he repeated, his voice now firm and commanding, as he had been taught in OCS.

With the thought of his OCS instructors, a whirlwind of disjointed memories flooded back. Images, sounds, feelings. *Departing Luna. Wormhole transit. Punching Renaldo in the arm for cutting in the chow line. Kasey's blonde hair, her smile. Suiting up in combat armor, checking ammo loads. Assault shuttle landing, being bashed into the shuttle's wall during reentry. Crashing through a door into a building. Terrorists. Children. Hostages. Fire. Blackness.*

"Easy there, Tomas," said the male voice. His crisp English diction with the Spanish lilt sounded soothing and reassuring. "You're liable to tear some sutures."

Katoa realized he had been struggling, the memories causing him to thrash about in his hospital bed. *Yes, hospital bed,* he thought. Explains the feel of sheets, the beeping. He tried to reach up with his left arm to remove whatever was covering his face, but his hand didn't reach.

"Please, wait," the voice said quietly. "We have a lot to discuss. You've sustained a great deal of injuries, and I'm afraid…" The voice trailed off.

Katoa's skin went cold. "What are you talking about?"

A hand touched his cheek and began to remove the bandages that had apparently been covering his eyes. Light streamed in and he squinted, turning his head away from what must have been a window. As the last of the bandages were removed, he opened his eyes, or eye as he felt, remembering the blood he wiped away from his other eye in the jungle.

"You were caught in an explosion, son. You nearly died," the voice replied. "One of my people found you buried in razorvine near the school. Your military neuretics were the only thing that kept you alive from the toxin, and controlled the blood loss from your face." The voice got quieter. "And from your arm."

Katoa shook his head to clear it. A fuzzy outline of a man standing near him started to take shape. He reached over to grab his left arm, and felt a wrapped stump, the arm ending just below the shoulder.

"Oh my God," he said, and a tear formed in his eye. Memories flooded back. *Children sobbing. Firing his pulse rifle. Men running, ceiling collapsing. Three prone figures, a man in street clothes standing over them. Fire. Blackness.*

"Listen, Tomas," the voice continued. The man's outline leaned in closer. "Yes, you've lost your arm, and your eye, and have some significant internal injuries. But we are equipped to help here. We don't quite have North American

Federation level facilities, but we have excellent people, and you will be just fine."

"Fine?" Katoa snapped. He looked up at the man; a tanned, goateed face peered back down on him. "With one eye and one arm?"

The man patted his good arm. "Yes, fine. You are alive, is that not what is important?"

Katoa slumped back into the bed, sheets ruffling. He stared at the ceiling. *Now what?* he thought. *I'm half a soldier, stuck on...*

"Wait," he said as he reached out and grabbed the man's arm. "Am I still on Eden?"

"Yes, of course, where did you think you were?"

Katoa gripped the arm tighter. "They left me," he said in a low voice.

"Who left you?" the man asked, prying his arm from Katoa's grip. "Tell me what happened. What do you remember?"

He closed his eye, letting the memories rush back, and tried to make sense of them.

"We, we...we came here because of a riot, there were hostages, children mostly. My squad got ambushed...dammit, they knew we were coming." A tear ran down his face, and another formed in its wake.

"Everyone was down. I thought I was the last, the shuttle was pulling the kids out — I, I went back in to the...gym, I think it was. Everything was burning..."

"Take your time, Tomas," the man said. "You're safe here."

Katoa blew out a noisy breath. "Safe, yeah. Now. But..." he reached for the man's hand and grabbed it, holding tight. "I went back in, and saw a man standing over a few members of my squad. They were down, dead. He...he was armed, and was about to shoot them." He squeezed the man's hand, lifting his head from the bed. "Why? They were already dead! What was he doing?"

A rapid beeping sounded, and the man used his other hand to ease Katoa's head gently back down onto the bed. "Please, Tomas, you must relax."

"My rifle was empty, I had lost my sidearm earlier," Katoa continued, trying to control his breathing. "But I couldn't let this, this terrorist desecrate their bodies, could I?" He took a long, deep breath. "I rushed him, slammed into him, knocked him down, out I think. I got up, and grabbed one of my squadmate's...bodies. I dragged his body to the door, and..." his voice trailed off. "That's it, that's all I remember."

"When my people found you, you were almost seventy yards away, up a small slope. It appears there was a massive explosion in the school, which threw you clear across the jungle. It's just...incredible that you even survived."

"Incredible," Katoa repeated in a low tone. "Sure. Lucky, right?" he asked. He waved his left stump, and a flash of pain shot through him. "They left me. They got one out, and left me." He sat bolt upright. "Someone survived," he said, staring at the goateed man. "They grabbed someone out of the building. It...it was the body I pulled out. He was alive...someone else survived!"

"Do you remember who it was?" the man asked.

Katoa closed his eye, searching his memory, trying to mentally zoom in on the stretcher. "It's...fuzzy," he said, scrunching his face up.

"Try, Tomas," the man replied. "It may help your recovery process if you know someone else made it."

He concentrated on the last vision from the hilltop: the pulsejets' blue exhaust rings blasting the blackened grass, the flames licking through the windows of the school, the troopers carrying the stretcher, the man on the stretcher, no helmet, head facing him. Close-cropped blond hair. The face became clear.

"Gabriel," he spat. His mind clouded over to black. "The one who led us into the ambush. That sonofabitch survived. And left me here."

The man leaned back and released Katoa's hand. "Okay. Gabriel. Let's work with that. That will be the start of your recovery, it will give you something to focus on while we rehabilitate your body." He walked over to the door, and Katoa saw him motion to someone outside the room.

"Right now, we're going to start rehabilitating your mind. There are some people I'd like you to meet, and I think we're all going to be great friends. I know we can help you, and I believe you can help us as well."

As a slim shadowy figure entered the room, Katoa eased back into the cool comfort of the sheets. The images of fire and blackness already felt less painful. *Gabriel,* he thought. *Gabriel.*

CHAPTER ONE

July 24, 2176

"That was an excellent piece of steak, boss. Appreciate the generosity," Galen Sowers said as he set his fork down on his folded napkin.

Evan Gabriel raised his iced tea. "My pleasure, Mister Sowers. I'm glad to see the gesture didn't go to waste." He motioned the glass towards the empty plate in front of Sowers. A sprig of broccoli was the only evidence left of a meal having been present.

Sowers smiled, raising his own glass in return. "No sir, not at all. Only so much vat grown meat a man can take, and Bussa's is one of what, five restaurants on Mars that import actual beef?" He looked at the large man sitting next to him for confirmation.

Harris Brevik polished off the last of his baked potato and wiped his lips with his napkin. "Six," he said.

Sowers laughed. "Right, six. But that's counting that shithole up north in Chryse Planitia, what was it called? Torrici, Tortorici, something like that? Real beef, sure. Just not sure what kind of cow they got it from."

Gabriel sipped from his glass and raised a finger from it, pointing at Sowers. "That was your mistake, if I remember correctly. What was it, a suspected prostitution ring, a couple thousand miles from any decent-sized city?"

"Whoa, sir, you got me all wrong," Sowers said. He held his hands up in mock surrender. "Those girls needed my help. How was I to know it was a ballet troupe that got lost?"

Brevik downed his water in a long gulp and set the glass down with an audible thunk. "Sir, you ready?"

Gabriel nodded. "Yes, Lieutenant, sure am. Sowers?"

"No dessert?" Sowers asked innocently.

"No, no dessert. Or coffee," Gabriel replied as he waved the waitress over. "You get jumpy with too much sugar and caffeine."

The waitress came over with the check and handed it to Gabriel with a smile. "Everything okay, gentlemen?"

"Yes, excellent," Gabriel replied, his eyes indicating the empty plates. "Compliments to the chef."

She smiled wider and turned to leave, but Gabriel touched her hand and set the bill folio down on the table. "We need to see Vasili, if you don't mind."

Her smile faded. "Who?"

"Vasili," he repeated. "The man in the back room surrounded by computers, probably in there with one or two other men, the door most likely guarded by a very large man. Vasili."

Her eyes gave her away. "I'm not sure who you mean," she said, starting to back away.

Gabriel withdrew a card from his inner jacket pocket. "If you find anyone who knows Vasili, can you please have them give this to him?"

Her eyes darted from Gabriel to Brevik to Sowers, then back to Gabriel and the card he was holding. She extended her hand and took it.

"Thank you," he said. He picked up the folio she had left and passed it across the table to Sowers. "My dinner companion will be taking care of this."

Sowers paused in mid-drink and set his glass back down. "Ah hell, sir. Again?"

"Rank hath its privileges, Petty Officer," Gabriel replied as he watched the nervous waitress head into the kitchen.

After a few minutes, the waitress returned and approached Gabriel. She leaned over and whispered, "Vasili has agreed to see you."

Gabriel stood up, Sowers and Brevik doing the same, and followed the waitress towards the back of the restaurant. Gabriel noticed the patrons watched them carefully as they wound their way through the dining room's tables. Part of him wondered if any of them were armed. He absently tapped the waistband of his cargo pants, feeling the reassuring bulge of his Heckart, and regretted he'd be losing it soon.

The four reached a curtained area just out of sight of the main bar. As Gabriel had expected, a very large man stood with hands clasped in front of the curtain, blocking the entrance to the room beyond.

Brevik walked up to the man and stared into his face at a slight upward angle. The guard didn't flinch, but simply smiled. "Weapons," he said, holding out a massive hand.

Sowers pulled his sidearm from his jacket pocket slowly, holding the handle with two fingers, and placed it in the outstretched hand. Gabriel did the same with his Heckart, while Brevik stood motionless. The guard tucked both handguns into his pants pocket and stared back at Brevik. "No weapons?"

"Don't need any, Tiny," he replied, earning a growl in return.

The guard inclined his chin towards the other two. "Arms out."

Both Sowers and Gabriel raised their arms, and the guard patted them down. He checked Gabriel first, and finding nothing, moved to Sowers. He patted him down roughly and stopped when he reached a bump in Sowers jacket pocket.

"Out," he said. He moved one hand to his own waist where Gabriel assumed he was carrying a weapon of his own.

"Just a comm." Sowers slowly reached into his pocket and withdrew the tiny device. He handed it to the guard, who looked at him quizzically. Sowers shrugged. "Old fashioned, I know. I'm not big on neuretic conversations."

The guard looked at the comm closely, turning it end over end and tapping a few keys. Apparently satisfied, he handed it back to Sowers, who replaced it in his pocket. The guard then turned to Brevik. "Arms."

Brevik raised his arms and allowed the guard to pat him down, never taking his eyes from the other man's. After a few seconds, the guard nodded. "Okay, you guys are clean. This way."

He turned and opened the curtain, revealing a small anteroom with another curtain on the other side. He led the three men through the room and parted the far curtain, then stepped back to allow them to enter.

Gabriel walked in first, followed by Sowers and Brevik. He was greeted by the sight of a tiny man, lips clamped around the stub of a cigarro, seated at a table, with four flatscreen monitors spread out before him. On the table in front of the monitors were multiple flexscreen tubes, most with the screens extended and various numbers and letters scrolling across them. Gabriel couldn't see what was on the flatscreens, but knowing what Vasili did for a living, he assumed they'd show the same scrolling numbers and letters.

At the table with Vasili sat a man with thick glasses. *Very anachronistic item in today's day and age*, Gabriel thought idly. Fish-like eyes stared and blinked at the newcomers.

A bay window was on one side of the room. The view of Orange Blossom Park was partially blocked by a man seated there, one foot up on the sill, one leg dangling above the floor. Gabriel immediately noted the open jacket and the bulge at his waist. Neither leg showed a backup weapon, only god-awful ugly argyle socks.

Gabriel and Sowers approached the table while Brevik hung back near the guard, who had stepped just inside the curtain to watch the proceedings.

Vasili smiled around his cigarro. "Well, hello at last, Lieutenant Commander Gabriel," he said in a nasally voice. "A pleasure to finally make your acquaintance." He pulled the cigarro from his mouth and stubbed it out in an ashtray in front of one of the monitors. He rose from his seat and extended his hand. "I trust your dinner was to your satisfaction?"

Gabriel stared expressionless at him, waiting.

Vasili dropped his hand after a few seconds, then cocked his head to one side. "Tsk, tsk. Tell me you did not try the steak?"

Sowers cleared his throat next to Gabriel. Vasili smiled again. "Yes, at least someone did." He stepped around to the front of the table. The man in the window stood up and walked closer, while Fish Eyes remained seated.

Gabriel had already performed a low-level shielded neuretics scan before even walking through the first curtain, and had picked up four separate energy weapons indications. He sent another scan, this one slightly more powerful, and pinned down that each man in the room was carrying a handgun. One additional energy source under the table told him that Vasili had a backup system, most likely a scatterray weapon triggered by neuretics if he needed it. The guard near Brevik carried a small kinetic assault rifle, a Heimark P-22 with a forty-round magazine of caseless 7mm projectiles, if the active scan was accurate. *Kinetic,* he thought. *Didn't expect that.* He sent a quick secure burst to Brevik with that information.

Vasili laughed. "Yes, Mister Gabriel, scan away. We have nothing to hide."

Gabriel was surprised that the numbers runner had access, or willingness, to have such high-grade neuretics implanted that he could pick up his shielded scans, but it wasn't entirely unexpected. Vasili was a major player in the cartel they had been systematically taking apart over the past month, and this cartel was far and away the best financed one on Mars.

"You know why we're here?" Gabriel asked, Vasili now standing within a few feet of him.

"Of course," the small man replied. "My friends have given me a heads-up that we may be seeing you. You've been busy," he said with a snort. He looked over his shoulder at Fish Eyes, who just stared back, blinking.

"Just doing a little housecleaning, or city cleaning in this case," Sowers said as he edged closer to the man who had risen from his window seat.

"But what do you expect us to do, Mister Gabriel? Come with you? Close the restaurant? Leave Mars?" Vasili said, smiling again. "Like an old American western, this planet isn't big enough for the both of us?" He gave a short laugh at his bad joke.

He turned to the man from the window and nodded. The other man pulled out a wicked looking gun from his waist and held it casually pointed at the floor. Gabriel's threat assessment window popped up in his Mindseye, flashing a warning and scrolling the details: Kunzman mag pistol, thirty pellet clip, heavy duty dual power cell. *Expected for organized crime*, he thought.

"Actually, Vasili, yes," he replied. "You'll be coming with us, and I'll be sending another team over to collect your equipment and data. I'm sure there is some…interesting information on your systems that Mars Central's AG will be very happy to see."

Vasili laughed out loud. Fish Eyes chuckled softly and reached into his own jacket pocket.

"You're unarmed. Surely you don't think we'll just hop in your car, do you?" Vasili looked over at the guard, who was now standing next to Brevik. "Gilberto, please escort the Lieutenant Commander and his friends out. They are no longer welcome in Bussa's."

The man from the window began to raise his weapon, and Gabriel sent the prearranged burst to Sowers and Brevik. Sowers immediately sent a signal to the device he carried in his jacket pocket, which was nothing like the old-fashioned comm he had made it out to be. It was a highly miniaturized and incredibly powerful homemade jammer Sowers had been working on in his spare time, one that Gabriel doubted would ever work, until he saw an impressive test Sowers accidentally conducted in an appliance shop. It sounded a small beep and activated.

Four loud, distinct *click-hiss* sounds were heard in the room, one from the window man's Kunzman, one from Fish Eyes's similar Kunzman he had just taken out, one from Vasili's jacket pocket where his handgun was residing, and one from under the table. The three men all knew exactly what a power cell overload sounded like, and panicked.

Both Kunzmans clattered to the floor, dropped immediately by the two men holding them. Vasili frantically grabbed into his jacket to withdraw his overloading weapon before the power cell could melt down, or worse explode against his chest. A pop was heard from under the table as the built-in scatterray gun overloaded and the power cell cracked.

As all of that was happening, Brevik turned and elbowed the guard under his chin as he was trying to pull the Heimark from a leg holster. The guard gasped and grabbed at his throat, sucking air in noisily through his damaged larynx. He dropped to his knees, and Brevik chopped him in the back of the neck. He collapsed on the floor, unconscious. Brevik reached down and pulled the assault rifle the rest of the way out of the holster and held it at port arms, staring back at the others in the room.

"Yes," said Gabriel to Vasili, who was staring down at his handgun, which was now in the process of melting into the floor. "As a matter of fact, I *do* think you'll just hop into our car."

CHAPTER TWO

"Jesus, Manny, I friggin' hate guard duty."

Manny looked up from his flexscreen, once again silently cursing the kid he'd been assigned to work with today. He squinted into the rising sun which was peeking through the pricklefruit and yellowbole trees surrounding the building the two guards leaned against. He gave a resigned sigh and closed the flexscreen, then slipped the tube into his shirt pocket and adjusted the strap of his rifle.

The day had started off well enough. Early morning breakfast of real chicken eggs and vat-grown ham, decent coffee, and a new graphic novel loaned to him by a friend. An hour into his watch at the Bioresearch Center, his new partner had already driven him to the brink of insanity. *If only Tori hadn't just up and left without telling anyone. At least she had the sense to keep quiet this early.*

"Listen, kid," Manny said. He spit out a wad of used kobo and reached into his other shirt pocket for a refill. "Guard duty is just that. Guarding. Not talking, not whistling, not shooting hoops. And certainly not bugging the hell out of me."

Manny watched as a moorant crawled towards the clump of wet kobo he had just added to the grass. A part of his brain wondered if the fat yellow insects got the same stim rush humans did from the native plant. He spit a stream of greenish juice towards the moorant, hitting it squarely on its hind segment. It skittered away in search of a less messy meal.

"Hey man, I know," said the skinny kid. "I mean, it's cool and all, getting to carry guns," he said as he waved his slung assault rifle around theatrically, "but it's boring as shit, you know? What's the point?"

Manny shifted the kobo from one cheek to the other, feeling the tingle the shredded leaves produced in his nerve endings. After a few seconds, he replied, "Terrorists, dumb ass." He spat again and pushed away from the wall he was leaning against. "Can't have Prophet and his boys waltzing into the labs."

"Ha!" said the kid, unslinging the rifle and aiming down the sights at a nearby yellowbole. "Terrorists. Bunch of hillbillies, from what I hear. Living in the jungle, eating bugs, stealing supplies. Seriously, how've they ever hurt us?"

"Have you seen Tori lately, huh?" Manny asked. "Ever wonder what happened to Baker, or that last shipment of medical supplies from Eden City?"

"C'mon," the kid replied, shifting his aim to a mottled green treemonkey high up in the yellowbole. "Rumors, nothing else. It ain't terrorists, man." He clicked the safety off and tucked the rifle closer into his shoulder.

Manny reached over and flicked the kid's safety back on and lightly smacked him in the back of the head. "So you think. Listen, before I shoot you myself for disturbing my reading, do a walk-around of the main building. I'll stay here."

"Fine, fine." He adjusted his cap that had fallen askew after the smack. "But after that..."

"Shh," said Manny. "Did you hear that?" He unslung his rifle and flicked the safety off, looking off into the jungle east of their position. *Something's not right,* he thought. The sound was like…a faint electronic whine. He narrowed his focus to the small rise about a hundred yards away. The sun caused a glare overhead, making it difficult to see.

The kid took a step in that same direction. "Where, the hill? I don't see…" His voice cut off as his face locked in a grimace, eyes rolling up in his head, and a strangled gurgle came from his throat. The rifle fell to the jungle floor, and he dropped to his knees, then keeled over face-forward into the grass. The gurgle ended abruptly.

"What the…" Manny began. He snapped his rifle up level and scanned his surroundings. Before he could call the watch desk, he felt a sharp pain in his stomach, then a white-hot needle stabbing into his heart. *Maser!* he thought with a detached panic. His hand moved to activate the emergency comm strapped to his belt. As his hand pressed the button, excruciating heat lanced his brain and he collapsed, brain-dead before his body even hit the ground.

A sticky moorant crawled up onto Manny's face, nibbling at the fresh kobo leaking from the dead man's mouth, as the treemonkey hooted laughter from above.

Idiot! the man thought, gritting his teeth at the stupidity of the team he had been chosen to lead. He reached over and smacked the sniper in the back of the head, knocking the man's hat off. He leaned over and placed his face next to the sniper's.

"What the hell was that?" he demanded. "I ordered simultaneous head shots, and you shoot late, *and* low?"

The sniper held up a hand, the other hand brushing the leaves off the heavy maser rifle in front of him. "Sorry, Captain Chaud, I'm not used to this Chinese model. Won't happen again."

Chaud ground his teeth again, reaching for his earbug. "Of course it won't, Maybeck. We only needed this shot. Think you'll do any better with a mag rifle?"

He tapped the earbug and opened a channel to the rest of his team. "Change of plans," he said. "Most likely the alarm has sounded and Eden Guard has been alerted. Everyone move in immediately, same assault positions, same points of entry. We've lost surprise, so assume the shelters will now be in play. Go now."

Chaud turned back to Maybeck. "Take rear guard, last man in. I don't need bad shooters on this op."

"Captain, how about me?" The other sniper had just finished packing up the maser into her duffel bag.

"Werth, take Maybeck's flanking position," Chaud replied. "Nice shot, by the way."

Werth gave a fierce grin and elbowed Maybeck, who was muttering under his breath as he packed up his maser.

"Let's go," said Chaud, powering up his mag rifle. "Prophet's expecting results, let's not let the man down."

The young man looked up from the test plate he had been studying at the sound of the buzzer. *Damn, what now?* He tossed the microtweezers onto the lab table with a clatter. *Every time I get somewhere with this experiment, something else interrupts.*

"What's going on?" he asked the girl sitting across from him. She was staring off into space, a look he recognized as intense Mindseye reading. The buzzing continued and was joined by a flashing red light at the far end of the lab space.

"Hey, Magali," he said, reaching over and grabbing her arm. She started, blinked her eyes a few times, and looked at him.

"What?"

"What's going on?" he repeated, pointing at the flashing light.

Magali turned from side to side, her eyes growing wide as she looked around the room. "Oh no, Jeromy, that's the perimeter alarm!" she said, standing up from the table. She grabbed several folders and a flexscreen tube. "We've got to get downstairs to the shelter!"

"No no no," he replied, shaking his head vigorously. "I'm right in the middle of this, I'm on the brink of getting this artificial skin to self-propagate. I can't leave now, seriously. The whole thing will fall apart."

She grabbed his shirt sleeve and tugged. "Then you'd better take it with you, 'cuz this is no joke. Remember the briefings? We *need* to get downstairs."

He banged his fist on the table in frustration, and several test tubes in a rack clinked in response. If this was a test, he was going to be livid. And if his culture died? He'd be going straight to the dean.

As he started for the door, it flew open and four Eden Guard troopers burst in, all wearing full riot gear. Jeromy opened his mouth to protest but was cut short by the stern look of the lead trooper.

"Out!" the trooper shouted. He waved one arm behind him where another trooper was holding open the door to the basement shelter. "Everyone out, now!"

The other fourteen students in the lab group, along with the two instructors, scrambled to comply. A mad dash of men and women snatched at e-notebooks and flexscreen tubes. Hardcopy pages spilled onto the floor from several tables. No one spoke; drills had instilled the need for complete silence and attention from the students when ordered to leave by the Guard.

Jeromy watched as one student, Hasid he remembered his name as, stopped to collect supplies from his algae experiment. One of the troopers grabbed his arm and physically shoved him to the shelter door. Hasid stumbled, dropping his flexscreen, and Jeromy thought for a moment he would put up a fight. Hasid looked back at the trooper, who stared him down, and the younger (and smaller) man thought better of it. He followed the last student to the door, grumbling under his breath.

"You two, what's the holdup?" asked the lead trooper, who was taking up a defensive position behind a large counter near the main door. He powered up his mag rifle; a soft whine sounded as he slapped the battery cell into place. "Get your asses downstairs, this is no drill!"

Magali tugged at Jeromy's shirt more insistently. "C'mon, let's go!" she said in a stern whisper. She let go of his sleeve and headed for the door, looking over her shoulder as she went.

Jeromy took a few steps after her, but stopped at the lead trooper, who was shouting instructions to his team. "What's going on, Corporal?"

The trooper looked down at him, being a solid six inches taller, and frowned. "What's going on is a perimeter breach, can't you hear the alarm? Go on, to the shelter." He took a hand off his rifle and pushed at Jeromy's shoulder.

Jeromy shrugged off his hand and stood fast. "Is it the terrorists? Or animals? I mean, we've got some major experiments going on here right now, and we can't afford time lost due to false alarms. Corporal, my mother is…"

The corporal cut him off. "We know who your mother is. Which is all the more reason you need to be in that shelter most quick." He paused and tipped his combat helmet back a fraction with his free hand. "We've lost contact with the two Guard personnel outside the complex, and we can only assume they're dead. Or taken. One raised an alarm, then nothing."

He glanced back at the main door, then around the room, seemingly to reassure himself that his men were in place. "You know we've lost people to the terrorists over the past month. They're getting more and more aggressive." He reached out and touched Jeromy's shoulder again, this time with less force. "We need all of you downstairs. In a few minutes this will all be over, and we'll come down and get you." He pushed a bit harder. "We're out of time. Downstairs, now, and we'll secure the door behind you."

Jeromy looked up at the trooper, seeing the fierce determination behind his eyes. He looked over to his lab table, where his precious experiment sat unguarded, alone, surrounded by hardcopy notes he had worked so hard on over the past semester. The trooper must have sensed his reluctance.

"Our first priority is the safety of the personnel," he said, "but you have my word we'll do our best to take care of the facility as well. Now with all due respect, get the hell out of here."

Jeromy nodded and headed to the door. "Going, Corporal. And thanks," he said over his shoulder. He stepped across the threshold and down the stairs. He heard the door slam behind him and the power locks engage. He continued down the stairs to where his other university classmates awaited the all-clear. He only hoped they'd get an all-clear, he thought with a twinge of worry, thinking back to the trooper's statement about the outside guards.

Jeromy sat down next to Magali and two other female students when he heard several loud crashes upstairs, followed by the unmistakable *crack-sizzle* of mag rifles being fired. Magali grabbed him and tucked her head into the crook of his arm, then covered her face with her other arm. He patted Magali's head reassuringly, watching the other students in the cramped shelter doing the same with their friends. No one shouted, or cried, or really made a sound at all.

The room shook with the concussion of an explosion upstairs, and an overhead lightstrip flickered, dust falling from the ceiling. One student on the other side of the room sobbed softly and was comforted by her companion with small shushes.

More rifle fire, a muffled crump of a grenade, Jeromy assumed, and now the sound of kinetic pistols. *Oh shit, the terrorists were inside,* he thought. The ceiling shook again, this time from heavy impacts, not explosions. Now came shouting, men's voices, more pistol fire. One more grenade thump, then quiet.

He looked up at the door at the top of the stairs, still sealed. Hoping the worst was over, he leaned down to whisper to Magali. Just as he started to speak, he heard a soft beep from above. He looked towards the door and watched as it began to slide aside. His spirits rose a bit; only the Guard would have code access to the door, and it would be retina scan only in times of lockdown. The terrorists would have had to blow it open.

The door opened fully, and he saw the hazy outline of the corporal at the top of the stairs, framed by smoke. Jeromy started to rise, feeling a huge sense of relief wash over him, when the corporal tumbled down the stairs, crashing to the bottom in a tangled mess of riot gear and limbs. His lifeless face was turned towards Jeromy. It only had one eye; where the other eye should have been was a bloody socket. Realization dawned on him instantly and he pressed Magali's head back down into the crook of his arm.

Another silhouette appeared at the top of the stairs, and a voice boomed out. "Hello, Eden University students and faculty. I am Captain Chaud, your tour guide for the day. Please join me on a little field trip. A special guest has requested your presence."

Magali began sobbing in Jeromy's arm, and he tried to soothe her by wrapping his arms around her.

"Oh God, Jeromy, what do we do?" she asked in a low voice, choked with tears.

He shook his head, gritting his teeth. This had all happened so quickly. Just this morning he was doing water tests at Moon Lake, and he remembered the smell of the newlilies that floated on top. Now, he sat in a dimly-lit shelter, surrounded by frightened classmates and friends. His nostrils were filled with the acrid scent of cordite, burned plastic, and flesh.

He squeezed Magali tighter. "Don't worry. Just do as they say, and we'll get through this."

She looked up at him, tears streaking her face, and gave a weak half-smile. "You promise?"

He returned her small smile. He hadn't realized until now that Magali thought of him as more than just a fellow student. Nor had he realized he felt the same. "Yes, I promise. We're too important to forget."

She buried her head into him once again and squeezed back. He looked up at the silhouette with a mix of apprehension and fury. *We'll get through this*, he thought. *My mother won't forget us.*

Steve Umstead

CHAPTER THREE

The outdoor café was a simple one, a two-wheeled cart equipped with a four-headed espresso machine, two self-service coffee carafes, cream and sugar dispensers, assorted sweets and cookies, and a sole proprietor, Luciolo Genrizzi. Lou, as his customers called him, was setting up the last of his six pop-up table & chair assemblies in the dome-filtered morning sun when Gabriel and Renay Gesselli arrived.

"This seat taken, Lou?" asked Gabriel, his hand on the back of one of the chairs at the table nearest the main street.

Lou looked up from his task with a smile. "Ah, *buongiorno*, Mister Evan and Miss Renay!" he said in a heavy Italian accent.

"Stop with the show, Lou," Gesselli said with a laugh. "We're the only ones here, the only ones dumb enough to be up at this hour on their day off."

"*Sí, sí,*" Lou replied. He twirled the end of his oversized handlebar mustache and adjusted his replica gondolier hat. "I know, just trying to stay in character," he said with no trace of accent. "The usual, even on the day off?"

"The usual, without the flair," Gabriel replied. He pulled out the chair for Renay and sat across from her. "But double for me. And make sure…"

"Decaf, of course!" Lou interrupted. "And Miss Renay, I have some excellent lemon scones today," he said with a flourish of his hand towards the cart.

"Hell no, never again," she replied, holding up both hands. "This desk job is going right to my hips. Espresso black, as always, *grazi*."

Lou set to work with a casual tip of his hat. The espresso machine hissed with the day's first order.

Evan Gabriel and Renay Gesselli made an unusual pair: the tall muscular Naval officer and the slight, almost demure Naval Intelligence agent, seated quietly at a roadside table. Gesselli already had her flexscreen out and was reading, while Gabriel sat with his arms crossed, gazing across the street to the buildings and shops along its far side.

Nuovo Portofino, or Porto to the locals, was one of the first settlements built in the Mars land rush of the mid-twenty-first century. New Hope, the first permanent colony, was built in 2056, soon after the official government charter had been put into effect. Porto followed in 2059, with the first Italian immigrants, construction workers, architects, laborers, and business owners arriving to a dusty parcel of land under the first dome. Porto shared the massive Arsia Mons dome with eight other townships, falling under the governance of the Arsia Dome Council. As Porto was one of the first townships to be established, it had prime choice of location within the dome. However the city planners chose not to build into one of the spacious natural caves the dome was built over, but rather on the shore of a long-dead sea, under the open sky — or at least as open as the transparent fabric dome could be considered.

Long before arriving, Nuovo Portofino's leaders had decided that they would bring the beauty of Italy to their new home on Mars. Porto was a near-perfect, albeit smaller, re-creation of the Italian Riviera village of Portofino. It boasted pastel-colored buildings and cobblestone streets running along the harbor, which had been carved out further to match the bay of the original village, right down to mockups of rowboats and sailboats that dotted the dry bed. The planners had hoped with the planned terraforming projects that in a few generations water would flow on Mars, and Porto would be a true harbor village. But with Mars's decay and the general loss of interest in overblown and overbudget projects that took money and resources away from exploring and colonizing other worlds, that turned out to be a sad pipe dream.

In the weak morning sun, if one could ignore the slight rainbow haze the dome created in the sky, the .6G under their feet, and the fact that there wasn't a drop of actual water in sight, a tourist could be forgiven for mistaking Porto for the original.

Gabriel could almost lose himself in Porto sometimes. For the past six months, this, along with a temporary initial assignment in Bradbury, had been his home. The locals, descendants of the original settlers from Italy, were cautious when the SpecFor team moved in after their reassignment from the NAF. The team was there ostensibly to help with security, but was feared by some residents as a new wave of enforcement and extortion. However, with the personalities and friendliness of the team, coupled with the dramatic drop in crime throughout the dome and beyond, they quickly became part of the community.

Gabriel watched one of the shops to the east end of the plaza open its front doors. An older woman came out and placed fresh hydroponic flowers in a small planter just outside the door. Standing up, she caught sight of Gabriel and Gesselli and waved. Gabriel waved back, leaning over to nudge Gesselli, who was still buried in her flexscreen.

"Mrs. LoDuca," he said to her, inclining his chin in the shop's direction.

Gesselli looked up, turned and spotted the woman, then returned the wave. "This her first day?" she asked as she turned back to Gabriel.

"Mmm hmm," he replied as Lou arrived with their drinks. "Her mother's shop. She worked long and hard to get that reopened."

Gesselli blew the steam off her espresso. "Thanks to you," she said with a wink over the edge of the cup.

Gabriel gave a small smile in return. He picked up his double-decaf skim-milk latte and took a small sip, cursing inwardly as the hot beverage burned his tongue. "We just cleared out some… undesirables. She did the hard part, getting that shop back up and running."

Gesselli kicked his leg under the table. Lou laughed in the background as Gabriel leaned over to rub his shin. "I don't think the Bruning brothers would agree that she did the hard work. Isn't Jurjen still in rehab?" she asked.

"He'll be fine. Just some nerve and ligament damage. He'll be up and running in no time," Gabriel replied, sipping his latte. "Running right to the prison transport to Ganymede, I believe that's his next stop."

A small girl rode by on her bike, a carbon wire frame model with wheels nearly as tall as she was standing. Her hair flapped behind her as she sped down the street. "Hi Miss Renay!" she yelled, her voice stuttering as the thin tires bounced over the Mars brick cobblestones. The bike hopped several inches on each bounce in the light gravity.

Gesselli waved to her, yelling back, "Bye Marissa!"

The girl pedaled faster, the active gearing on the bike tripling her leg energy and propelling her quickly out of sight around the end of the street. Gabriel leaned back in the chair and looked over at Gesselli. He felt the same thing come over him he did every few days, an odd feeling of detachment, one he found hitting him more and more often in recent weeks.

"Listen, Renay, I don't know…" he started.

"I do," she said, cutting him off. She took a sip of the cooling espresso and set the cup down on the table, and to Gabriel's surprise, closed her flexscreen tube and set it down next to the cup.

"You were about to say that this isn't you," she continued. "Right? That this work, this police work, security work, whatever you want to call it… the forms to fill out, the council to report to, the… *job*. It isn't you."

Gabriel's jaw dropped a millimeter and he stared at Gesselli for a long few seconds before starting to reply. "How did…"

"It's written all over your face, it's in your body language, it's in the way you talk, walk, eat, drink."

He sat forward, holding his cup with both hands. "But no one else…"

"No one else is with you twenty-four hours thirty-seven minutes a day, seven days a week, and no one else," she said, fixing him with her gaze, "is sharing your bed."

"But how can…"

"I can because I know you, Evan. I know…"

"Cripes, will you stop cutting me off?" he said, exasperation evident in his tone.

Gesselli smiled. "I'm a woman, it's my job. And one of the jobs here I rather enjoy." She picked up the espresso and finished it, then called Lou over with a slight upward tip of her head.

"I don't know, Renay. It's just…it's not what I was made for. Does that make any sense?"

"Yes…and no," she replied. "It's not what you've done before, no. But look at what you guys have done here, in just six months. Look at Mrs. LoDuca and her shop reopening. Look at Marissa, able to ride her bike down the street by herself. Look at Lou." She pointed behind Gabriel as the proprietor walked over. "Do you think any of that, any of this," she said, waving around her, "could have happened without you and your team?"

Gabriel frowned. "I think you're making too much out of that, what we've done. It's helped, but anyone could have helped with the right support."

"But that's you and your team, again," she said, pointing at his chest. "You're not just police, you're part of this township, this community. You've made friends, and you've gotten rid of the trash. And people like you, and respect you. Not just fear you, like before."

"*Grazi*, Mister Evan and Miss Renay, always a pleasure," Lou said as he left a bill folio on the table. "See you soon?" he asked with a broad smile.

"Every morning, Lou," Gesselli replied, pushing the folio towards Gabriel. He picked it up and opened it, but it was empty.

"Lou," Gabriel growled. "When are we actually allowed to pay for coffee?"

Lou laughed as he walked away. "Next time the sun doesn't come up, you come find me. I'll take your money then. But until then, I owe you more than free coffee can repay."

Gabriel shook his head in resignation. Good people here, and great potential for the future. A beautiful city, getting more beautiful by the day. Sometimes hard to believe it was on a cold lifeless planet millions of miles from…home. He watched Mrs. LoDuca bringing more brightly colored flowers out of the shop to display outside as the township's inhabitants rose from their beds and walked out to the street to walk to work, shop, or relax in the small park. Next to the flower shop, the butcher turned his Closed sign to Open, making Gabriel's mouth water with thoughts of ribs, even vat-grown, for dinner this evening. Next to the butcher was a boarded up shop, and another next to it. Still more work to be done. *But is this really what I was made for?* he thought.

As he was about to rise from the table, the neuretics comm buzzed in his head. The ID showed as coming from the governor's office, so he took it immediately in Mindseye. The governor's avatar appeared and Gabriel held up his hand to Renay, who had also risen. She sat back down, recognizing the far off stare of an incoming call.

"Lieutenant Commander, this is Governor Tarif," the avatar said, a perfect replica of the Saudi Arabian woman who ran Arsia Mons. The computer-generated image was perfectly detailed, right down to the threads on the traditional gray half-burqa she wore in public. "I know this is an off day for you, but a drone just came through the Ryokou wormhole carrying a very unusual message, and it's meant for you. Can you please join us at the governor's residence as soon as possible?"

Gabriel pursed his lips and took a deep breath through his nose, glad the gesture and sound wouldn't be transmitted over the comm. He looked at Gesselli and mouthed, "Governor." She rolled her eyes in response, and he nodded in agreement. The governor was a huge supporter of the SpecFor team and their activities throughout the dome, and had given them nearly carte blanche to clean up the criminal elements, well in excess of standard charter law. But Gabriel always thought of her as high-maintenance, sometimes impossible to please.

He checked his internal clock, and went through his calendar for the day just to stall for time. Unfortunately, he found nothing pressing enough to get out of a visit to the governor's house.

"Yes," he said, broadcasting his voice through the comm to the avatar. "I can be there in an hour or so. I just need to get a car and…"

"No need," the avatar said. "I've sent one for you. I'll see you and Lieutenant Gesselli in twenty."

The transmission cut off, and Gabriel grimaced. As he was about to relay the abrupt conversation to Gesselli, a black government-issue electric stretch transport pulled up at the curb and the rear door swung open. Gabriel's neuretics acknowledged the receipt of the proper passcode from the governor's office, confirming the car's identity and purpose.

"Guess this is our ride?" Gesselli asked. She wore a wry smile on her face, reminding Gabriel of the smirk she wore when he first met her in Toronto. Back then, it struck him as condescending. Now, after six months together on Mars, it meant something entirely different.

"Our chariot awaits, I suppose," he said. Standing up, he turned back to Lou, who was waiting on two new customers. "See you tomorrow, my friend," he called.

"Hope so, Mister Gabriel!" the barista replied as he tipped his hat, momentarily forgetting his accent.

Yeah, hope so, Gabriel thought. But something about this call gave him an itch between his shoulder blades. Something that made him think a double-decaf latte with skim milk wasn't going to be on the menu for a while.

CHAPTER FOUR

The room was dimly lit, the only illumination coming from a weak overhead glow. Pale light, broken apart into individual beams by the thick diamondglass of the skylight, cast stark shadows on the faces of the four men seated around a small table. The table was cluttered with wine glasses, ashtrays filled with cigarette butts, and small plates with remnants of buttered bread and oil. A low haze of smoke hung in the air, further shading the light from the men's faces.

"Six months," one man said. He reached an overflowing ashtray in front of him and stubbed out another cigarette. Ashes spilled onto the fabric tablecloth. "Six months staying behind the scenes, while the dust cleared, so you say."

He brought another cigarette to his lips and lit it. The flare of the lighter was like a miniature star in the dark room, lighting up the shadowed faces. He took a deep puff, and the end of his cigarette glowed orange. He flipped the lighter closed and leaned back in his chair, blowing several smoke rings into the gathering clouds above.

"Hiding. Let's not pull any punches, Rafael. We have been hiding," he said, drawing on the cigarette again.

The man he addressed took a sip of wine and set his nearly empty glass back on the table. The younger man to his right took the cue and poured more red into the glass from a large crystal carafe.

"*Gracias*, Chimo," Rafael said. He tapped the filled glass with a long fingernail, making a soft, low chime. "One can never have too much tempranillo, eh?"

Chimo smiled and returned the carafe to the center of the table. "*Claro*, señor," he said, lowering his head in acknowledgement.

"Yes, six months, Isidoro," Rafael said. "Six careful months, wouldn't you say? We could not afford to have the North American Federation crashing down our doors, interrupting our operations, could we?"

Isidoro snorted. "Operations? Rafa, by hiding for six months, our operations are grinding to a halt." He picked up his own wine glass and downed it in one gulp. "All of our operations, not just here on Luna."

The fourth man at the table dipped a piece of bread in what remained of the oil on the plate in front of him and swirled it around in the spices. "Would you rather we be in prison, or perhaps dead?" he asked. He carefully put the bread into his mouth and wiped his lips with a napkin.

"No, of course not," Isidoro replied. "That's not what I'm saying. I'm saying it's time we resume control of our interests. The firestorm over Tevez's idiotic plan has died down." He picked up the carafe and filled his own glass, then splashed a few drops into the fourth man's nearly-full glass as a token gesture.

Rafael chuckled. "Tevez's idiotic plan? If I recall correctly, that was your plan to begin with, wasn't it?"

Isidoro crushed his cigarette into the ashtray, then picked up the pack from the table and shook it. Finding it empty, he rummaged through his jacket pocket and pulled out a fresh pack and tore open the vacuum seal with a quiet hiss. "Not quite, my friend," he said as he lit up. "Tevez pushed the envelope and got careless, brought in the wrong people. *My* plan," he emphasized *my* by rapping the table with his lighter, "would have worked just fine. With the full support of La Republica de Sudamérica."

"In any case," Rafael replied, "we, not the RDS, are here now because of that fat bastard. But while we are out of sight, we are also out of mind, and I think you'll agree we are not exactly scrounging up there, in the Buenos Aires gutter, for food, are we?" He pointed upwards, where Earth was just starting to appear in a corner of the skylight.

"And it wasn't just Tevez's bumbling, I think you'll agree," Isidoro said. "The NAF special forces team turned out to be unexpectedly...resourceful."

"Yes, there was that," Rafael agreed, sipping from his glass. "Commander Evan Gabriel."

"*Lieutenant* Commander, *señor*," Chimo chimed in.

Rafa smiled and handed Chimo his glass for a refill. "I stand corrected. Court martialed, demoted, and banished to Mars. Our standing could be worse, no?"

"Again, *caballeros*, all I am saying is..." Isidoro began.

"Enough," said the fourth man, gravel in his voice. He leaned forward and pushed his wine glass away from him, scattering butts and ashes from one of the ashtrays in the process. "I agree with both of you. Rafa, we are safe and secure, and for the most part, comfortable. Isi, Tevez was a fool, his ambitions too large for even his obese size. We did not gain control of a valuable world, and its discoveries, and that is extremely disappointing. I believe the root of all the problems was Gabriel." He picked up the last piece of onion bread from his plate and idly pushed it around the oil and spice mixture. "With all of that being said, the question is, what is our next move?"

"*Señor*, if I may?" asked Chimo, his voice cracking slightly.

As one, the three men turned to the subordinate at the table with curious looks.

Chimo cleared his throat and continued. "I have been doing a lot of research. That is why I am here, no?" He waited for a response, and receiving nothing but stern stares, went on. "There is a very valuable world, with priceless resources and technology, that is much closer to home, and I believe much more ripe for the picking, as the North Americans would say."

"Go on," said the fourth man as he set the bread back down on his plate.

Chimo leaned forward and pulled a flexscreen tube from his shirt pocket, extending the screen. He quickly tapped at the surface and brought up a rotating image of a dusty orange ball.

"Mars?" said Isidoro with a smirk. "It's a dead-end, a failed experiment. Who the hell would want any part of that? Doesn't even have a functioning government."

"That's just the point," Chimo replied. He pulled up a scrolling list of figures on the flexscreen. "There is no central government to speak of, only local and regional governance, no central army, and certainly no space naval forces. Tevez's thug Santander was running a very successful dew operation there, which was financing part of the, ah, previous plan." He glanced at Isidoro before continuing. "That operation was shut down, but all the infrastructure is still in place."

"Shut down by Gabriel and his team, isn't that correct? The same Gabriel who is, as we were just discussing, still on Mars?" asked Rafael, a dubious look on his face.

"I will get to that in a minute," he replied as he continued to tap on the flexscreen. Rafael's eyes widened a bit, but he said nothing.

Chimo continued. "Mars has functioning skyhooks, multiple domed cities, mining operations, living areas, established transportation systems, water at the poles, and a population used to complete anarchy. Why not step in and provide stability? Our companies have more than enough experience in management, and more than enough personnel to maintain an active presence across the planet. It's a small enough population to control, even with minimal military forces. My projections have shown that if we can persuade just two of the most powerful regional governors to accept our, ah, assistance in setting up a central government, the other seven will follow, and the agreement will trickle down to the local mayor level. And then we gain access to all of Mars's resources and technology, as well as a major foothold for pushing further out into the solar system and beyond. It's really a win-win for us, and for Mars. Plus, no one else wants it."

"Of course no one wants it," Isidoro snapped. He stubbed out another cigarette. "Like I said, a failed..."

"Tell me about Gabriel," said the fourth man, cutting off Isidoro.

Chimo smiled. "I have something in mind for Lieutenant Commander Gabriel and his team. Something that will not only get him out of the way, but also allow us to exact a little...retribution for his interference in our previous plan."

The fourth man nodded in admiration. "Chimo, I like this new assertive side of you. Please, tell us more."

Isidoro and Rafael leaned back in their seats and sipped their wine, listening to Chimo's plan being spelled out, and glanced across the table at each other. Isidoro raised an eyebrow, and Rafael shook his head almost imperceptibly. *Later,* he sent in a secure neuretics burst to the other man. *Our time will come.*

Isidoro nodded and continued sipping his wine as Earth grew larger in the skylight overhead.

CHAPTER FIVE

The ride to the governor's residence was uneventful, short, and quiet. Gabriel looked across the back of the stretch at Gesselli, who was, as always, buried in her flexscreen. He wondered if she was reading a novel or solving a genetic equation; he could never tell by her stoic expression. She had always projected a tough exterior, but perhaps that's what had initially attracted him. He looked back out of the tinted window, watching the townships end and the government sector begin.

The dome was built in a natural valley near the 12-mile high extinct Arsia Mons volcano, the southernmost volcano of the three on the massive Tharsis bulge, near Mars's equator. The valley itself was ringed by small hills pockmarked with dozens of caves and ancient lava tubes. Most of the dome was over the open area of the valley, where much of the real estate was located. However the original colonists, who called themselves *Arsians* (a name the large UK contingent in Pavonis Mons got a huge kick out of), built the first structures right into the cave and tube system provided by the valley walls.

The government offices, called Cavus Central, had originally been designed as living quarters for the hundreds of technicians and laborers who had arrived in the mid-twenty-first century to build the dome and its townships. As the population grew and spread out throughout the valley, the original structures were converted into a central government location for the dome.

The governor's residence the transport pulled up in front of was officially called Cavus House, but was known to local Arsians as the Can. From the outside it was quite unassuming: a round concrete-faced wall built into the rock of the hill, fitted inside a long-extinct lava tube. It stood close to forty feet tall and sixty feet wide, a squashed oval, and bore a handful of ground floor windows and several smaller upper floor windows in addition to its double main doors. It sat level with the floor of the valley, so it lacked the grand steps one would expect from a typical government building. The doors were flanked by flagstands: one for the Mars Republic, a deep purple background with a red orb surrounded by two white moons, and the other for the Arsia Mons Dome city, a multi-colored woven quilt representing the various backgrounds, colors, and ethnicities of one of Mars's first cities.

The reason locals called it the Can was that inside, the same squashed cylinder continued for over two hundred yards; if it were all open without walls separating rooms, it would have looked just like an oversized empty can of vegetables lying on its side.

The transport crunched to a stop in front of the Can and a doorman-slash-guard greeted them as the door swung open. "Right this way, Lieutenant, Lieutenant Commander," he said as he held out one hand to help Gesselli from the car.

Gabriel climbed out behind her and threw a look at the doorman, who quickly averted his eyes from Gesselli. The doorman led them to the entrance and opened one side of the double doors, allowing them to enter. "Ma'am," he said as he tipped his cap to Gesselli, earning a throat-clearing from Gabriel.

The open entry foyer was impressive, having been converted over eighty years ago from a housing complex cafeteria and check-in desk into a grand lobby, with polished stone floor, hanging wall tapestries representing individual townships in Arsia Mons, and holographic projections from the ceiling showing rotating images of Mars's history. It seemed to Gabriel that he saw a different one every time he set foot here; today he saw Radimirov's first steps on the surface of Mars, the tiny Russian lander in the background. Familiar ones, such as the first space elevator car's ascent, the ribbon cutting at the Phobos mining facility, the landing of the first Arsia Mons colonists, and the erecting of the dome fabric for the first time, appeared and disappeared as they walked across the lobby.

Arriving at the far end, ninety feet from the entrance, Gabriel and Gesselli stood at the main desk and waited while the receptionist finished his call.

"Lieutenant Renay Gesselli, Lieutenant Commander Evan Gabriel, here to see Governor Tarif as requested," Gesselli said as the man tapped his ear to end the conversation.

The receptionist, a new hire Gabriel thought, stood up quickly, straightening his jacket. "Ah, yes, of course. Please," he said, extending his arm towards the glass doors to his right. "This way, I'll take you to the security area."

"No need," replied Gabriel. "Not our first time." He and Gesselli walked around the desk to the doors and stepped through, leaving the receptionist standing open-mouthed.

As they stepped through the doors, they were greeted by a guard, who smiled. "Miss Gesselli, Mister Gabriel, a pleasure to see you again," he said. He stepped back out of the way to allow them by.

"Hello, Jasper, how's the wife?" Gabriel asked as he deposited his sidearm, wallet, and flexscreen tube in the plastic bin. Gesselli did the same with her items.

"Oh, she's great sir, thank you for asking," Jasper replied. He ushered them through the detector arch, which blanketed them with sniffer puffs and electronic waves, then signaled green as they passed through. "She's in her third trimester, we're looking forward to the big day. And," he said with a laugh as Gabriel retrieved the plastic bin from the other side of the detector, "she swore we'd never be on Mars long enough to have kids."

"Never say never, right?" Gesselli said as she tucked her flexscreen tube into her skirt pocket.

"And you two?" Jasper asked as they continued down the hall.

"Don't push it, buddy," Gabriel called over his shoulder. "Hard enough being her boss." Gesselli's stare ended any further discussion on that topic.

<<<<<>>>>>

The governor's office was located at the far end of the long building; whether by design or by accident, Gabriel couldn't be sure, but he suspected it had something to do with impressing visitors with the architecture of the cylindrical building. The outer walls were smooth and polished, but not covered, leaving the natural rock exposed, yet sealed in a transparent silica/plastic shell to prevent erosion and to shore up the stability of the lava tube. The walls themselves were spectacular, bearing colorful ripples and ridges hinting at the massive lava flow hundreds of millions of years before humans ever set foot on the planet. With the dull shine from the sealant giving the walls an eerie, almost living glow, it had always reminded Gabriel of what it would be like to walk through the trunk of a massive redwood tree. Only this one had dozens of people working in it, day and night.

Stepping through a door into an anteroom, Gabriel and Gesselli acknowledged the armed aide waiting for them, who scanned their neuretics to confirm identity. Satisfied, the aide opened the door to the governor's office.

Governor Mubina Tarif sat behind a synthoak desk, phone bug in her left ear, tapping away at a flexscreen keyboard. As the pair entered, she held up her hand without taking her gaze away from the monitor in front of her. In the room were two other people: a tall man wearing the uniform of the Mars Defense Force, and a plump woman dressed in an ill-fitting business suit. Both were standing at the head of Tarif's desk, apparently waiting for the governor to end her conversation.

Gabriel noted the phone bug and wondered again why the governor had never decided to have neuretic implants. Religious reasons, physical reasons, she never explained it, and he never pursued it, just went along with the slow and laborious methods of avatar-to-neuretics calls she made to him from time to time.

"No, no, no!" Tarif said, shaking her head and banging more energetically at the keyboard. "We will not allow them a work stoppage. Explain to them again, if they walk out, we will find others to take their place. No questions asked." With that, she tapped her ear and cut off the call.

"Sorry about that, Lieutenant Commander, Lieutenant," she said. She took the phone bug out of her ear and leaned back in the chair. "Thank you for accommodating my request on such short notice."

"Didn't think we had much of a choice, Governor," Gabriel said with a small shrug.

Tarif smiled, breaking the tense atmosphere. "No, probably not. Please, pull up those chairs," she said to the two others. "I'll get some coffee."

Gesselli held up a hand. "None for us, thank you ma'am, just came from the café."

"Well, I'm sure you won't mind if I indulge," she replied as the tall man dragged chairs over to her desk. She pressed a button on the comm unit on her desk. "Radja, can you have coffee brought in?" A voice acknowledged the request and she clicked the unit off.

"Now," Tarif said. She walked around from behind her desk to join the other four, all of whom had seated themselves in a loose circle around a low table. "Down to business. Evan, my call earlier referenced a message we received. A message that specifically asked for you."

Gabriel nodded. "Yes ma'am, but I'm still very much in the dark. No one contacted me directly."

"I'll let my guests fill you in on the details," Tarif replied. "This is Major Andon from MDF Intelligence, and this is Lila Vasuda from our Communications office."

Andon leaned forward. "Lieutenant Commander, the message was sent outside of normal channels. It piggybacked on a standard frequency used by diplomats and was only routed to the governor's office because of the header tag. The message was sent to you, although because it addressed you as 'Commander' Gabriel, our assessment is that it's from someone who has been out of the loop for a while."

Gabriel frowned, looking at Gesselli, who remained impassive. "Go on," he said.

Vasuda spoke up. "Sir, it took us a while to decode the message itself. Apparently it used a one-time key used by only a handful of departments, one of which was your former command."

Gabriel cocked his head at her. "What does that mean?"

Vasuda swallowed. "Sir, the message came from Eden, and it's from one of your former squad."

Gabriel felt shock, then denial, then disbelief, his emotions running the full gamut in seconds. He looked from Vasuda to Andon, who nodded his head in agreement, then to Tarif, and finally to Gesselli, whose eyes showed concern as Gabriel digested the news. He sat back in his chair heavily, rubbing his temple.

"That doesn't make any sense, Miss Vasuda. There was no one left from my squad, no one who could have possibly had that key," he said slowly. "Could this have been faked?"

"We thought of that right away," Andon said. "My analysts concur with Miss Vasuda, the message is genuine, and the voice analysis confirms the identity of the sender. Do you know a Tomas Katoa?"

A lump formed in Gabriel's throat, and Gesselli reached over and put her hand on his arm. The emotions, the raw memories, flooded over him, overloaded him, and his head swayed. Flashes of Eden rushed back, images of fire, burning buildings, children. The sound of Tamander's screams as the Geltex burned through his armor. Petty Officer Tomas Katoa's terrified look as the burning ceiling collapsed on him. Santander standing over Gabriel with a gun.

He shook his head, squeezing his eyes closed to push away the memories, the nightmares. After a few seconds he looked up at the others. "That's not possible. He's dead. Everyone was dead. I was the only one to get out. I *know* that." He shook his head again. "Not possible," he repeated in a lower tone.

"It's confirmed, as far as we are concerned," Andon repeated. "Why don't we just play the message for the Lieutenant Commander," he said to Vasuda.

She nodded and set down the small device she had been holding, a portable comm unit, and activated the speaker. A scratchy voice filled the room.

"Commander Gabriel, this is Petty Officer Tomas Katoa. I don't know if you'll get this message, or where you are, but you're the only person I could think to send this to. Sir, I'm being held on Eden. It's been…five years, I think, I don't… There's…there's a group of rebels, they're still fighting the Eden government, and they took me. Right after the firefight. Five years…"

A burst of static came from the comm unit, then the voice continued.

"Sir, these rebels, they're planning something. I was able to bribe one of them to get me to the transmitter, but they killed him, and they're coming for me now. Something big's going down here, you gotta tell someone. It's big, they've got bio…"

Another burst of static, and Vasuda picked up the comm unit, switching it off. "It ends there," she said. "No other transmissions, no other message tags or indications of any other data encoded in the stream."

The governor held up her hands. "Evan, before you do or say anything, I need to clear some things up," she said. "We are apparently the only ones to receive this message. I talked to some of my contacts back on Earth in the NAF, and they are not aware of any distress call from Eden, or any type of organized uprising. There is no official authorization for anyone to go out there under the pretense of military action. Do you understand?"

Gabriel's head continued to spin, more images of Katoa and his other squadmates, flames, burning metal and plastic. He stared at the coffee table, dazed, wondering how someone could have survived for five years, captive, all alone. And how he had even lived through the carnage of the operation, the failed attempt to capture the terrorists, the explosions, the treachery. The massacre.

"Evan?" Tarif said.

Gabriel looked up, blinking his eyes rapidly. "What?"

"Did you hear me?"

He ran back through her words, words he had heard but didn't listen to, catching on her last statement.

"Official authorization, ma'am?" he asked.

"Correct," the governor replied. "There is no sanctioned operation being planned. My contacts say the NAF does not believe this transmission constitutes an actual, on-paper threat, and are unwilling to send troops in. They are simply unwilling to risk a diplomatic incident over speculation." Gabriel saw her jaw clench.

"However," Andon cut in, "we're concerned with the last word Katoa said, and my analysts believe he is referring to possible bioweapons. But *we* aren't concerned about a diplomatic incident, and are prepared to act on speculation. There are Mars natives on Eden in various positions, some with families here, that we are...worried about." Gabriel caught a glance Andon gave the governor.

Andon pulled a flexscreen tube from his jacket pocket and extended it. "You have extensive knowledge of the facilities there, more so than anyone else on Mars. You also have a friend there, someone who's asking for your help."

He tapped at the flexscreen, and Gabriel's neuretics confirmed receipt of a data packet. His security system scanned it and allowed it to open. Schematics of a ship and scrolling data popped up in the corner of his Mindseye as Andon continued.

"We have a ship scheduled to depart tomorrow morning for Hodgson, one gate away from Eden. We can have it add the extra leg, ostensibly for delivering Mars minerals to Eden, as we do have regularly scheduled cargo runs there."

Andon turned to the governor, who nodded in return. "Lieutenant Commander, unofficially, we'd like you and your team to be on board that ship to investigate. And find your man."

Gabriel leaned back in the chair, resting his head on the high back, and stared at the far wall. Eden, the mission that had caused his life to spin out of control. The death, the destruction, the massacre. It all seemed to be coming back full circle. Almost like it was meant to be, he thought, remembering back to the conversation with Renay at the café. *Maybe it really is what I'm made for*, he thought to himself.

He looked over at the governor, who sat quietly with her eyes cast on the coffee table. There was something there, he thought, something beneath the surface. Something they weren't telling him.

"Governor," he said. Her head came up and she looked him in the eye. He saw the steely stare he was accustomed to, but also a weakness, a sad far-off look buried inside. "Is there anything else?"

Tarif gave a sad smile. "Leave it to you." She crossed her hands in her lap, and Gabriel noticed she tugged at a bracelet she wore. He hadn't noticed that she rarely wore jewelry; this piece appeared to be special to her.

"This?" she said, noticing his look. "My son sent this to me a few months ago. It came in on a ship from Eden."

Gabriel cocked his head, wondering where she was going with this.

"My son…is a university student on Eden. He's doing a medical research internship for his doctorate, and has been on Eden for the past four months." She looked down at the bracelet, twisting it around her wrist. "Just before we received the transmission from Katoa, I took a call from Prime Minister Howarth. It seems that these terrorists, as he calls them, attacked the lab facilities where Jeromy was studying. Several Eden Guard were killed, and Jeromy and seventeen others are listed as missing, and presumed kidnapped by the terrorists."

Gesselli leaned forward and took Tarif's hand in hers. "Oh, Mubina, I'm so sorry," she said.

Tarif squeezed her hand in return. "Thank you. I'm sure he's alive, I truly am. But that is part of the reason I called you." She looked at Gabriel with pleading eyes. "I trust you, and I'm one hundred percent behind you. The Prime Minister knows I wield a great deal of political power and is more than willing to accept my unofficial help. And I must send my best people in. I'm sure you understand that?"

Gabriel tilted his head forward. A memory of the meeting in Toronto over six months ago with his former commanding officer Llewelyn "Dredge" MacFarland, where he was called back to active duty. It felt like that all over again. But this time…this was different. The governor, someone who believed in him and his team, someone who supported them through tough times when they arrived on Mars, was in trouble. And Katoa. *Jesus Christ, Katoa. How the hell?*

"I do understand," he said after a moment. "And I will help." He fixed her with a stare. "If I go, my entire team goes, and I want full equipment and personnel support. As much as an 'unofficial' visit can have."

"Done," she said without hesitation. "Some of Andon's people will be on the ship with you and will accompany you to Eden. You'll have the best we can offer. Unofficially, of course. The NAF won't get involved, but has authorized a provisional promotion back to full Commander for you."

Gabriel's eyes widened just a bit. He hadn't expected that to happen so quickly... or smoothly.

"And your jobs here," the governor continued with a small smile, "will be safe."

Gesselli tightened her grip on his arm, and he looked over at her.

"I want to go with you," she said. "I know this is a hard thing to do. I want to be there for you."

He shook his head emphatically. "Absolutely not, out of the question," he said. He covered her hand with his. "The last thing I need is for you to be in any danger at all. I don't think that's going to make it any easier for me." He looked her in the eyes and lowered his voice. "Knowing you're here safe and sound... trust me."

She frowned, but eased her grip on his arm. She stared into his eyes for several long moments before replying. "I understand, I do. But you'd better take care of yourself, mister."

"Yes ma'am," he replied. "You know me."

"Exactly," she said, her frown deepening.

Gabriel gave her hand a squeeze, then turned back to the other three. "Governor, I think I'd like that coffee now. And might as well make it regular. Decaf isn't going to cut it this time."

CHAPTER SIX

"Alphabetical, gentlemen, so first round's on Brevik."

The team had gathered in their usual meeting place, the Canali Brewpub in Porto, origin of the Mars-famous Deimos Ale, one of the planet's few successful exports to Earth. The five men, plus Gesselli, were seated around one of the pub's many kidney-shaped extruded plastic tables.

Brevik shifted his bulk in an undersized chair. "Not quite, Petty Officer Third Class Jimenez. I believe A for Arturo precedes H for Harris."

Keven Takahashi snorted from the end of the table. "You walked into that one, Arturo."

"Round's on me, guys," a voice said. Everyone's heads turned at once.

Galen Sowers, normally the team's least-likely-to-pick-up-a-round member, sat with his arms folded at the end of the kidney opposite Takahashi, a Cheshire cat grin from ear to ear.

After a few seconds, it was Gabriel who broke the silence. "Well? Spill it, Sowers, why the sudden generosity?"

Sowers spread his hands wide. "Let's just say an investment paid off handsomely the other day."

"What invest…you know what," said Gabriel, shaking his head. "Belay that. I don't really want to know. Anyway, this is a one-round evening. We've got business to discuss."

The conversation ceased as the waiter brought five bottles of Deimos Ale and a glass of Long Range Vineyards pinot noir to the table. He passed out the drinks and left the check with Sowers.

"Lost friends," said Takahashi, raising his bottle. The others chimed in with the same toast and the group clinked glass, each taking a sip and pausing for a quick moment of remembrance. Gabriel took a second sip, the memories of Eden still bouncing around in his head, now with the added weight of this new mission.

"Well boss?" said Jimenez. He set his bottle down on the table, glass striking plastic with a hollow *thunk*. "You say we have a trip tomorrow?"

Gabriel took a long pull of his beer and looked over at Gesselli, who returned his look with a sad smile over her wine glass. The smirk he remembered from months ago. Only this time he knew what it truly meant. Separating.

"Yes we do, but this is on a strictly volunteer basis," he replied. "I spoke to the governor this morning, and there's some trouble a few systems away. Possible rebel activity, possible bioweapons, possible hostage or hostages, including the governor's son."

Sowers clapped his hands together. "Hot damn," he said. "I'm in, possible or no. How about it, Arturo? Getting a little cabin fever down here like me, old buddy?"

Gabriel held up a palm. "Not so fast, Mister Sowers. This one is unsanctioned. Off the books, so to speak."

"And?" Sowers motioned with the mouth of his bottle for Gabriel to continue.

"And," Gabriel said, "it's not under NAF, or Mars, regulations, so I can't order anyone to go." He paused before continuing. "Listen, the mission…is to Eden."

The silence around the table was palpable. It was Brevik that finally broke it.

"Sir, I believe I speak for everyone around this table," he said, looking at the others. "It doesn't matter where or when, we're with you."

"And Eden especially, sir," said Takahashi.

"Thank you guys," said Gesselli. She sipped her red wine, holding the glass with both hands. "I'm staying here." She glanced at Gabriel with a stern look. "I trust you'll all keep an eye out for each other."

Sowers laughed. "Yes ma'am, we certainly don't want to face your wrath for leaving him behind."

The rest of the men joined in the laugh, but stopped at seeing the look on Gabriel's face.

"Sir?" asked Jimenez, cocking his head.

Gabriel paused, trying unsuccessfully to tamp down the memories and emotions welling up inside. He looked around the table at the men, his men, and took a deep breath.

"Someone was left behind. One of my men from the original mission, five years ago, survived, and he's being held against his will. That's part of the reason we're going in."

"Holy shit, sir," said Sowers in a low voice. "A survivor? After all this time? My God..."

"He knows," Gesselli cut in. "No need to remind him."

"Ah, right, ma'am," Sowers said. He lowered his eyes and swigged his beer.

"Don't worry about it," Gabriel said with a flick of his hand. "Strange situation all around. Especially with the addition of possible bioweapons. Which brings me to this." He pulled out a piece of hardcopy from his shirt pocket.

"We're gaining three new team members for this to bring us up to full eight-man squad strength. That is, assuming the lieutenant was correct in his assessment that everyone is in for this?"

A chorus of "hell yeahs" greeted his statement.

"Excellent. I appreciate your support, seriously," he said, glancing down at the hardcopy. "They are MDF..."

"Oh no, sir, you can't be serious?" asked Sowers. "Mars Defense? Like, regular conscript Army pukes?"

"Maybe we *should* order a second round," muttered Jimenez under his breath.

"Hold on," said Gabriel. "Let's give them the benefit of the doubt, shall we? At the very least, meeting them? I believe just a few months ago, I was the newbie, right?"

Brevik cleared his throat. "Absolutely, sir. What's the plan?"

Brevik's change of subject quieted the other three men immediately. Gabriel looked around at each man one by one, getting nods from each, and continued.

"They're headed to the *Lady Cydonia* as we speak, so they'll already be on board when we arrive at the orbital transfer station tomorrow. We can go over the personnel folios during the elevator ride. I have been assured by the governor," he glanced at Gesselli, who had been confirming logistics with the governor's office all afternoon, "that we'll have all the equipment we need already in place. We'll brief the details of the mission during the flight, so for now we can just kick back and relax for the evening. Tomorrow morning, I need you all at the skyhook terminal no later than oh-seven hundred hours with your standard kits. And Mister Sowers," he said, looking at the man at the end of the table. "No basketball this time."

"Amen," said Takahashi, and toasted Jimenez.

Sowers started to protest, but Gabriel cut him off with a gesture. "No basketball, but go ahead and pick up another round for the table."

Sowers rolled his eyes dramatically, but seemed more than happy to flag down the waiter.

"*Señor*, may I enter?"

The man looked up from his flexscreen and put his wine glass down on the side table. Closing the flexscreen tube, he answered, "*Sí*, Chimo."

The door to the office slid open at Chimo's touch, admitting him to the small alcove. He stepped inside and palmed the door closed behind him. He waited patiently as the man finished his wine and stood up.

"Chimo, good to see you again. May I offer you some wine?" the man asked. He indicated the carafe on the table next to his empty glass.

"No, uncle, *gracias*, but you know that I do not drink," the younger man replied.

The man nodded in approval. Excellent, he thought. His parents raised him well, no need for the distractions of stimulants. The man's brother, killed by an NAF sniper during the Brazilian water crisis several years ago, would have been proud of his son, he thought with a twinge of sadness.

"Please," he said as he waved Chimo over to the couch against one wall of the office. "Have a seat. You have brought information for me?"

"*Sí*, I have," Chimo replied. He walked carefully in the low gravity and sat on the couch, then accepted a glass of water from his uncle. "My contacts have reported that Gabriel and his team are scheduled to depart Mars tomorrow morning on a civilian cargo freighter, bound for Eden. As we expected, and planned."

The man smiled as he refilled his wine glass from the carafe. He turned back to his nephew. "And Gabriel does not suspect anything out of the ordinary?"

"Not as far as my contacts can see, *señor*," Chimo replied, sipping at the water. He cocked his head and looked at the glass as if it surprised him.

The man chuckled at Chimo's reaction to the taste of the water. "Yes, my nephew, real water, pure iceberg water, imported from our Antarctic operation, not reconstituted lunar moisture." He sipped his wine and continued. "I still have access to many luxuries, even marooned here on the moon. I don't think Isidoro and Rafael appreciate the…

opportunities that present themselves when no one is looking for you."

"Not many icebergs left, though," the younger man replied. "How did you…"

"Being in the right place at the right time and knowing the right people. Remember this, Chimo. There is no such thing as luck. It is only being prepared when an opportunity presents itself. I have lived by those words, and very comfortably I might add, my entire life."

Chimo nodded, sipping more of the water. "Our people are in place on Eden, and on Mars, should the situation work out the way we need it to. The timing and nature of the very personal distress call could not have worked out better for us. We were very lucky… no, *lo siento*, we were prepared when this opportunity came up at the right time, and it's going to work to our advantage."

"*Sí*, I believe it will. Please keep me informed of any changes, I will make preparations for the second part of your plan," the man said. He tapped Chimo's glass with his own. "I'm proud of you, you've really become quite the young man. Your father would be proud as well."

Chimo beamed. "*Gracias*, uncle, I don't know what to say."

The man took another sip of wine and smiled. "Thank me when this is all over. I believe there is a prominent position awaiting you on Mars."

CHAPTER SEVEN

"Are you a soldier?"

Gabriel looked up from his reading towards the voice, finding a small boy, maybe five or six years old, standing in front of him, wearing a Mars Mariners minor league baseball t-shirt and cap.

"Hmmm, what?" he said as he stretched his arms out. Both shoulders popped at the strain.

"Are you a soldier?" the boy repeated, taking a small step closer. "You look like a soldier."

Gesselli laughed softly next to Gabriel. She elbowed him in the ribs. "Well, are you going to answer the young man?"

Gabriel rolled his eyes and closed the flexscreen with a snap. Moravec Station was starting to fill up, he noticed. Families with children headed off-planet, probably vacationing on Phobos in one of the low-grav parks, one of the more affordable, nearby destinations for cash-poor Mars inhabitants. School had just let out for the season, so the crowd was filled with parents dragging tired teens, who were in turn dragging even more tired younger siblings, who were then in turn dragging small carry-on bags. He wondered how many of them had to travel over three hours from Arsia Dome, and again a distant part of his mind puzzled as to why Mars's largest dome didn't have a skyhook, and the less-populated Pavonis Mons dome did. *People still afraid the cable might fall*, he guessed.

They had arrived quite a bit early for the eight o'clock elevator departure, Gesselli insisting on it so they'd not be the last ones in. Upon finding that Customs & Immigration personnel didn't show up until an hour after they arrived, Gabriel grumbled his way to a cup of coffee and borrowed her flexscreen to read a novel. The coffee didn't agree with his stomach this early, and now the reading wasn't working out either.

"Hey there, little man," he said to the boy, holding out his hand for a high-five.

"I said are you a soldier," the boy repeated. He left Gabriel's hand hanging in mid-air.

"Hush, Ty, be polite," a woman seated near Gesselli said, a sleeping baby on her lap. The boy's mother, Gabriel assumed.

"Yes, I am a soldier," Gabriel replied. "How did you guess? I'm not wearing a uniform."

The boy bit his lip and took a step backwards. "Are you a good soldier?"

Gabriel cocked his head, a puzzled look on his face. "Well, yes, of course. What do you mean?"

"Ty," his mother warned.

"You're big like a soldier, and your hair looks like a soldier, but you're not mean like other soldiers. So I think you must be a good soldier." The boy's eyes took on a distant look. "My daddy got shot by a bad soldier." He looked at the floor. "My daddy's gone now."

Sadness punched Gabriel in the chest, and he felt a lump form in his throat. He looked over at Gesselli, whose face reflected his own feelings. Years of anarchy and lawlessness on Mars had created such an ingrained feeling of dread and despair among the population, now even the children expected the worst. He looked around the terminal, seeing dozens of families wandering to their gates, or to breakfast, or to the rest room, towing tired or crying children. He shook his head sadly. Only six months here, not enough time to make enough of a change for everyone to benefit. But the programs, the policies, were in place. Mars could, and would, provide a brighter future for these kids.

He swallowed, fighting down a growing lump in his throat. "Yes, Ty, I'm a good soldier," he said. He leaned over and offered his palm again.

"A very good one," Gesselli chimed in next to him, smiling.

The boy looked at his mother, who nodded, then back to Gabriel. "Promise?" he asked with a hopeful look.

Gabriel smiled broadly. "Promise."

The boy stepped forward hesitantly, then reached out his hand and slapped a loud high-five, laughing at the sound.

Gabriel laughed in return and shook his hand dramatically. "You like soldiers?"

"Well, good ones, I guess," the boy replied as he rubbed his own hand.

"Here," said Gabriel. He reached into a thigh pocket and pulled out a small patch. "I'm supposed to wear this, but I've got nowhere to put it. It's for really, *really* good soldiers. Will you take it and wear it?"

The boy reached out his hand and Gabriel placed the square piece of cloth in it. "This is the special patch worn by good soldiers of the North American Federation Navy. See the blue background? That's for the oceans on Earth, where my navy used to be most of the time. Now almost all of us are in space, which is the black circle in the center. And the white tee symbol in the very middle? That's for the very best soldiers. It's called the Navy Cross. My boss gave it to me many years ago."

The boy stared open-mouthed at the patch in his hand.

"Sir, you don't have to..." his mother began, tears forming in her eyes.

"No, no, don't worry," Gabriel replied. He turned back to the boy. "It's a special patch, but I know I'm a good soldier, so I don't need it anymore. Take this patch and keep it with you, and remember I gave it to you. Maybe one day, when you grow up, you can be a good soldier too, and give it to another boy you meet."

The boy's mouth opened farther still, and he turned to his mother. "Mama, can I keep it? It's... it's awesome!"

The mother smiled back at her son. The baby in her lap was just beginning to wake up. "If he says so, then yes. But you have to promise him you'll keep it safe."

"Yes, yes!" he said, and reached out his hand to give Gabriel another high-five. "I promise!" he said as he slapped his palm. He hopped over to his mother and baby sister, waving the patch in the air, and began spinning around in the aisle.

Gesselli leaned over and kissed Gabriel on the cheek. "You are some kind of guy, you know that? You old softie...I love you."

He leaned back in his seat, watching Ty dance around chanting, "Navy, Navy!"

"Yeah, softie. Just don't let the other guys..."

His eye caught sight of the massive Brevik walking towards him, chewing on a double-stuffed breakfast burrito, followed by Takahashi, Sowers, and Jimenez, all eating some type of fast food, and sighed. "So much for the moment, huh?" he said ruefully, looking at Gesselli.

"Hey boss," Sowers said. Crumbs of egg-substitute cascaded down his chest like a miniature, yellow avalanche. "Who's your fan club?" he asked, pointing with his muffin at the singing boy.

"Never mind that, Petty Officer," Gabriel said as he stood up. "You boys all full up for the ride to zero-G?" he asked. He looked at Takahashi sideways.

The ensign answered by pointing to a pink sticker behind one ear. "Bought it online this week, guaranteed to work."

"I'm not sitting next to him this time, forget it," said Jimenez, shaking his head.

"Zip it and line up," said Brevik. He polished off his breakfast and dropped the trash into a nearby receptacle. "Sir," he added to Gabriel in polite deference to rank.

Gabriel turned to Gesselli as the team made their way past him to the gate, which was flashing a boarding signal. "You take care of yourself, you hear me?" he said, giving her a hug. Behind her Ty was looking up at the two of them, and Gabriel flashed a thumbs up and a wink. The boy returned the gestures with a smile and a feeble attempt at his own wink.

"You too, good soldier," Gesselli whispered in his ear. "Come back safe."

The embrace lasted another few seconds, ending when Sowers walked by and cleared his throat.

Gabriel looked into her eyes. "I promise."

She pecked him on the lips, then pushed him away. "Get going. Don't be late now, after dragging me out here at some ungodly hour this morning."

He started to protest, but saw her smile. "I love you too. See you in a couple of weeks."

With that he turned and waved good bye to Ty, who gave a small salute. "Be careful sir," he said.

"Aye aye, soldier. Take care of your little sister, and have fun on vacation."

Gabriel walked past Ty and down the aisle between benches, following the team to the boarding gate, leaving Mars behind.

<<<<<>>>>>

Across the terminal, a man in a Moscow Thrashers baseball cap finished his coffee, which had gotten ice cold after sitting for over an hour. He stood up from the plastic chair he had been sitting in for the better part of that same hour. Walking out of the Bagel Shack, he glanced at the gate and watched the last of the SpecFor team pass through security. Once the last of them departed, he placed a neuretics call using the prearranged code he had been given.

"They're gone," he subvocalized. He waited until he received the confirmation code. When it came back, he disconnected the call, and the codes dissolved into static in his Mindseye. He tossed the empty cup into the same trash receptacle Brevik had used and walked out of the skyhook terminal.

The team was seated on the upper A level of the Skyhook Alpha elevator car. The seats had been specially requested by Sowers, apparently in an attempt to make Takahashi as sick as possible. The transparent ceiling provided an excellent view of their transit up the thin carbon-carbon nanotube cable to orbit, and would provide an even more spectacular view of the surface of Mars halfway through the journey when the car flipped over prior to arriving at the orbital station.

Gabriel sat near the back and began going over the personnel reports for their new team members. He took a quick look around the car's cabin, noting very few empty seats on a busy travel day. Jimenez sat near Gabriel in the back, as far away from Takahashi as possible, wearing oversized headphones. Sowers was sitting next to Takahashi, perhaps in an attempt to watch the festivities should the ensign's infomercial patch fail to work as advertised. Brevik, as was his nature, was seated in the very front and was fast asleep before the car even lurched into motion.

The ride up was quiet, taking just under two hours, the only sounds coming from a few laughing children watching a movie on their parents' flexscreen. No one paid much attention to the five men spread throughout the cabin, except for a few wide-eyed stares at Brevik's size from small children. Gabriel was glad the trip had been arranged this way; he'd much rather take standard civilian transportation as opposed to a logged military flight. *The less people that know we're leaving, the better.*

He idly scrolled through the personnel reports of their new members, skimming the overview of service records, achievements, skills, and the like. *Better to see it in their eyes,* he thought. Sabra and Lamber looked great on paper, but there was something in each of their eyes that never rubbed him the right way. He only found out their true nature when it was too late, and St. Laurent had paid the price. *Tee.* He took a deep breath and put her memory, and the memory of her death out of his head, and skipped ahead to the ship statistics.

The *Lady Cydonia* was a standard inter-system cargo hauler, fitted for equipment and machinery as opposed to minerals or fuel like many haulers. It had a crew of seventeen civilian transportation workers, and made runs throughout the wormhole network several times a month. Today she was scheduled to depart for a twelve-day round-trip voyage to Jericho, Farpoint Station, Hodgson, then back. Late last night, a stop after Hodgson to Eden was added for the purposes of trading additional atmosphere processors. It would add two days to the overall flight plan, and would have their R & R layover at Eden instead of the water world of Hodgson, but the crew was given time and a half bonus for the extra leg, so no complaints were heard, and no questions were asked.

Gabriel read on. What the *Lady Cydonia* lacked in beauty, he noticed, it more than made up for with complete lack of creature comforts. It was a slight upgrade from the rust-bucket Mars-to-Earth shuttle he was on a few weeks ago, but it certainly wasn't a luxury liner. The crew of seventeen hot-bunked in four staterooms, each fitted with two beds and a sink, with a common area in between, all in the standard rotating torus starships were equipped with to provide artificial gravity. Adding the five of them, plus the three additional MDF soldiers they were meeting, was going to be an interesting exercise in logistics.

He closed his eyes for a brief second, trying to remember the story he had started to read in the terminal. A thump in his seat caused his eyes to fly open. He looked around the cabin; passengers were starting to unbuckle their seat belts and push up from their seats in the microgravity.

"Sir, you awake?" asked Jimenez, who was floating next to him in the aisle, stretching his back.

Gabriel yawned to pop his ears, realizing he had dozed off for the trip and the car had arrived at the station.

"Yup," he answered. He looked around at the others headed his way. "I'm up. Everyone all set?"

"Present and accounted for," said Takahashi cheerfully. "Worked like a charm, sir!" He tapped the sticker behind his ear.

Sowers was next to him, frowning. "Yeah, like a charm. Fun's over now," he said. He headed for the cabin door, pushing his carry bag in front of him. Brevik followed, nodding at Gabriel. Takahashi turned to follow him, and Gabriel patted Jimenez on the back.

"Let's hit it, Mister Jimenez. We've got a long flight in very uncomfortable digs," he said. "Last one there gets last choice on bunks."

With that, Jimenez shoved off hard from one of the seat backs towards the cabin door. Gabriel gave a small smile and followed.

CHAPTER EIGHT

"So, let me see if I have this straight, Karl," Gabriel said. He was holding a personnel folio, and tapping it on the table. "They call you 'Chaos'?"

The young man who sat across from him in the rec center sported a baseball cap worn backwards, a long-sleeved Mars Defense Force tunic with the sleeves rolled up, and a wide smile, which grew broader at Gabriel's question.

"Absolutely, sir, but with a K," he answered.

"Corporal Sennett, how exactly do they call you Chaos with a K?" Gabriel asked. "Is it pronounced differently?" He continued to tap the folio, the sound like a metronome. His eyes bored into the other man.

"Uh, well, no sir, it's not pronounced differently," he replied, his earlier confidence showing a slight crack. He sat forward in his chair. "Ah, I just know..."

"Do all MDF soldiers have... nicknames?" Gabriel said. The folio noise increased in volume.

Sennett watched the folio rising and falling. He cleared his throat and removed the baseball cap. "Uh, some of us sir. We, ah, feel that it gives us a sort of... special brotherhood, you know? Like a club?"

The folio stopped in mid-tap. Gabriel stared at Sennett for a long minute. A bead of sweat appeared on the young man's brow and he licked his lips.

"Sir, I…"

Gabriel held up a hand, silencing him. Another long minute passed. He slapped the folio onto the plastic table, the noise sharp in the quiet room.

"Corporal," he said. "This is an NAF Special Forces operation you've been attached to. Do you understand?"

"Yes sir, of course."

"You have excellent qualifications. Test scores, range marks, the works. But you know what you don't have?"

Sennett swallowed. "A nickname?"

"Correct," Gabriel said flatly. "There will be no 'Chaos' on my mission."

He stood up from the table and walked around to where Sennett was sitting. Sennett looked up at him and swallowed again. Gabriel sat on the edge of the table and folded his hands in his lap, looking the corporal in the eye.

"Listen, son. Doing drills, dressing up for parades, hanging out with the buds in the bar after patrol… none of those have anything to do with an actual mission, and neither does a nickname. And in this squad, we don't have a club. But we do have brothers, and sisters, that look out for each other, like a true family does."

Sennett's eyes opened wider and he unconsciously squeezed the baseball cap in his hand. "Sir, I never suggested…"

Gabriel held up a hand again. "That's not the point of this. I've already talked to Private Olszewski and Specialist Negassi, and they understand the seriousness of what we're doing, and the danger we may be heading into. I've given you the overview of what our mission is, and I think you're qualified enough to help us. But I need to know if you can help us, or if your attitude, or any overconfidence, will be a liability. Enough of a liability that I'll need to leave you onboard when we land."

Sennett stood up, leaving the crumpled cap on the table, and came to parade rest, hands clasped behind his back.

"Yes sir, I can help. You have my word."

Gabriel let a few seconds pass, watching Sennett stand rigidly with his eyes locked on the far wall. According to his file, and from what Major Andon had briefed him on, the corporal had top-notch marks in every area. But he was brash, he thought. Cocky, full of attitude. *Remind you of anyone?*

"I need more than your word, son," Gabriel said, standing up. "I need your skills, your talents, your hard work, and your willingness to follow my orders. No matter what they are. Are we clear?"

"Yes, sir!" Sennett said in a sharp voice.

Gabriel stood in front of the younger man, who was within a hair of his own height (*and probably in much better shape*, he thought wryly), and nodded. "Get out of here. Transit is in a few hours. We'll meet up in the mess at fourteen-hundred hours."

Sennett stood still, eyes still locked on the far wall.

"Dismissed, Corporal," Gabriel said, turning back to his chair.

As Sennett left the room, Gabriel sat down heavily in his chair. He picked up the personnel folio and resumed his tapping. *Kids. I'm getting too old for this.*

The mess hall was a tiny compartment compared to most he had seen. *Barely deserved of the moniker of hall,* Gabriel thought. He nursed a weak cup of decaf coffee at the hall's tiny lone table, and wondered how even half of the seventeen-member crew could possibly squeeze around it for a community meal. *Two hours to final transit,* he thought. *About time we can get out of this cramped tin can.*

Over the past two days, the *Lady Cydonia* had made quick drop off and pickup runs in three different systems. She had left Mars on a Tuesday with a full cargo hold. After a few hours of acceleration & deceleration, she dropped off mining machinery for the Tao Chien mining facility in the Belt and picked up iron ore. This cargo was carried through the solar system's lone wormhole, called Ryokou, into Nu Ophiuchi, a dead binary system which was the first destination of any extrasolar flight plan. While in Nu Ophiuchi she resupplied the T-Gate station with fresh grain and vegetables from Mars's expansive Valles Marineris domed farms, exchanging the foodstuffs for locally-mined natural diamonds that had been traded down the line from Jericho.

The next wormhole transit took her into their current location, the Canaan system, a trinary system devoid of any life or permanent colonies. After a quick supply stop at the T-Gate station immediately after transit, where they exchanged full nuclear fuel cells they were carrying for the station's empty ones, it was a long, uninterrupted day of travel. A day that Gabriel used getting to know the new members assigned to them by the Mars Defense Force, and in effect, Governor Tarif directly. A day he also paused to remember his last trip through Canaan, where he spent an afternoon in the observation lounge of the NAFS *Richard Marcinko*, chatting with Teresita St. Laurent about her future plans, just days before she was killed. He hoped, counted on in fact, this being a different mission entirely.

He had just left Corporal Karl Sennett in the rec center. *Another barely deserving moniker*, Gabriel thought. The term rec center invoked images of fit men and women playing indoor squash, swimming laps, playing basketball. The *Lady Cydonia's* rec center was a card table, four folding chairs, a 40 inch 2-D wallscreen, and a couple of ancient board games. Fortunately, the mess hall, like the rec center, was in the rotating torus, so at the very least, some semblance of comfort was afforded by the .45G.

Sennett was a known quantity. To all outwards appearances, he was an obnoxious, rebellious youngster, but Gabriel had seen through all of that with one look. In

Sennett's eyes, he had seen fire, determination, loyalty. Combined with wisecracks and goofing off, yes, but a solid soldier inside. Reading that his father was NAF Army Brigadier General Hayward Sennett, Deputy Chief of Staff and Army representative to the Joint Fleet Chiefs of Staff, Gabriel knew the young man would be reliable, through and through. He just made a note not to pair him up with Sowers at any time. The two of them, he thought with a shudder, would either bring the house down with jokes, or drive each other so crazy they'd end up shooting one another.

Private Stanislav Olszewski, or Stan-O, as he introduced himself (quickly rebuked by Gabriel), was, by his own accounts, a ninth generation Polish grunt. Grandfather after father after son were Army men during various incarnations of the country's government, dating all the way back to Major Jarek Olszewski, a hero of one of the very few victories Poland scored over Hitler's invading armies in 1939. He was very proud to say his great-great-etc. grandfather Jarek had singlehandedly defeated an armor attack in the Battle of the Bzura using backpack explosives and fast feet. The next day, said Olszewski with a sad, distant look in his eye, Grandpa Jarek and the rest of his platoon were overrun by additional panzers and Poland fell.

Gabriel watched while the private described the scene as if he were standing there himself, narrating, using his hands to show movements. By the end of the story Olszewski was sweating profusely, as if he had been the one sprinting across a barbed wire strewn field carrying sixty pounds of unstable explosives. He was eager, enthusiastic, nervous, bright, and very inexperienced, Gabriel saw. But he had a lot of potential; his folio showed perfect marksmanship scores, and he had tested highly proficient in long range sniper rifles. He was the youngest current holder of the European Commonwealth Distinguished International Shooter badge, and he wore the gold medal with hanging globe on his shipboard tunic proudly.

Specialist Leilani Negassi hailed from the Republic of Eritrea, which had just recently annexed the Republic of Sudan several years after annexing Ethiopia, making it one of the largest countries in Africa. With the discovery of massive uranium and cesium deposits in southern Sudan, it was now also one of the most prosperous. Her family was in the mining business and had done very well for themselves. Negassi had explained to Gabriel that they were so unhappy with her decision not only to enlist in the local army, and to go off-planet to join the Mars Defense Force, they had disowned her, both in name and financially. Negassi was her middle, or second name; her *Habesha* name she said. Her true surname was Haylom, which her family no longer permitted her to use. Gabriel listened as she detailed her childhood, an incredibly difficult life she had gone through, all the way up to training for infantry on Mars.

All in all, Andon had provided his team with three excellent, if young, soldiers to fill out his ranks for the upcoming mission. He felt a pang of regret, thinking about the missing team members they were replacing. Marco Lamber, the former Marine, and Mikaela Sabra, the sniper, both of whom had turned out to be traitors. Both were killed in the Poliahu mission; Lamber by Gabriel's doing, and Sabra in a poetic justice attack by the natives of the planet.

And then there was Teresita St. Laurent. Gabriel had become very attached to her during the short mission. Nothing physical; Gesselli had grilled him on more than one occasion about that. More of... *older brother, younger sister*, he thought. Something about her inner paradox had fascinated him. Medic and sniper, soldier and aspiring wine entrepreneur. Killed by a raging Lamber on the frozen planet of Poliahu, buried by her team and family on her small vineyard in Oregon.

He knew inside that the temporarily assigned replacements weren't true replacements, but just thinking about Tee again, and the emotions he saw from his team during the funeral six months ago, made him wonder how the new family would work together. *Only one way to find out,* he thought. He checked his neuretics for the time to transit and queried the *Lady Cydonia's* systems for a status update. One hour, ten minutes until they reached the Canaan One gate, which would take them into Calypso for their Jericho stop, then on past Hodgson, then Eden.

Picking up his coffee cup and draining the cold, stale liquid in one quick gulp, he called up the copy of the novel Gesselli had flashed to his neuretics in the airport before he left, and dove back into it.

CHAPTER NINE

The sun was just dipping below Eden's horizon as Captain Jamar Chaud escorted his team to an unmarked prefab building near the back of the compound. The eight men and women had just returned from another supply raid and were still coming down off an adrenaline high when Chaud had received a call from Prophet's right hand man, Zeno.

He had mixed emotions after disconnecting the call. He had known Zeno for many years, even before Prophet had taken over leadership of their group, and his voice sounded... distant, almost scared. Prophet had requested the team's presence for a quick meeting after the supply raid, to "celebrate the success of the university mission" as he had put it. Chaud had known Prophet a few years as well, but certainly wasn't within the man's inner circle, so he felt a bit of turmoil about the summons.

His team walked quietly between the smaller huts and tents of the compound. *Professionals, every one of them,* he thought again with an inner pride. Near-perfect mission the other day, zero casualties on their own side, and successful retrieval of the special package Prophet had asked for. *So why the odd feeling in the pit of the stomach?*

He reached the building and rapped on the door. His team came to a loose parade rest behind him.

"Come," a voice answered, muffled behind the plasteel.

Chaud palmed the lockpad and the door hissed open. No one was standing there to greet them, so he walked in, the team following on his heels.

The inside of the building was poorly lit. He considered switching on his IR implant, or calling out, but shook the thought off. *No sense in jumping the gun and looking nervous.* As his eyes adjusted, he saw he was standing in a large room, no separating walls or furniture, other than a long banquet-style table in the middle, ten chairs around it, and two men seated facing them. Zeno, and Prophet.

Chaud looked at their leader. Prophet had only recently risen to power in the rebel hierarchy, assuming command of the hundred-odd freedom fighters just a few years ago after the untimely assassination of their former head. He was ruthless, Chaud had seen, but not stupid. Able to see both tactically and strategically, Prophet had quickly enabled their group, one of five splintered bands of thieves for the most part, to assimilate the others and grow to their current size. He rewarded the loyal, purged the weak, and brutally eliminated the disloyal. He had been given the name Prophet, Chaud remembered, for a very good reason. No one else could have possibly foreseen how much more powerful a single group could be than a spread-out handful of terrorists. Chaud followed willingly; he had seen his own brother killed at the hands of the fascist Eden government puppets, and swore revenge years ago.

Zeno stood up from his seat alongside Prophet and walked over to Chaud. "Jamar, my friend," he said, extending a hand. "I'm so glad to hear of your success. Thank you for bringing your team over so soon after another mission."

Chaud took the shorter man's hand in his own and shook it. "Of course, we are honored to be here." He turned and waved towards his team. "I believe you know everyone?"

Zeno nodded. "Yes. Especially Miss Werth," he said, casting a longing glance at the team's sniper. Werth didn't respond, keeping her eyes fixed on the dim wall above Prophet's head.

"Anyway," Zeno continued. "Please, all of you have a seat." He walked to the table and motioned for the rest to follow him. He pointed each team member one by one to a seat, almost as if they were numbered. He took a few extra seconds to help pull out Werth's chair for her. He walked around to the other side of the table and took his seat next to Prophet, the portly Zeno a physical antithesis to his slim leader.

Chaud sat down and pulled his chair in a few inches, leaning his elbows on the synthoak table. He was seated directly across from Prophet and stared into his face; he was sure Zeno sat him there for that reason. Prophet, an unassuming man of medium build and average looks, would never have struck fear into the heart of anyone. Until they saw what he was capable of. It was all there behind the emotionless face.

"Captain Chaud," Prophet said in a low tone. "Thank you very much for your successful mission at the university the other day." He nodded to Zeno, who stood again and picked up a large decanter of what appeared to be red wine from the center of the table. Just then Chaud noticed there were wine glasses set in front of every person, but no napkins, utensils, or plates. *Good thing we ate before walking over,* he thought.

Chaud caught the scent of the locally-produced merlot as it splashed into his glass. Once the glasses were full, Zeno filled Prophet's, then his own, and resumed his seat.

Prophet raised his glass. "Congratulations, one and all. We've made progress in not only hurting the fascists, but have also acquired a significant asset in our fight towards toppling the governmental system, and the people in power."

Nine more glasses joined Prophet's in the air with a chorus of *hear, hears.*

Chaud took a small sip of the wine, not wanting to appear rude, but not wanting to imbibe too much so soon after combat. He remembered many a mission where he drowned his highs and lows in the bottle afterwards, and the next morning was never pretty. His team, he noticed, didn't share any of his reservations. Most glasses were set back down on the table with scarcely a drop of red left in them.

"Now I have additional information. You," Prophet said, motioning around the table with his wine glass, "are my top team. My most trusted team. We have very important people to make happy, and very special guests on their way."

Maybeck, sitting to Zeno's right, coughed into his hand. "Sorry, sir," he said, clearing his throat.

Prophet continued as if he hadn't heard the man. "Our financial backers, who you folks have so kindly helped out with the mission, will be providing us with significantly more in the way of matériel and supplies in the coming months. The asset we acquired makes that all possible, as our backers have plans far larger than our little civil war."

Maybeck coughed again. Chaud looked over at the man, whose face had started to turn a lighter shade of white. He gritted his teeth. *Idiot*, he thought for the second time in the past few days.

"There is a team on their way from Mars, sent to reacquire that asset from us," Prophet said. "If...no, *when*. When we eliminate that team, we will be provided with additional personnel, both military and political, by said backers, to once and for all get rid of the status quo, and rebuild Eden the proper way."

He set his empty glass down on the table with a loud thunk. "However, we cannot afford any missteps. Any at all. Even the smallest ones, with the team I know is coming, could prove fatal to our entire group."

Maybeck coughed loudly, his breath now laboring.

Chillemi, seated on Maybeck's right, leaned over and grabbed his shoulder. "Hey man, you okay?" he asked.

Maybeck gasped, scratching at his throat. Chaud started to rise from the table to find out what was going on with the man, but stopped when he saw Prophet's look.

"We cannot afford any missteps," he repeated, staring into Chaud's eyes.

Chaud sat back in his chair, his mouth coming open a fraction. Prophet continued to stare at him, and a wave of queasiness hit.

"Mister Maybeck," Prophet said, finally breaking the stare with Chaud to look down at the wheezing man. "Do you know of the jerumba plant?"

Maybeck's eyes grew wide, and he clawed at his throat. His fingernails left red furrows as he gasped for breath.

"The native jerumba plant, as some of you are probably aware," Prophet continued, "secretes a highly-lethal toxin from its flower at the very end of its life each year to dissuade predators from eating it before it goes into hibernation. It's odorless, colorless, and perhaps most deadly, tasteless. Curiously enough, we've found it dissolves in wine even faster than in water, and enters the bloodstream much more quickly with alcohol as the catalyst."

Maybeck struggled to speak. "But...but," he coughed. "Every...body...had...wine..."

Prophet gave a tired smile. "It was already in your glass."

Maybeck gasped again, coughing as his airway spasmed. He looked wildly at the others around him; no one wanted to meet his gaze. Chaud watched helplessly as his man struggled to breathe.

Prophet continued. "The toxin acts on the respiratory system of the predator, and constricts air flow. Which is what you're feeling now." He looked at Zeno and indicated with a small wave for him to refill his glass, which he hastily did.

"After that, to prevent the predator from continuing to eat the plant, the toxin attacks the nervous system. This effectively paralyzes the animal, which then dies slowly from asphyxiation. However," he said as he took a sip of the wine, "with humans being larger than the plant's natural predators, the toxin works much more slowly on the nervous system. So what happens is the predator, in this case you, simply chokes to death, fully aware and cognizant of the situation, able to experience every last painful feeling to its fullest."

Maybeck was pulling at his shirt collar in a desperate attempt to breathe. Chaud watched him as he grabbed Chillemi for support. He stood up from the table and gasped for breath through his closed throat.

Chaud swallowed, but knew deep down it was a necessary demonstration of power and intolerance for poor performance. Maybeck had screwed up the shoot at the university, and if things had gone differently after that, they may have lost some people. And it wasn't his first mistake. As Chaud watched the dying man fall to the floor, gurgling his last breaths, he knew it would be his last mistake.

"Now," Prophet said, looking back at Chaud, "where were we?"

CHAPTER TEN

Gabriel rubbed his eyes as the cobalt blue flash subsided, just a few lingering sparks finishing their last dance in his vision. He worked his jaw until it popped and began to stand up from his cramped seat in the mess, but stopped when he felt a wetness on his shoulder under a weight he didn't remember being there.

"Petty Officer Jimenez!" he said loudly, pushing the man's drooling face away from him and standing.

Jimenez snorted, then tried to shake himself awake, pawing at his face in a daze. Sowers came up behind the groggy man and gave a friendly, though not light, smack on the back of his head.

"Arturo, my man, c'mon," Sowers said. "Can't be napping on the boss. You need to choose your transit seating arrangement better, Sleeping Beauty." He watched as the other man tried to stand up on wobbly knees. "Or is that Bambi?"

Gabriel looked at the spot on the shoulder of his shirt with a grimace. *At least it wasn't Takahashi sitting next to me,* he thought.

As if on cue, retching was heard from the back of the mess, and the team as one turned around to find the ensign bent over the trash can. After a few more painfully loud seconds, he stood up, wiping his mouth with a napkin.

"Stupid infomercials," he said. He pulled the small pink sticker off from behind his ear and flicked it into the trash can.

Gabriel shook his head as he picked up a napkin of his own from the table they sat around and dabbed at the spot. *Here we are,* he thought as he stared at the tiny wallscreen showing a computer-generated image of the green planet at the end of their journey. *Eden.* More memories flooded through his mind, memories he had tried so painfully hard to eliminate. Memories of fire, blackness, loss. Too many men lost. And now he was leading another team back.

He bit down on the skin on the inside of his cheek, hard enough to draw blood. The coppery taste brought back more memories. Images of a screaming child held by one of the terrorists, then the red spray as Tamander's bullet destroyed the terrorist's face. The child rushing into Tamander's arms. The child being escorted from the building to safety. The sound of Tamander's screams as the Geltex burned through his armor.

"Sir?"

The voice next to him shook him from the memories, and he looked over at Specialist Negassi, who was staring at him with a concerned look. He looked over her shoulder at the rest of the team, who were cleaning up scattered plates and cups in preparation to leave the mess. With the exception of Negassi, and a quick glance from Olszewski, none were paying any attention to him. *Most of them are used to my little daydreams,* he thought.

"Sorry, Specialist, just thinking," he said. He didn't get the impression she was buying his answer, so he changed the subject before she could pursue it any further. *No need for the new guys to think the man in charge has issues.*

"Ever been out this far, Negassi?" he asked, pointing to the wallscreen.

"Ah, no sir," she replied, her curiosity forgotten. "Actually, sir, as soon as we cleared the Belt, I was as far as I'd ever been. The only wormholes I've been through, every one of them was on this trip."

Gabriel was caught off guard a bit by her answer. He didn't remember her folio mentioning her lack of interstellar experience. Then again, when one hasn't done something, very rarely would one put that fact on their resumé.

"My goodness, Specialist," he said as he clapped her on the shoulder. "I had no idea. Gentlemen," he called out to the others. "We have in our midst an honest-to-goodness pollywog."

The NAF Navy personnel in the room immediately stopped what they were doing and turned to Negassi with wide smiles. Even Brevik, Gabriel noted, had more of a smile than he had seen on him in a long time.

"Uh oh, sir," she said, staring at the four grinning faces. "Did I do something wrong? What in the world is a pollywog?"

Sowers opened his mouth, his eyes wide with excitement. Gabriel held up a hand before he could speak.

"Hold on, everyone," he said. "This is a combat mission, and we've just entered the target system. We've got some shuteye to grab and a mission briefing in a few hours. We do not have time for the standard Crossing the Line ceremony. Or," he said, fixing Sowers with his gaze, "any other ridiculous, non-sanctioned events you may have in mind."

Sowers snapped his mouth shut and blew through his lips in a raspberry. "Aw, sir, it's tradition!"

Gabriel nodded. "Indeed it is, and we'll do something a little special before we get started with the briefing. But there will be zero tolerance for things like shots of hot sauce, or bathing in pickle juice, or hanging her from a yardarm, if there's even one on board this bucket. And the alcohol will have to be saved for the return flight, understand?"

Three yes sirs answered him. Gabriel looked pointedly at Sowers, who hadn't spoken up. "Mister Sowers?"

"Yes sir," he said reluctantly. "But I get first dibs on the, ah, events, on the return." He looked around the room. "Agreed?" Nodding heads answered him, and a warning stare came from Brevik.

"Wait, what is all this about?" asked Sennett.

"It's just a Navy tradition," Takahashi answered. He took a long drink of water from the bottle he held. "In the old surface Navy, when a sailor crossed a certain point of the globe for the first time, like the equator, prime meridian, Arctic Circle, among others, his or her ship's crew held a ceremony. They called it something along the lines of 'converting the slimy pollywogs to trusty shellbacks', and it just naturally carried over into space." He paused to take another drink. "So now, when a Navy crewman or woman transits a wormhole for the first time, they are initiated into the shellback fraternity. So to speak."

Negassi looked concerned. "But I'm not Navy," she protested.

"Technically, you are, Specialist Negassi," Gabriel said. "You've been attached to this Navy mission, released by the MDF for said mission, so for all intents and purposes, you are Navy. And the two of you?" he asked, looking at the other two MDF soldiers.

Olszewski shook his head. "Did a tour last year as security on a diplomatic mission to Farpoint."

Sennett held up his hands, palms forward. "Same, sir. I've done two wormhole runs, one as a passenger, one as MDF."

Negassi's face fell. "I don't think I like the sound of this."

Sowers laughed. "No worries, we'll be nice. Just think, you'll be an official Navy puke, just like the rest of us."

Gabriel smiled, the memory flashes of Eden finally slipping from his clouded mind. *This trip will be different*, he thought. He was going in with not only a solid team, but also good intel, and actual political backing.

"Wrap it up, folks," he said, waving them to the door. "I need everyone sacking out for at least five hours." He held up his hand at the protests. "Yes, we're all a little cramped.

Make the best of the sleeping arrangements. Take a cue from Mister Jimenez, just fall asleep wherever there's an open shoulder."

Jimenez grimaced. "Yeah, yeah. Sir," he added, tossing off a quick salute as he left the mess. The others followed him as Gabriel called out, "Meet in the rec room at oh-nine-hundred hours ship time for the briefing. And Specialist Negassi, you may want to wear your chest armor."

Negassi looked at him quizzically and opened her mouth, but apparently thought better of it, and simply turned and walked from the mess, shaking her head.

Gabriel gave a small chuckle and followed her out. He palmed the door plate as he left, and the door slid closed behind him.

A soft knock sounded at the man's door. He looked up from his meal in annoyance and set his fork and knife down on the ceramic plate. He took his time in answering, dabbing at his lips with a cloth napkin. Setting the napkin down on the plate, he picked up the glass of red wine and took a sip. *Excellent Argentinian vintage shiraz*, he thought, and a corner of his mouth curled into a small smile. Leaning back in his chair, he looked through the skylight at the three-quarter Earth hanging above. *Soon, we can return. But we must be patient.*

"*Venga*," he said as he set the wine glass down and stood up from his small table. He brushed a few crumbs of bread from his shirt as the door slid aside, admitting Chimo first, followed by Isidoro and Rafael. With the research and planning, and strong will, Chimo had shown over the past several days, he was not surprised to see the two older men showing him more respect than usual.

The man walked over to the living area of his suite, quite lavish by lunar standards, with three overstuffed sofas, a coffee table already set with a samovar of tea and four porcelain teacups. A wallscreen showed a live video feed from the sun setting over the mountains of Patagonia. He sat in the smallest of the three sofas, implying he wished to sit alone, and indicated the other men seat themselves in the others.

Isidoro sat with Rafael on the largest of the sofas, while Chimo politely remained standing.

"Chimo, please have a seat," the man said.

"I'd be happy to serve the tea, uncle," he replied, hands clasped in front of him.

"Nonsense," the man said. He waved at Rafael, who sat closest to the samovar. "Rafa would be more than happy to pour." He caught a glance between Isidoro and Rafael and waited for an argument, but the look disappeared quickly. Rafael picked up the samovar and began pouring tea into each cup. He waited to pour Chimo's last, the man saw. *No matter,* he thought. *Plans unfold according to the plan itself, not the personalities involved.*

The men sipped in silence for several minutes, watching the deep oranges of the sunset turn into red, then purple, then flashing to a deep indigo haze before the mountains disappeared from view.

"Beautiful," Rafael said as he set his teacup down. "Nothing like we have here, that's for sure."

"And nothing like they have on Mars," Isidoro said with a quiet snort.

"And that brings us to the reason I summoned you here," the man said. "Chimo informs me that the first part of his plan…" He paused when he caught another glance from the other two men, but continued. "The first part of his plan has begun as expected. Mars has sent a team, including our esteemed Evan Gabriel, to Eden, because of a combination of good fortune and timing. Chimo?"

The younger man leaned forward, setting his teacup back on its saucer, and looked at the other two men. "Our operation on Eden, as you know, has just been a side project. One we have financed for future interests, in the hope that one day we can gain control of the planet.

However it has been less than successful, until very recently."

He picked up a biscuit from the tray and nibbled at it. "A leader who goes by the name Prophet has organized the individual groups of rebels into a cohesive force, one that over the past few months has made significant inroads. Much more so than just hassling shipments and scaring inhabitants, they have hurt the Eden Guard and have taken several valuable political prisoners. And now, under my, ah, our orders, they have successfully kidnapped the son of the most powerful governor on Mars, Tarif. All this has come together at the right time, and we were prepared for the opportunity. Not lucky." He glanced over at his uncle at the last statement.

The man nodded, again proud of how Chimo had grown, and of his willingness to put himself out there in front of the established players without fear or hesitancy. He watched as his young nephew casually ate the biscuit, and saw the hooded looks from the others. *I'll handle that soon enough.*

"Yes, we are aware of all of this, or at least most of it," said Rafael with a frown. "What does this do for us? What is our next step?"

Chimo smiled. "Tarif is the key. She is the most influential governor of any of the nine. She wields tremendous power within the Mars Central government. She also has the largest population center, Arsia Mons. Put that all together with the fact that she's female, it gives her incredible control over what goes on on Mars."

"What does being female have to do with anything?" Isidoro said testily. He reached over and poured himself more tea.

"Being female gives her power within the female community, by seeing her as a sympathetic underdog, and within the male community by being someone they think they can control. These two vastly different views of her have given her a pillar second to none from which she governs, and from what I've been able to research and find out from our contacts on Mars, the other governors follow her lead, almost unflinchingly."

"And we have her son," said Rafael with a small smile.

"Yes, in a manner of speaking," said Chimo. "The rebel group has him, but they are almost completely financed by us and are dependent on us for new equipment and supplies we smuggle in. We asked them to do this, and they did. So yes, now essentially we hold her son."

"And Gabriel?" asked Isidoro as he reached for a biscuit. "What of him and his team?"

"I won't dismiss him out of hand," said Chimo. "He has proven to be resourceful. However, I have corresponded with this Prophet personally, and I believe they are well-equipped to handle an eight-man squad. We know for a fact the NAF is not sanctioning this mission, and is not providing any matériel or personnel because of political wrangling back on Earth. Tarif wants to send in a small team to extract her son quietly, and she does not expect much resistance. However, we know what the rebels have available to them, and the numbers they possess, two things Tarif does not, so I do believe Gabriel is walking into a situation he will not be able to walk out of alive."

The man leaned forward. "It is time to implement the second phase of the plan. Mars. I will need trusted people to handle this, as it will be a delicate negotiation with the governors to ensure a smooth transition. After all, financial and military backing from the RDS may not be seen by the people already there as the panacea Mars needs. In addition to carefully talking with Tarif about her son's safety, the other governors will need assurances from us. Whether financial, or... motivational."

A few seconds passed before Isidoro realized what the man was saying. "Wait, you are sending us, aren't you?"

The man nodded. "Trusted people," he repeated.

Isidoro tossed his half-eaten biscuit back onto the tray and sat back in the sofa. "Not exactly what I had in mind for this grand plan."

"Nevertheless, you'll be leaving tomorrow morning on a diplomatic shuttle," the man said. "Both of you be ready at the spaceport by eight."

Rafael and Isidoro looked at each other with frustrated expressions. Before either could say a word, Chimo spoke up.

"I have arranged a meeting with Governor Seidell of Eos Chasma for tomorrow evening. You'll be on an HV shuttle, so the flight time is less than ten hours. You'll dock and transfer down on Skyhook Beta into Hartog Station, where a car will be waiting for you to take you to the governor's residence. All of the details of our... offer will be waiting for you on the shuttle. The plan is that Governor Seidell, who is a friend of the RDS from long ago, will arrange the meeting with Tarif. At which time you will present our main offer."

Rafael was rubbing his brow with one hand while crushing a napkin in the other, the man saw. Isidoro sat quietly, a clenched jaw and throbbing vein in his forehead the only indications of his reaction to the news.

"Fine," said Rafael. He flicked the crushed napkin onto the table. "We will handle this. However, as this progresses, I expect to be kept more in the loop on these... these plans." His last words were punctuated by the waving of his hand in the general direction of Chimo.

Isidoro stood up, jaw still clenched. "I'll need to pack, so by your leave?" He turned to the door without waiting for an answer.

Rafael stood up as well, taking a last sip of the cold tea. "Please let us know of any other... changes." He turned and followed Isidoro out of the room.

After the door closed behind them, Chimo turned to his uncle. "I think that went as well as expected, don't you?"

The man had returned his gaze to the wallscreen, which now displayed the stars as seen from the southern hemisphere on Earth. He chose to end every evening with the serene view of the Southern Cross constellation, tonight being no different. As he watched Alpha Crux twinkle, he took one last sip of tea before returning the cup to its saucer on the table.

"Yes, my nephew, as well as could have been expected," he said. "Plans are plans, independent of the people. Make sure this one progresses as we need it to."

"Of course, uncle," replied Chimo. He stood up. "May I help clean up?"

The man smiled. *Always respectful.* His father would be proud of him, if perhaps not so proud of the plot he had put together. A man must throw his own clay. Others may help shape it and contribute to it from time to time, but the final pot would always be created by the man himself. And Chimo was growing to become quite his own man.

"No, Chimo, I will take care of it," he said. "Please, get some rest. Tomorrow may be a slow day for the two of us, but we will have all we can handle in the days to come."

Chimo nodded with a smile. "Good night, uncle. *Buenos sueños.*"

"*Buenos sueños* to you as well."

Chimo left the room, the door sliding closed behind him. The man looked back at the wallscreen and the Southern Cross. The RDS had been hiding for too long, Isidoro was right in that. Now, the sleeping giant begins to awaken. He smiled and poured another cup of tea.

CHAPTER ELEVEN

"Know ye, that Leilani Negassi, heretofore from the Republic of Eritrea, and heretofore from the Mars Defense Force, and lawfully attached to a somewhat-official North American Federation Navy voyage, on this the second day of August in the year of our Lord two thousand, one hundred, and seventy six, aboard the spacious and well-appointed luxury vessel *Lady Cydonia*, did two days ago appear at the wormhole Ryokou, entering into Our Royal Domain, and having been inspected and found worthy by My Royal Staff, was initiated into the Solemn Mysteries of the Ancient Order of Deep Space. I command my subjects to honor and respect her as a true fellow trusty shellback."

Gabriel stepped forward to where Negassi stood in front of the small wallscreen in the rec center. A nearly imperceptible smile was on her face. The rest of the team were at parade-rest, spread out, or as spread out as the cramped rec center could accommodate them, behind him. He reached out and carefully pinned a small badge to Negassi's tunic above her left breast.

"The Royal Staff hereby presents the rare and exclusive Transit Trident in honor of good King Neptune, who even in this waterless void we sail through, always watches over us."

Negassi looked down at the badge, a raised golden three-pronged spear on a black sphere, then back at Gabriel.

"Thank you sir, it will be my honor to wear it proudly."

Gabriel smiled. "Don't thank me yet. The others must show their respect. You did take my advice on the chest armor?"

Negassi's eyes narrowed. "Ah, no sir, I thought…"

Gabriel held up his hand, cutting her off, and stepped back. "Gentlemen, as you please."

One by one the others came forward and gave Negassi a firm but not overly-powerful punch to the badge, after which they shook her hand to welcome her to the fraternity. Brevik went last, and Gabriel watched Negassi's eyes widen as the huge man stepped forward.

"Specialist," Brevik growled. He held up a clenched fist. "Welcome to the club." He opened his fist and reached down and shook her hand.

Negassi smiled, bright white gleaming in her dark face. "Thank you, Lieutenant. In more ways than one." She rubbed her chest with a wince.

Gabriel could have sworn he saw Brevik wink at her, but shook that off as flickering from the ancient wallscreen that had just come to life.

"And with that," Gabriel said, pointing to the screen, "we must begin the official part of this meeting. Briefing you shellbacks on Eden."

The group shuffled to try to arrange themselves around the small card table facing the screen. Brevik stood against the back wall, as did Sowers and Sennett. Gabriel cast an extra glance towards the latter two, hoping no shenanigans would go on. It had only been a couple of days, but already he could sense the beginnings of a potentially dangerous friendship between the two. *At least Jimenez kept Sowers grounded… somewhat.*

Gabriel pressed a button on the remote control he held, and not for the first time, wondered when they'd get decent ship accommodations. The *Marcinko* was ultra-modern, the Chinese ship coming home was a mess, and everything else was just in between for the last six months. As he stabbed harder at the button, trying to get the POS screen to respond, he had a flash of his apartment, lying in the plush bed, the holovision flicking on at a signal from his neuretics. *Damn.*

The screen finally obeyed and Eden appeared. It was a hazy green sphere, criss-crossed with wide rivers, or narrow oceans, depending on how one looked at it. Only a few mountain ranges; Gabriel remembered from his original briefing several years ago that the planet had very little tectonic activity, so no real subduction zones or volcanoes to push up the terrain. Small snow-capped poles were the only other color besides the dominant green landmasses and lines of deep blue. From a distance, it truly lived up to its namesake, at least in the eyes of the team that discovered it over a hundred years ago. However, up close, Gabriel knew it to be much different than it appeared.

"Eden," he said. He pressed another button on the remote, hoping the screen responded. It did, and zoomed in on a large continent in the northern hemisphere. "Not quite as beautiful as it looks from orbit. Or as safe."

He noticed Sennett's eyebrows rise a bit. *Good, he had his attention.*

"Eden, as the original colonists found out the hard way, has a very... unusual flora system. It's hard to explain, but essentially, it's alive," he said.

Several seconds passed before anyone spoke. It was Jimenez who broke the silence. "Uh sir, am I missing something here?"

Gabriel shook his head in response. "No, not necessarily. A lot of us on the first mission asked the same question. The 'of course the flora is alive' reaction." He pressed the button on the remote again, hoping it continued to function. The screen changed to show a shot of a densely-packed jungle: tall trees with brightly-colored leaves, thick tangled vines surrounding the base of each one, with several medium-sized plants scattered between. The jungle floor was made up of random patches of bluish-green thick grass on a brown soil. All in all a peaceful scene, one Gabriel remembered from his briefing years ago. He had thought it looked as if it came off an artist's palette. A scene he knew all too well was incongruous with the onsite experiences he had.

"This shot belies the true nature of the planet, something the long range surveys and probes never picked up. Only when the original colony planners and builders arrived did they find out the jungle that spans most of the habitable part of the planet was very protective of its home. The Eden colony has had a greater percentage of deaths attributed to the jungle itself than any other colony has, for any reason. And that includes the Farpoint conflict that killed a third of the population."

Gabriel knew he had their attention now. Seven faces stared intently at the wallscreen, waiting patiently for him to continue. He pressed the remote button and the image changed, splitting into several equally-sized frames, each showing a different form of plant life. He used the remote's laser pointer function to indicate each frame one by one.

"Razorvine secretes a paralyzing toxin to immobilize its prey, then slowly extracts its bodily fluids. Yellowboles have a symbiotic relationship with their scouts the treemonkeys, who throw the tree's acidic sap at other animals, then bring back the bodies for the trees to absorb into large openings in their trunks. Eden mantraps, similar to flytraps on Earth, only ten times larger, and able to swallow an unprotected person whole. Pincushions, small puffy flowers that can fire poison projectiles over thirty feet when disturbed. Just two or three impacts can bring down a fully-grown man. Babylon creepers, hanging vines that drip a sticky fluid that infects the nasal membranes, causing a severe reaction that can sometimes lead to suffocation. Swamp violets, purplish lilypad type plants that work together to tangle and trip up animals walking through, drown them, and then feed off the nutrients the body leaves as it dissolves in the high pH swamp water."

"Holy shit," said Sowers. "And people live here?"

"Exactly," replied Gabriel. "None of these were spotted in the initial surveys, only the scenic foliage, the world-spanning sea rivers, the cute little furry animals and abundance of sea life, and the nitro/oxy atmosphere. Which is why the colony chose the name of Eden. Now we know better." He looked around the room. "And these are only the six major flora threats. There are countless more minor ones, nuisances mostly, but all potential problems for a ground force."

Several moments of silence passed as the team absorbed the information and stared at the images. Gabriel hoped they were taking it seriously. A fleeting memory flickered across his mind. Campbell's pincushion dart-riddled face as he choked to death, the massive dose of poison too much for his suit's medical systems. The smells returned: the cloying scent of rotting vegetation mixed with burning plastic and metal. He lowered Campbell's lifeless body to the jungle floor, reaching down and closing the young man's eyes. He felt the sting of a dart hit his neck, felt wooziness…

"Commander?" asked Takahashi.

Gabriel shook his head to clear it, realizing he had closed his eyes at the memory. Opening them, he found the entire team now staring at him and not the wallscreen.

"Sir, you okay?" said Sowers, concern creeping into his normally-light voice.

Gabriel took a deep breath and willed the images from his mind. *Dammit,* he thought. *The closer we get to Eden, the more these come back. Too much death…*

"I'm fine, just going over some mistakes we made the first time. No worries," he said, holding up a hand. "We won't be making the same mistakes."

Sennett spoke up. "I know I'm new here, so I may be speaking out of turn, but what happened on the first mission, sir?"

"At ease, Corporal," Brevik rumbled. "It's none of your concern."

Sennett opened his mouth to reply when Gabriel cut in. "No, Lieutenant, it's okay. Matter of fact, I don't think any of you know the full story of the first mission. Not that I've ever bothered to tell you, which is my fault. Honestly," he said, taking another deep breath, "I've never really talked about it with anyone. A shrink would probably have a field day in my head."

"Sir, it doesn't matter…" Takahashi began.

"It does matter." Gabriel interrupted. "We're going in as a team, and you should at the very least know what I went through the first time. What I was dishonorably discharged for." He checked his internal clock. "We've got a few minutes. Grab some coffee."

The seven men and one woman were arranged loosely around the tiny table in the rec room: Brevik standing, the others seated as best they could with the limited space available. The wallscreen had been shut off. Sowers had brought the coffee pot from the mess along with a handful of plastic cups, Jimenez had dragged in a few extra chairs to the protests of the *Lady Cydonia's* crew trying to eat breakfast, and Takahashi had pilfered bagels from a source unknown.

"It was five years ago," said Gabriel as he took sip of coffee. He winced at the taste and the thought of the caffeine he'd be regretting later. "A separatist group had gotten a hold of some heavy weaponry and took over a primary school on Eden, wiping out the small police force Eden had in place. Their stated goal, if I remember the wording correctly, was the 'liberation of our brothers in arms throughout the galaxy.' They were never more specific with their demands, only that they wouldn't hesitate to kill every last child in the school if the NAF didn't release all political prisoners on all known worlds. Pretty lofty goal, I think you'll agree."

He set the cup down and waved off Sowers's attempt to refill it. "There were thirty-seven kids in the school, between the ages of six and eleven, and four teachers. All four teachers were killed...murdered...within five minutes of the assault, and the bodies were thrown into the courtyard of the school as a warning. They gave the NAF forty-eight hours to produce proof that the prisoners had been freed, or they'd start killing the kids."

Olszewski cursed under his breath. Gabriel saw seven sets of eyes all reflecting the anger he had felt hearing the news. It was a universal feeling, he knew. Don't mess with kids.

"My team and I were doing a training mission in the Hodgson system, one gate away, and were by far the closest NAF force to Eden. Word was that the police force on Eden were either dead or in on the assault, so the only choice was for us to be sent in. MacFarland," he spat out the name, "ordered us in, and we boarded the *Damocles* headed for Eden within an hour of the demands being issued. Seven hours later, we were orbiting the planet, and two hours after that, a stealth shuttle landed us a couple of miles from the school." He paused, gritting his teeth. "But we went in without all the proper data."

"The Geltex?" Jimenez asked.

Gabriel nodded. "Yes, I'm sure you heard that in the news. But not all of it." He looked at the three MDF soldiers, who were listening with rapt attention. "We went in unaware of the separatists' ace in the hole. Geltex in its normal form is a fairly-stable solid gelatin explosive, highly powerful but manageable, only able to be detonated with a very specific electric signal," he said. He picked up his coffee cup and downed the cold acidic contents in a quick gulp. "However, what we were not informed of was that they possessed a massive quantity of it, and had somehow been able to modify its molecular structure to form it into a thick, viscous liquid able to be ignited. And they used it against us. Very effectively. We had no defense against it."

He looked down into the empty coffee cup, a distant sound in his mind reminding him of the assault. Tamander's screams as the flaming Geltex poured down onto him from the gymnasium rafters. Flames. Screams. Smoke. Blackness. He shook his head again to clear it. *I have a new team now, I can't let the past affect this mission, or put them in any jeopardy.*

"Of our team of twenty men and women, ten were killed outright by the modified Geltex in the first five minutes of our assault. If we... if I had known about it, the assault would have been done much differently. Five more died inside, two from heavy railgun rounds, another weapon MacFarland so conveniently left out of the briefing. Four more died getting the last of the kids out of the school, and I got pulled out. I thought I was the only survivor, but obviously that wasn't the case."

Jesus, Katoa. How must he have felt, left behind, stranded on Eden for five years, now hostage? Gabriel chewed on his inner cheek, staring at the table top.

"Why would your commander leave out that information?" asked Negassi.

Gabriel looked up from the table, gritting his teeth once again. "Because he was politically ambitious. Come to find out later he had practically begged to lead the mission, even though he knew that with the equipment we had available to us, we stood a very strong chance of being wiped out. He held back that weapon intel from us and destroyed any paper trails that showed he knew in advance, and sent us in. He knew that if the Geltex information was fully known to all parties, the NAF would have either sent in an infantry invasion, or even bombarded from orbit to prevent the terrorists from getting off-planet with it. He couldn't let that happen, or he'd miss out on the glory. He managed from above, never setting foot on the planet, and not only took credit for the success of the rescue, but blamed the deaths of my people on me as commander on the ground."

He reached over and picked up half a bagel, biting into the stale crust and chewing slowly before he continued.

"He was playing both ends from the very beginning. He created his own win-win situation, and came out looking like the savior with a convenient scapegoat. Nothing I was able to prove, so after I asked for a formal investigation, he very publicly ushered me out of active service, while shining his own reputation. His father-in-law's political connections ensured my discharge, and two months later he was awarded his first star as Rear Admiral."

The silence was palpable. Gabriel finished his bagel and looked up at his team. "But we got every last kid out of there," he said. "And I just found out last week that the oldest of them, a boy named Finn, graduated high school two years ahead of schedule and was accepted into my brother's alma mater, Princeton. It's impossible to justify the deaths of nineteen...no, eighteen...of my men and women, not to mention the teachers and police force, but sometimes I suppose there's a little silver lining."

"Wow, sir, that's just..." said Takahashi.

"It's in the past, and we learn from it." Gabriel paused. "I'm actually feeling a little better now that that's out on the table, instead of you guys wondering if I'm going to lose it at any time."

He stood up from the table and brushed the bagel crumbs from his shirt, then refilled his coffee cup.

"Now, speaking of learning from it, let's get into the nuts and bolts of the mission."

He picked up the remote and switched the screen to a satellite image of a compound in the jungle on the banks of one of Eden's massive sea rivers. "This is the terrorist camp, our main objective."

Gabriel saw the other seven all paid close attention to the screen, and Sowers had even pulled out a small paper notebook and pen. "But we're not landing anywhere near it…"

CHAPTER TWELVE

"I don't like this at all, Rafa."

Isidoro floated at the viewport of the high velocity shuttle, staring out into space. Their flight had just come out of the acceleration phase, and the two men in the personnel lounge had eighteen minutes of weightless relief before the shuttle completed its flipover and fired engines for decel. The halfway point of an HV schedule was always the most comfortable; the four hours of 1.4G on either end of it made for a very unpleasant experience, which was why passengers rarely traveled HV runs. The small sparsely-furnished lounge reflected that, with two acceleration couches, a twenty-year old 2D wallscreen, tiny food dispenser, and a cramped head.

Rafael snorted and touched a panel on the arm of the couch, which turned off the wallscreen movie that had been on in the background. "At least we are away from that *cabrón* Chimo," he said. He pushed up from the couch to float towards the ceiling. He reached up and touched the metal surface, planting his feet on the back of the couch, and stretched his back and shoulders. After several pops, he pushed off the ceiling and let his velcroed deck shoes grab the carpet. He reached down to the small table in front of his couch and picked up the tea bulb. He squeezed the last remnants of Earl Grey into his mouth.

Isidoro turned from the viewport, still holding onto the bar beneath it with one hand. "I am still not happy with this. We are clearly being shunted off to the side in this... this grand plan they have." He pushed off the bar and grabbed the arm of one of the couches, then pulled himself down into a seated position.

Rafael flicked the now-empty tea bulb towards the far wall, where it bounced lazily away, floating into the corner of the small lounge. "I'm not happy either. However, that does not mean we are not part of the plan," he said, looking down at the other man. "Nor does it mean we cannot affect the outcome to our benefit."

Isidoro reached for a tube of food paste clipped to the table. "And how do you propose we affect anything they have planned? We will be well over a hundred million miles away."

"Yes, but we will also be in prime position to make valuable contacts with the Mars government. Firsthand. Over a hundred million miles from the two of them, and their plan. That prime position will allow us to modify it, to run the plan as we see fit."

Isidoro swallowed the paste with a grimace. "And what then?"

Rafael looked towards the viewport. A tiny pinpoint of bluish light was all that remained of Earth as the shuttle completed its turn. He exhaled through his nose, regretting again being paired up with the hot-headed Isidoro. He had been a longtime friend since childhood, and they had risen through the ranks of La Republica de Sudamérica together, but while he considered himself more of an intellectual, a planner, Isi was more of a... doer. Follower. And not one for long term thinking.

"We have a meeting set up with Governor Seidell. He is an influential man, but a weak one, one with vices. He has several friends in high places, including Governor Tarif. We need to convince Seidell that it is in his best interest to side with us. Not necessarily the RDS, but us personally. From there, we meet with Tarif and present our demands."

"And?" Isidoro asked again.

"And," Rafael said patiently, "you and I take over the positions of power on Mars, ousting Tarif and Seidell peacefully. Not the RDS under a new charter, but us as governors of the two largest and most influential cities. We can then cut off diplomatic ties with Chimo and his uncle, and as we would then control a significant portion of the population, and ostensibly the military, we can do this legally. What it comes down to is less of a coup and more of an orderly transition in government."

Isidoro frowned, and Rafael could imagine the wheels turning in his head, giving off smoke. "So what you're saying is we proceed with the plan as it was presented to us, but instead of the RDS gaining control, the two of us do? Just the two of us?"

"Precisely, my friend. From there, we can negotiate terms of trade and supply with the RDS, the NAF, and any other government or corporation who wishes to do business with us."

Isidoro still had a dubious look on his face. "But what of Chimo and his uncle?"

Rafael smiled as a tone sounded overhead, indicating two minutes to engine start. "They are stranded on Luna with little to no resources, and down two important men. What could they possibly do?"

Rafael sat down in the adjacent couch and cinched his straps, Isidoro doing the same in his couch.

"You will see," said Rafael. "With Gabriel and his team off-planet, and the governor's son hostage, this will be the quickest change in government in history."

A double tone sounded, and the engines rumbled to life, pressing the two men into the acceleration couches. The empty tea bulb that was discarded earlier flew past Isidoro's ear and impacted on the wall behind him. Conversation ceased as gravity increased, and Rafael closed his eyes to try to get some semblance of sleep before the long evening ahead.

"Welcome to Mars!" said the portly Delmer Seidell, extending his hand as the two stepped through the glass entry doors into Hartog Station's private arrivals lounge. Rafael raised his free hand in greeting, his other towing his carry bag. Isidoro followed, struggling with two awkward wheeled suitcases.

Rafael looked around the sparse lounge, noticing it looked nearly unused. Several spotless chairs and a modern wallscreen in one section, a bar and bistro in another, all devoid of people. He remembered his first trip to Mars, coming in through Skyhook Alpha just outside of Bradbury, and how absurdly busy the terminal was. Here in Beta, it almost appeared they had arrived through Delta, the third and only partially-completed skyhook. But considering that was located nearly halfway across the planet in Huygens, he knew that couldn't be the case.

"Get their bags, will you?" Seidell said over his shoulder to the two men standing behind him, shooing them forward. They rushed around Seidell and grabbed the luggage. One took both of Isidoro's, the other took Rafael's smaller carry bag, then they turned and headed for the lounge exit door.

"Pleasant flight?" asked the governor as he lowered his chubby hand to his side.

Isidoro snorted. "Not quite, but we'll manage. How long until we're at our hotel?"

Seidell's smile widened. "No hotel for you esteemed *caballeros*," he said. He pronounced both L's, making Rafael wince. "You will be my honored guests in the governor's mansion."

Rafael rolled his eyes, not caring if Seidell saw. If he wanted to call the top floor of a residential tenement with the walls blown out between rooms a mansion, so be it. He had done his research on Seidell before departing Luna, and not only did it give him the background he needed to effect the first part of the plan, but also showed him to be a man who preferred to live beyond his means, and over-exaggerate a great many things. Including the loose term of mansion for studio apartments.

He activated his full neuretic systems, making sure they were linked into Mars's network, and checked the local time. "It's four-thirty now. We have a dinner meeting at seven, correct?" he asked.

"Yes, yes, of course," the governor answered. "My car will take you to the mansion, less than twenty minutes away. There we have two suites set up for you with full amenities, even running water showers." He smiled in pride. "Nothing but the best for our Republica de Sudamérica *amigos*, you will see."

Rafael again winced at the man's butchery of the Spanish accent. He had heard grade school children with better pronunciation.

"Ah, a shower. We would be most grateful," said Isidoro. "Can we at least grab a drink on the way?" He cast a longing glance at the bar.

Seidell put his arm on Isidoro's back and led him to the exit door. "My friend, we have the best Mars tequila you have ever laid your taste buds on. And I just so happen to have a bottle of our finest in my car."

He looked back at Rafael, who was walking several steps behind the two. "I am so happy and honored to have you two here. I can't wait to hear your plans for our expansion. I believe we have a very profitable future ahead of us."

Rafael frowned as Seidell turned back and pushed the door open for them. With the information they had on this governor, he'd be an easy mark. Maybe too easy. Perhaps so easy that other governors, including the all-important Tarif, may not hold him in such regard that their plan could proceed smoothly. He only hoped he was wrong on that account. And he certainly wasn't looking forward to Mars-produced tequila.

Dinner was scheduled for seven o'clock local, which meant the weak sun was just setting over the horizon of Eos Chasma, one of Mars's largest cities. Rafael stood on the balcony of his tenth-floor suite, looking out at the dome. It glowed with a purple shimmer, a unique effect generated from a combination of the low sun angle, the low elevation and equatorial location of the city, and the composition of the layered transparent fabric. The local Chasmans, with a large contingent of Dutch settlers, called it *saars nacht*, or purple night. Watching the glow ripple across the sky, he could understand why.

As the sun dipped below the horizon, a deep indigo flash, the *blauw licht*, lit up the sky for a brief few seconds, illuminating the other tenement buildings in the area. That was the traditional time for supper in the city, and a distant bell sounded. For a split second, he was back in his hometown outside of Corrientes, standing on the shore of the Parana River washing clothes, as his grandmother rang the village bell to call the local Catholics to worship. Before the Dark Days' tidal surges had wiped the city from the face of the planet.

Rafael's door buzzed, and the memory faded. He turned and stepped back into his suite, sliding the glass door closed behind him. *Perhaps Mars wasn't such a cesspool,* he thought as he walked across the deep-pile synthetic carpet to the door. *It has potential... I could get used to this.*

He palmed the door plate and it slid aside, revealing Isidoro, face red with rage.

"Come in *mi amigo*," Rafael said. He stepped aside to let the sputtering man in.

"What the hell is going on here, Rafa?" Isidoro said as he paced back and forth in the suite, gesturing with his hands.

Rafael walked over to the bar arrangement Seidell had installed for him and picked up his glass of bourbon. "Whatever do you mean?

"This! All of this!" Isidoro said, pointing to the bar. "He's falling over himself to please us. And now we have to drop the hammer, as they say? How is that supposed to work? Are we being set up? *Dios mio*, I have rose petals on my bed!"

"Relax, Isi," he replied. He sipped the bourbon. Imitation, most likely synthesized locally from molysugar and aged in plastic containers lined with a handful of oak chips imported from Earth, but not bad considering. "Seidell is a moron and a malleable one at that. Ignore the frivolities he is providing us with. We have business to attend to this evening, and he will agree to our terms, regardless of what he is giving us. He is under the impression we will be partners, and he wants the RDS money to continue to flow."

Isidoro stood with his hands on his hips. "But how are we going to go forward with the Tarif request if we crush Seidell now?"

"Leave that to me," Rafael said. He finished off his bourbon and set the glass back on the bar. "Straighten your tie. We need to leave."

Isidoro frowned. He walked to the mirror over the bar and adjusted his tie and collar. "This had better work," he said.

"Don't worry. Just don't drink too much."

Rafael walked back to the door and palmed it open, and the two men walked out into the hall.

Steve Umstead

CHAPTER THIRTEEN

The *Lady Cydonia's* surface shuttle screamed across the atmosphere of Eden, leaving a trail of superheated ions in its wake. Gabriel sat in the rearmost row of the twelve-seater craft, looking out one of the few tiny viewports. He imagined treemonkeys chattering and pointing upwards at the fiery line as the shuttle streaked overhead. Treemonkeys. And the acid sap. He idly rubbed at the back of his neck. The small burn mark, raised just slightly from the rest of his skin, was another physical reminder of his last trip here.

The shuttle rumbled and creaked, shaking violently every few seconds as the air thickened. He looked around the cabin at the rest of his team. Several of them had their faces pressed up against the plasteel ports, peering down at the planet. He saw Sowers in the adjacent row peering around Takahashi's head to get a view, Olszewski in the row ahead of them staring out with his mouth open, and Brevik, as usual, fast asleep in the front row. *The man could sleep through anything,* he thought. He looked at the back of Sennett's head, and for a second a brief image of Tamander flashed through his mind, a young man very similar in appearance and age to the corporal, one who had died in horrific manner in the initial assault five years ago.

The images were coming harder and faster the closer they got to landing. The memory removal surgeries he underwent several years ago had proved themselves terribly unreliable. However, the images didn't burn, didn't ache, the way they once did. Perhaps because he had exorcised many of those demons, including Santander himself (helped along greatly with the assistance of his brother Zack on Poliahu), but also because he had finally decided to talk about it, and talk about it to the people he trusted the most. He had discussed generalities with Renay a while back, but not specifics. He still wasn't sure if he'd ever get into those details with her, but telling his team, letting those images be shared with others who understood the death, the confusion, the chaos of battle... helped. Even the scar on his leg from the assault didn't itch anymore.

"All hands, prepare for landing!" called the pilot. A loud beeping tone was sounding in the background of the static-filled intercom before it clicked off. The shuttle banged from side to side, and an overhead compartment opened, allowing a bundle of equipment to crash to the floor.

Sowers turned from his craned view out the window to face Gabriel, a theatrical look of horror on his face. "Sir, tell my wife... tell Naomi I love her!"

"Her name was Nairomi, and I don't think she'll miss you, considering you were in the company of Talitha when you asked for her hand." Gabriel shook his head. "Settle down, Petty Officer, plenty of excitement ahead of us."

"Ah, Talitha," Sowers said, pressing his head back into the headrest as the shuttle dropped in a pocket of low density air. "I should have asked her instead."

Gabriel looked back out of his viewport and watched as the jungle coalesced from a high-speed blur into individual trees as the shuttle slowed to landing speed and engaged its ventral thrusters. With the exception of a few newly-constructed buildings in and around the small spaceport in Eden City, the view from above was eerily similar to his last landing. But unlike last time, he had all the information he needed. *At least I hope I do.*

The shuttle's forward movement ceased, and it settled vertically on its thrusters onto the landing pad. With an audible thump and one last shake of the cabin, landing was complete, and the team one by one stood and retrieved their belongings. The hatch door slid open with a hiss, and thick steamy air wafted into the cabin. Gabriel brought up the rear exiting as the six other men and one woman walked through the hatchway, into Eden.

The main terminal in Eden City Spaceport hadn't changed a bit in the five years since Gabriel had been there. Small, sparse, and barely worth the title of terminal, let alone main. One small desk where the immigration officer sat, one threat detector arch for arrivals and departures to walk through, two Eden Guards on duty, and a few dozen folding metal chairs arranged haphazardly facing a large window overlooking the solitary landing platform. Even the term spaceport was a little grandiose, Gabriel had thought the first time he had arrived.

As the eight walked in from the pad area, Gabriel closed the manual door behind him, shutting out the sounds of the shuttle engines spooling back up for the return flight. The *Lady Cydonia* was sticking around in orbit, ostensibly for R&R, but the team didn't want the shuttle on the ground in case the operation went south. As pessimistic as the policy sounded to Gabriel, it was prudent: the less evidence on-site, the better.

The immigration officer glanced up from his flexscreen with a look of surprise on his face.

"Ah, excuse me folks," he said. He rose from his seat and set down the flexscreen on the small desk. "Who are you?"

The Eden Guards that had been lounging near the arch stood up straight, eyeing the newcomers. Gabriel took a quick glance around the terminal, noting that barely a handful of passengers were in chairs awaiting departing flights or arriving friends and family, and was thankful for their early morning local time arrival.

He stepped to the front of the group and up to the man's desk, extending his hand. "Commander Evan Gabriel, NAF Navy. My team and I are here at the request of Prime Minister Howarth, personal reasons. Not an official visit."

The immigration officer eyed Gabriel's hand warily, then finally shook it. Gabriel glanced over at the Guards, who were both standing with their hands resting on the trigger pads of the assault rifles slung across their chests. Safeties still on, he noticed, but that could quickly change. He needed to handle this as quickly as possible; several eyes in the waiting area were watching them now.

"We were not informed of any visit, personal or official, Commander," the officer said. "The only thing I have on the schedule for your flight is one deliveryman and about fifteen hundred pounds of meat cargo."

"I would be your deliveryman, and this," he waved over his shoulder at the other seven members of the team, all standing in relaxed positions holding various bags, "would be fifteen hundred pounds of meat."

One of the Guards snorted out a laugh, then coughed to cover it up, earning a warning glance from the other.

"Ah, Commander," the officer replied as he looked over at the seven soldiers. "I'm going to need to call this in."

Gabriel nodded. "Of course. Actually, I'd appreciate it if you can call the Prime Minister directly, as again this is a personal matter."

"I can't…"

"Here," said Gabriel. He handed him a small sheet of hardcopy. "This is his comm code. He's expecting your call."

The officer took the sheet and looked at it with a frown. He looked over at the Guards, who stood expressionless, then back at Gabriel. "Well, I suppose…"

"Thank you, again I appreciate that. If you would be so kind as to call now? We are in a bit of a hurry."

The officer took one last glance at the other seven, then nodded. "Certainly, sir." He turned back to his desk, picked up the comm, and placed the phone bug in his ear.

Gabriel walked over to the two Guards just on the other side of the detector arch. "No worries, gentlemen. We'll be out of your hair in no time."

The ranking Guard, a sergeant Gabriel noted by the three stripes, replied, "I don't mind, sir. It's been a little slow in terms of arrivals, as you can imagine."

The other Guard spoke in hushed tones. "Are you here because of the... terrorists?"

Gabriel shook his head. "You know I can't discuss that. We're here to see the Prime Minister for personal reasons. Anything else is just speculation." He leaned in closer to the two men, all three of them now congregated around the arch: two on one side, one on the other. "How are the Guards holding up?"

The sergeant frowned. "As well as we can, considering. We've lost six men and women in the past month, and the government hasn't even declared this as an official conflict. You're the first support we're receiving. I know," he held up his hand, "unofficially. But unofficially, we appreciate you being here."

Gabriel had his neuretics run a quick scan of the two men. The results popped up in his Mindseye. "You both have Level Three mil-rets. Do me a favor and open up a pipe. I'd like to set up a secure link with the two of you, along with a few other Guards we are scheduled to meet up with. Unofficially, of course."

The two men complied, and Gabriel had his systems create a cipher comm link. Both men nodded as they received the codes.

"Thank you, sir," the sergeant said as he extended his hand through the arch. Gabriel took it. The detector remained dormant, not picking up any sign of his enhanced combat muscles or upgraded neuretics.

"Absolutely, Sergeant, we're all in this together."

The immigration officer set the comm back down on his desk. "Commander, you're all set," he said as he waved the other seven forward. "You've been cleared to proceed, and the Prime Minister sends his regards, as well as a groundtruck for you."

"Thank you again for your expediency," Gabriel said. Turning back to the two Guards, he pointed casually to the arch. "Any reason we need to strip down?"

The sergeant gave a small laugh. "No sir, it hasn't been that slow that we need that type of show. Please, you and your men…"

"Ahem," Negassi said from the middle of the group.

"Sorry, you and your men, and *lady*," the sergeant continued, nodding his head in her direction, "head on through."

"Appreciate it, Sergeant. Let's go folks, we've got a truck waiting for us." He waved them forward and through the arch, which beeped softly as each passed. As Brevik brought up the rear, Gabriel shook the immigration officer's hand again. "Thanks again."

"No problem, Commander. Right outside the main door, you'll find…"

"I've got it," Gabriel said as he turned to the arch. "It's like old times." Speaking these words, an image of a burning gymnasium flashed through his head. *Not this time*, he thought.

<<<<<>>>>>

As the outer terminal door closed behind the group, a man seated in one of the folding chairs got up and made his way to the rest room, stepping around a sleeping woman. He pushed open the door to the rest room, entered, and opened one of the stall doors.

Sitting on the commode, he pulled out a pencil-thin plastic comm unit and activated it. After a few seconds, a tiny red light on the unit illuminated. The man spoke softly into it.

"They have arrived. Team of eight, cargo undetermined. Private transport to Government House."

He waited until the light turned a pale blue. He switched off the unit, stood up from the commode, dropped the unit into it, and flushed. He watched until the comm disappeared completely before exiting the stall.

He turned on the water, rinsed his hands under the stream, and splashed some on his face. Looking in the mirror, he saw the drawn, haggard, sad face that stared back at him. This was his last mission, Prophet had promised. No more spying, no more deceit. His family would be released, he had assured him. He blew out a breath and picked up a towel from the rack, drying his face.

He turned to leave and tossed the towel into the receptacle near the door, then was nearly hit by the door opening inwards.

"Oh, sorry," he mumbled as he stepped back. He was surprised to see it was the sleeping woman he had passed by earlier in the waiting area.

"Uh, ma'am, I think you have the wrong..."

The woman reached out and touched his neck, and he felt a sharp sting. He reached up to grab her hand, but it felt like he was moving underwater.

"What..." he said as his knees gave out on him, sending him crashing to the floor. He looked out from heavy-lidded eyes to see the door close behind the woman as she left. He thought of his family as his vision faded to black.

Steve Umstead

CHAPTER FOURTEEN

"Eleven hours," said Chaud, highlighting an icon on the flatscreen.

Chaud and three other men were in Prophet's quarters, going over the data received from covert probes scattered throughout Eden City and the surrounding areas. Chaud had received the call from their man in the airport, who had served his final mission well. They knew now that Gabriel and his team had arrived, and were on their way to Government House.

"Eleven hours," he repeated. "That's our best estimate of when Gabriel would be here, if we assume they leave first thing tomorrow morning."

"Estimate?" asked Prophet, arching an eyebrow.

Chaud nodded. "Yes, sir, that's the best we can do. Our man inside Government House should be able to notify us when they depart. And obviously they'll be coming on foot. Dusk would be the earliest they can get here, and we're basing that on the assumption that they will not want to be walking the jungle after dark."

Prophet rubbed his chin as he looked down at the table's flatscreen the five men stood around. Chaud watched him stare at the screen, and could almost hear the gears turning in the man's head. Their leader had shown a knack for timing, a very important facet of planning, which had helped them tremendously in the past few years. Chaud worried that he'd be overruled on the timing estimate, his biggest worry when putting together the plan earlier in the evening.

Chaud looked over at Zeno, standing to Prophet's right, and caught him glancing back. Like before the previous night's dinner incident, he got the impression Zeno was afraid, worried about something. He gave a small nod to the other man, who returned it, then cast his gaze back to the table.

After a few seconds more of rubbing his chin, Prophet finally spoke. "I concur. Captain, I believe your estimate of eleven hours is right on target. I'd probably say more like twelve, but we can err on the side of caution. Having read up on Commander Gabriel, I think it's safe to say he'll want to get on the road. What little roads there are. And yes, I agree. They will not move at night." He turned to Zeno. "The captain has taken care of the onsite personnel. Zeno, please fill us in on what you have put together for Gabriel and his team during their journey."

Zeno cleared his throat. "Well, sir, we have several barriers in place, in addition to our sensors. They will have only one passable route in from Eden City."

He leaned over and tapped a few icons on the table's surface. On the screen, an image of the surface of Eden appeared, and zoomed in on Eden City. It panned back slightly, showing their compound on the banks of the Gihon Sea River. A jagged white line appeared between the two, meandering through the jungle, skirting a few small tributaries of the Gihon as well as the edge of the Cherubim Mountains.

"It will be slow going for them, no doubt, as we all know from our own strikes on Eden City and the surrounding area. It's thick jungle all the way, no chance of groundcar transport, and with the heavy yellowbole canopy, no chance of an airdrop either. Captain Chaud is correct in saying it'll be many hours until they reach us."

He tapped a few more icons, and small yellow dots illuminated along the route.

"These are our active sensors, and these," he said as several more dots glowed red, "are our automated sentries. Fully armed, I believe they'll give Gabriel more than enough to handle. With those supplementing the natural forces inherent in Eden's jungle, I don't believe many will make it through to even surrender to Chaud's men."

Prophet stared at the screen for over a minute, during which no one spoke. Chaud looked at the other faces around the table: Zeno, Davitz, Chillemi, and Harvin. Long time trusted allies of his, all of whom, including himself, having pledged their loyalty to Prophet several years ago. Something about this operation, something about Gabriel's reputation, had Chaud worried, and perhaps that's what Zeno was afraid of. Maybe not necessarily Gabriel and his team, but maybe more of what Prophet would do, how he would react, who he would take his frustrations out on, if the operation failed in any way.

"Fine," said Prophet. "I like the plan. Make sure that everything is in place here with the systems, and tomorrow afternoon, Davitz, I want you to bring Jeromy Tarif here. I want him nearby when the operation is complete. I have a message that needs to be sent not only to Eden's government but further along as well."

Prophet stepped back from the table and the door opened, Chaud assumed, by neuretic command.

"Thank you for coming. I trust that everything will go off without a hitch. I'm going to get some rest, I suggest you have your men do the same. Tomorrow will be a long day. Chaud," he said, looking at the captain. "Take Davitz and go check on the hostages. I don't want anything happening to our precious cargo before our friends arrive."

With that, he turned from the others and walked into an adjoining room, signaling the end of the meeting.

"Jeromy, I still don't understand."

Jeromy looked up from the book he was reading at the sound of Magali's weak voice. She sat to his right, squatting on the dirt floor of the dilapidated prefab housing unit the thirty some-odd hostages had called home for the past week. She stared at the ground, as he had watched her do since they had been escorted into the building. The tear tracks on her face were dry now, but struck him as being almost permanent. He had gotten used to her crying, used to comforting her, but he didn't think he'd ever get used to her sad, tear-streaked face.

He glanced around the cramped common room; eight others were in the room in similar states of apathy. Of the group, Jeromy was most worried about the young Mowab, who sat in a corner rocking back and forth, mumbling something in his native Hebrew tongue, eyes squeezed shut. He hadn't eaten since they arrived, only drank water. *Even Magali was in better shape than he was,* he thought.

He set the book, a worn paperback he had found stuffed under a bedroll in the sleeping quarters, down on the ground. *Loose Ends*, the faded yellow title said. He idly wondered, and not for the first time, what happened to its original owner. Perhaps he was a loose end.

He reached over and took Magali's cold hand. Her gaze didn't shift from the floor, but he felt her hand squeeze.

"You still with me?" he said, squeezing back.

A corner of her mouth ticked up briefly, then settled back into the grim line it had been set in for many days. "Why are they holding us? What can we possibly offer them?"

He shuffled his body over to sit in front of her, taking her other hand. "Mag, we talked about this. They're terrorists, barbarians. Nothing more. We're just leverage."

She shook her head vigorously. "No, no, no. Not we. It's you, isn't it? They're going to kill you."

He sat back on his haunches, feeling slightly stunned. This was the first time her misery had gone in this direction, and it caught him off guard. He let go of one of her hands, and reached up to her chin, pulling her face up to meet his.

"Shhh, don't say that," he said. "We're going to be fine. Remember I promised?"

She took his hand from her chin and put it on her cheek, at last lifting her gaze from the ground.

"Yes you did, and I'm holding you to that," she said, and a vestige of a smile leaked through. "But who will take care of you? It's your mother's position, right?"

He nodded. "Most likely, but she's light years away. I can't imagine…"

A loud "*Yeshua*!" came from Mowab, and Jeromy winced. The prayers were one thing, but the random shouts were putting the entire group on edge. He started to rise to talk to the young student, but Magali held his hands fast, pulling him back.

"Don't," she said softly. "Just let him go. We're all dealing with this in different ways."

He looked into her red-rimmed hazel eyes. "And you?"

A genuine smile creased her dirty face. "I'm… better. I trust you, Jeromy. No one else here. You. And you promised."

He returned the smile, feeling warmth seep back into her hands. "And here I thought we were just lab partners."

He started to lean in to give her a hug, but the main door crashed open, and the greenish filtered light of the jungle spilled into the windowless room. He turned to see the silhouette of Chaud, reminding him of the same doorway silhouette he had seen at the university a few days ago. Right after his men killed the Guard corporal and threw his body down the steps.

Another man accompanied Chaud; Jeromy knew from day one that none of the terrorists ever came in alone.

Another hostage named Baker, an Eden Guard that had been captured several weeks prior, told him that he and a fellow Guard had jumped one of the terrorists who had come in by himself, and laid a pretty good beating on him before others had rushed in and subdued the two Guards. Baker said he never saw the other Eden Guard again, and Jeromy remembered the terrible angle at which one of Baker's arms hung, and the difficulty he had in speaking through a cracked jaw. He had spread the word to his fellow students and two instructors to not stir up any trouble. If Eden Guards couldn't break out of here, what good could a bunch of college kids do?

Chaud took a couple of steps into the room, allowing the other in behind him.

"Davitz," Chaud said, hands on hips. "Watch them, I need to do a head count of the military prisoners."

The other man gave Jeromy a sneer as Chaud walked through the open doorway into the sleeping quarters and disappeared from sight.

"*Goel!*" yelled Mowab, continuing to rock.

Davitz cast an annoyed glance at the student, shaking his head. "Mister Tarif," he said as he strode up to where Jeromy and Magali sat.

Jeromy looked up at him, then back at Magali. He gave her a reassuring smile and squeezed her hands, then stood up to face the other man. Davitz outweighed him by a solid fifty pounds and at least four inches, so even drawing himself up to full height didn't make much of a show of force. Davitz peered down on him with a tired look.

"Tarif, you'll be accompanying us tomorrow afternoon, as a special guest of Prophet," he said. "Consider yourself lucky, you won't need to sleep in this rathole tomorrow night."

Jeromy looked up at Davitz. "I'd prefer this rathole to your rats any day. If it's all the same to you, I'll stay here."

Davitz laughed. "Brave little man. No, it's not all the same to me," he said. He gave Jeromy a light shove in the chest.

Jeromy moved quickly, more quickly than even he himself thought possible. His left hand flashed out and grabbed Davitz's forearm as the other man's hand touched his chest, and he turned his body the opposite direction. His right hand shot forward to Davitz's throat, fingers tightly locked in a chop. As his fingertips approached the vulnerable soft spot below the chin, Davitz's other hand snapped up and caught Jeromy's wrist, twisting it violently. He staggered backwards, trying to ease the pain of the twisting motion, and dropped to one knee.

"Jeromy!" screamed Magali as his vision clouded over with pain. The twisting continued for another long second, then eased. He looked up at Davitz, only to see the other man's fist crash into his cheek. He collapsed to the floor, stars swimming in his eyes.

Magali screamed again and crawled over to him. He felt a stickiness on his lips and a numbness in his jaw. A brief flash of Baker's mangled jaw crossed his mind as he pushed himself up to all fours. He ran his tongue around the inside of his mouth, then spit out a bloody tooth.

"Don't screw with me, kid," Davitz said, giving him a solid kick in the ribs.

Jeromy rolled over on his side. He gasped for breath as the impact of Davitz's foot reverberated throughout his stomach and chest. Magali leaned over him and cradled his head on her knees. He looked up into her face, and saw fresh tears running down the familiar dried streaks. He coughed and looked back at Davitz, who stood rubbing his fist.

"You...need...me," he said, wincing with each word.

Chaud came in from the other room. "Davitz, stand down!" he yelled. Walking up to the groaning Tarif, he said, "You overestimate your worth, kid." He looked around the room, then back at Davitz. "Leave him be," he said. He pointed at Mowab, who was mumbling under his breath. "Take the loud one out to the workout area. Some of the others could use some hand-to-hand combat training."

"No!" screamed Magali as she grabbed Jeromy's shoulders.

Jeromy looked up helplessly, his breath still coming in gasps. "Don't...he's...just..."

"You're correct Tarif, we need you," Chaud said as he turned for the door. "But I don't need most of the others. Do what I say, you hear me?"

Davitz walked over to Mowab and picked the smaller man up by his upper arms. His legs wobbled, and Jeromy's woozy mind noted that was the first time he had seen him stand since they arrived. Mowab continued to chant and mumble, now looking up at the ceiling and swaying his head back and forth. Jeromy watched as Davitz marched the young man out the main door behind Chaud, and rage grew like a wildfire in his chest.

CHAPTER FIFTEEN

Isidoro and Rafael walked into the governor's office promptly at seven o'clock Mars time, as requested. The governor sat at his desk in front of a large picture window. It looked out over the Eos Chasma plain and monorail tube that connected the dome with the massive scientific complex and farms located closer to the center of Valles Marineris. He was sipping a cup of coffee, Rafael assumed from the steam rising from the small cup, and had a plate covered in crumbs at his other hand.

Upon seeing the two men enter, Seidell set the cup down on the saucer with an audible clink and stood from the desk, brushing a few stray crumbs from his shirt. He stepped around the desk and extended his hand.

"*Señors*, thank you for coming," he said. "I trust your accommodations are satisfactory?"

Rafael took the chubby hand, looking with disdain at the governor's crumb-covered, untucked shirt and ugly tie. *This is our valued contact?* he thought.

"*Sí*, of course, Governor. They are quite satisfactory."

"Perhaps too much so," said Isidoro next to him.

The governor laughed. "Ah, I'm guessing you took advantage of the in-suite massage therapist?"

Rafael felt more than saw his partner's frown, noticing the other man shifting his feet impatiently.

"No, I did not, and that's not necessary," Isidoro said gruffly. "And for that matter..."

Rafael cleared his throat. "Governor, we do have some business to attend to. Do you mind?"

"Ah yes," Seidell said. "Business." He indicated plush chairs surrounding a stone coffee table. "Have a seat, my SAR... er, RDS amigos. Sorry, I get those letters confused... you say things backwards."

The three men sat, and Rafael noticed Seidell's far-off look. Neuretic comm, he guessed. Within a few seconds, the door they had come in through opened again, and the young assistant they had passed outside entered, carrying a tray of coffees, teas, and biscuits. She set the tray on the table and left without a word.

Rafael watched as Seidell's eyes followed the young woman from the room. Hungry eyes. Predator eyes. His insides churned at the memory of the briefing they had gone over during the shuttle flight. The information Chimo had provided on their...ally...was curious at best, disgusting at worst. It was this information that was the beginning of their plan. Rafael was not comfortable discussing it but knew it to be necessary.

"Governor," Rafael said as he reached for a coffee cup. "We have come a long way, in a most uncomfortable fashion, to speak to you about an issue of great importance. An issue regarding your governance of Eos Chasma."

He sprinkled a packet of real cane sugar into his cup, idly noting the governor had certainly not been spending their support money wisely. In-suite bars and massage therapists, silver coffee tray and imported sugar, Mars granite table, crushed velvet chair cushions. The man had a taste for the expensive. And that taste made him an excellent first contact.

"My governance?" Seidell asked, cocking his head to one side. The rolls of fat around his jowls bunched up like a deflated inner tube.

Rafael sipped from the cup. Colombian. *Yes, a taste for the expensive.*

"Yes, governance. It has come to our attention that you have certain... debts. Debts with La Republica de Sudamérica, with some known felons, and probably unknown felons."

He reached into his jacket pocket and withdrew a flexscreen tube. Seidell's eyes grew larger as he watched Rafael extend the screen.

Rafael tapped at a few virtual icons on the screen, then turned the screen around and placed it on the table in front of Seidell. Isidoro idly munched at a biscuit, watching the scene play out. Rafael hoped Isi would maintain a level of composure as they went through this. One false step, one ill-timed angry yell, and it could all fall apart, and they'd find themselves being shoved out of an airlock onto Mars's dusty red surface.

Seidell leaned over to look at the screen. A few crumbs that remained on his shirt fell onto the table. Rafael watched as the man's eyes scanned back and forth over the readouts he had called up. After a few seconds, the governor leaned back in his chair.

"I can explain," he said. "Those are routine transactions, carried out by people in my staff, and are for necessary equipment and personnel to keep the city running." He ran a finger around inside his tight collar, then unbuttoned the top button and loosened his tie. "There are invoices for weapons, supplies, the usual."

Rafael reached out and took the flexscreen back. "Some are, yes. However, many of those line items are codes. Substitutions for the actual product you are using our money for."

Seidell cleared his throat as he reached for his cup of coffee. "No, that's not true. I'm not sure where you got your information from, but I can assure you, all of the monies you have so generously sent to us have been used properly. Things like..."

"Things like covering gambling debts?" Isidoro asked in a sharp tone.

Rafael raised his hand to settle Isidoro down. "My friend is correct. Many of these invoices are for vaporware. And you know it, Governor. We have full paper trails on over half a million in gambling losses that you have billed us for under various false items, burying them within larger, normal invoices."

Seidell started to speak, but Rafael cut him off. "Stop. I'm not here to screw around. We have more important things to talk about. I need you to realize that we know of these lies. However, these lies are minor compared to the other piece of information I have. Information that could not only destroy you, but bring down your entire government and the city around it."

"Sick bastard," Isidoro muttered.

Seidell looked from one man to the other, his eyes growing even wider. "What are you talking about?"

Rafael tapped an icon on the flexscreen and passed it back to him. "Your habits."

Seidell took the flexscreen and brought it closer to his face. Rafael wondered if his eyes would pop right out of the man's head, they were so wide. He watched as the governor stared at the screen, and saw sweat begin to bead on the man's upper lip.

"Scroll to the left. There are many more," said Rafael in a low voice.

Seidell swiped his fingers across the screen as more and more sweat appeared on his face. His forehead was now soaked.

"Where...where did you get these?" he asked weakly. The flexscreen shook in his hands.

"Doesn't really matter, does it?" Rafael replied. "The point is, we have them. As do our people back on Luna and

Earth. And we won't hesitate to use them if it becomes necessary. Pictures like these, in full color, full holo glory, could ruin everything you've worked for here. And everything you've done your entire career."

"Not to mention what it would do to your wife and children," Isidoro rumbled.

Seidell closed the flexscreen and handed it back to Rafael. He sat back in the chair and dabbed at his face with a napkin. Rafael could feel the tension in the room, the palpable silence as he waited for the governor to respond. As always in negotiations, Rafael knew, once the offer, or in this case the evidence, was presented, the next person to speak loses.

Seconds turned into minutes as Seidell stared at the table. Rafael had his neuretic security system monitor for any outgoing comm calls, but the airwaves were as silent as the conversation.

Finally, the governor spoke. "I understand," he said, his voice barely above a whisper. "You want me out. I will go. Just... just give me a few days."

Isidoro barked a laugh. "No, you fat son of a bitch, we don't want you out. We're here to be your new partners!"

Rafael grimaced at the outburst, but the tone and angry words didn't faze Seidell, who continued to stare at the table. More long seconds ticked by, then Seidell's head came up in a jerk.

"Wait, what? Partners?" he asked, his voice coming back.

Rafael pocketed the flexscreen tube and pulled out a paper envelope from his other jacket pocket. He opened it slowly, enjoying the nervous Seidell's face watching his every move.

"Yes, Governor. Partners," Rafael said. "I have with me a formal Transition of Power document, which will cede the governorship of the Eos Chasma Dome to Isidoro Montañez, effective immediately. The reason for this, as stated on the document, is you have decided to step down because of personal and health issues, and wish to spend more time with your family. Señor Montañez, as a representative of Eos Chasma's strong allies in the RDS, will take over the responsibilities and tasks of the Governor's Office and will continue to weed out corruption, create jobs, and help grow the dome to its fullest potential. You will continue as an adviser to the governor, and will retain the nominal title of Vice Governor."

Seidell's mouth had dropped open at Rafael's mention of the transition document, something Rafael knew had only been used in a handful of rare cases in colonial history. Again, he waited for Seidell.

"I don't understand. You want to keep me here?"

"Yes, yes," said Isidoro impatiently. "Are you not getting this?" He reached for another biscuit. "We need you around to smooth over your people. This is a peaceful transition, not a coup. Get it? And we trust you now, fully. Now that you know what we have on you, I do believe we'll be very strong partners, *sí*?"

Seidell rolled his head back over the top of the chair, staring at the ceiling. Rafael noticed blotchy red patches beginning to appear on the man's skin, and hoped a heart attack wasn't imminent. They needed the fat man around, at least for a little while. He had one more job to do.

"Governor. Or should I say Vice Governor," said Rafael. "There is one more thing. After you sign the document, of course."

Seidell groaned, continuing to stare at the ceiling. "What?"

"We need you to set up a meeting with Governor Tarif."

Seidell's head popped upright. The color ran from his face, and the blotchy patches cleared up almost instantly.

"Wh..why? You're not going to tell her all of this, are you?"

Rafael smiled a toothy smile. "No, not unless you force our hand, no." He picked up his coffee cup. "We need to meet with her about a similar subject."

For the first time since the two men walked in, Seidell smiled. "Tarif? She's untouchable. She's the true power on Mars. What could you or the RDS possibly have on her?"

Isidoro smiled back, and Seidell's disappeared quickly. "Oh, I think you'd be surprised. What we have on you is damaging to say the least. What we have to discuss with Governor Tarif, however, is potentially devastating."

"Get it set up," Rafael said sternly. "Right away. I don't care what you have to do, what strings you have to pull, what courier you need to send, or what diplomat you need to buy off. Get it set up. For tomorrow night. Are we clear?"

Seidell gritted his teeth, and Rafael saw his temple throbbing, the red returning to his face. After a long pause, the governor, soon to be ex-governor, replied, "I'll take care of it."

He stood up from the table and took the document from Rafael, then turned back to his desk.

"Now, if you... gentlemen will excuse me, I have some papers to take care of. Please," he said, waving over his shoulder, "let yourselves out."

Rafael stood from the table and set his coffee cup down, Isidoro doing the same.

"A pleasure doing business with you, Vice Governor," Rafael said, and the two men turned for the door, leaving a visibly distraught Seidell sitting at his custom-made Marswood desk.

Steve Umstead

CHAPTER SIXTEEN

The groundtruck was nothing more than an open-air version of an ancient twenty-first century electric delivery truck, but instead of cargo or mail, this one delivered personnel. The cab up front seated three across, but for this trip only the driver and Gabriel took up the bench seat. In the open bed of the truck, two benches ran down either side with railings protecting the occupants, in this case the other seven members of the team, from falling out. And considering the condition of the roadway they drove on, Gabriel was glad his team had the railings.

At first glance, the road appeared to be a wooden boardwalk from an old seaside resort on Earth. In actuality, Gabriel remembered from his last trip here, it was solid steelroot planking laid down on top of hard-packed soil. Eden was extremely mineral-poor; most of the infrastructure of the city was either created using easy-to-manufacture plastics or drawn from the living jungle. The wood of the steelroot tree was as hard as carbon steel, and nearly as durable as ceramacrete. Considering the exorbitant cost to transport large quantities of heavy ceramacrete ingredients across several star systems, wooden decking was an easy choice. However, as the truck bounced over another worn patch, Gabriel wondered if it was the smartest long-term plan.

The driver seemed to read his mind. "Sorry, sir, we're long overdue for a road refurbishment. Just don't have the cash, know what I mean?"

Gabriel watched as they passed a small prefab housing area, where several children played soccer in a laser-fenced yard. "Why is that?" he asked.

The driver yanked the steering yoke to one side in an attempt to avoid another bounce before replying. Gabriel heard a shout of surprise from behind him; Jimenez it sounded like.

"Tourism kinda fell off, know what I mean?" he said. "High hopes when people first arrived. Big plans for ziplining parks, swimming with riverwhales, ecotours, that kinda stuff, know what I mean?" He shifted the truck into a higher gear as they left the residential area and sped up. "But with the living jungle, not so much. Not much money flowing in anymore. Not much to sell off-world, know what…"

"Yes, I know what you mean," Gabriel said, cutting him off with a sharp tone. He stared out the open window at a stand of yellowboles they were passing and idly rubbed at the acid-burned patch on the back of his neck. *No, tourism certainly wouldn't work here.* Laser stun fences not to keep kids in, but creeping razorvine and parweasels out. Electric nets strung above common areas not to hang lights from, but to protect inhabitants from poisonous pipeflies and carnivorous spiderbats. Armed guards at every public facility not to check ID badges, but to keep the population from being kidnapped or killed by terrorists. *No,* he thought, *Eden wasn't what the original settlers had expected.*

The driver remained quiet as the truck entered the commercial area of Eden City. The buildings here were similar in appearance to the residential area: plastic extruded prefab units arranged in blocks, larger buildings having multiple units connected to each other. But unlike the residential blocks, the commercial blocks were built in multiple levels. Many buildings reached several stories into the air, but still far short of even the smallest of the yellowboles surrounding them.

A banging sounded behind Gabriel, followed by a voice. "Hey boss, we there yet? With this piss-poor excuse for a road, I gotta piss."

"Settle down, Mister Sowers," Gabriel yelled back over the whine of the straining electric motor. "Kids," he muttered under his breath.

The driver laughed and pointed out the front windscreen of the groundtruck. "We're here, sir."

Gabriel looked at Government House as they approached, a nondescript four-story prefab unit at the end of the roadway, flanked on each side by smaller units; communications office and courthouse, if he remembered his past trip. Government House looked nearly the same. The fourth story had been added sometime very recently judging by the lack of vines attached to it, and the government officials were all completely different, but he still couldn't get the feeling of dread out of his head, like history was repeating itself.

The groundtruck pulled up in front of the entrance to Government House and the driver shut off the motor. "This is your stop, sir."

Gabriel stepped out of the cab and nodded to the driver as the rest of the team jumped from the back of the truck. "Thanks for the ride."

Sowers walked up next to Gabriel and leaned in the window. "Listen, on the way back, you mind taking the road and not through the missile testing grounds?"

The driver held up his hands in mock surrender. "Hey man, I just work here."

Brevik pushed Sowers by the shoulder towards the main doors. "I've got him, Commander."

"Just as long as you show me where the head is, LT," said Sowers as he stumbled away.

"Sir, is he like this all the time?" asked Olszewski, who was the last person to leave the truck.

Gabriel watched Brevik pushing the petty officer and listened to Sowers's weak protests. "Yes, Private, I'm afraid he is."

"Do you trust him?"

Gabriel looked the MDF soldier in the eye. "With my life," he said.

Olszewski nodded. "All I needed to know, sir. I certainly don't need another babysitting duty on this mission."

Gabriel started to reach out a hand to stop the private as he walked past, but paused, reflecting on his last words. *Another?* he thought. That bears some looking into. He let Olszewski continue on, then turned and cast a quick wave to the driver, who returned the wave and engaged the motor. The truck pulled away in a cloud of steelroot wood flakes and dust to drop their gear off at Eden Guard headquarters.

Gabriel turned and followed the rest of his team up to the main doors and entered Government House, wondering, probably not for the last time, if he knew enough about his new team members.

"Sir, you can't *all* go in there!"

The woman's tone matched her stern look. The tall brunette stood in front of the double doors to the Prime Minister's office, arms crossed, effectively blocking entry.

Gabriel sighed, a feeling of impatience washing over him. It had been a long five days transit across four star systems, a bumpy shuttle landing, and a torturous ride through the jungle just to get to this point. And now an underpaid, overworked assistant was misunderstanding their intentions.

"Ma'am, we don't all mean to go in," he said in a soothing voice. "Mister Sowers gets…ahead of himself at times. You do have a restroom, yes?"

The assistant narrowed her eyes, looking at Sowers. "Yes, of course. Back out into the hall, next to the Finance Minister's office."

"Thank you, milady!" Sowers said and dashed out of the anteroom.

The assistant frowned and looked around her cramped space at the remaining seven soldiers. "Prime Minister Howarth was expecting just you, Commander Gabriel. Not seven… er, eight people."

"I understand," he replied, holding up a hand. "It will be me and my second-in-command meeting with the Prime Minister. If that's okay with you?"

She uncrossed her arms and placed her hands on her hips. Gabriel felt the slight thaw in tension and let his own hands drop to his side. "The rest of my people will remain in the lobby area," he said.

A few seconds passed, then she reached one hand up and smoothed her hair. "Fine," she said and walked back to her desk, jostling Jimenez to the side in the process.

She reached over and pressed a button on the antiquated intercom. "Sir," she said into the microphone pickup. "Commander Gabriel, and… guest are here to see you." A double beep sounded in return.

Gabriel saw Brevik's eyebrows twitch upwards at the word guest.

"Much appreciated, Mrs…?"

"Agustsdottir," she replied. The corner of her mouth rose slightly. "And it's Miss. Just Adele, actually," she added as she smoothed her hair again.

A cough sounded from behind Gabriel. With Sowers out of the room, he wasn't sure who may have issued it. He started to mentally run through the people present, but his impatience finally got the best of him.

"May we?" he asked Adele, his eyes indicating the double doors.

"Hmm? Oh, yes, my apologies," she said. She pressed another button on the intercom, and the doors swung wide. "Please enter, Commander. I'll be here if you need me."

Gabriel turned back to his people, noticing a wide grin on Takahashi's face, and pegged him as the inadvertent cougher. He cleared his throat. "At ease, everyone. Back to the main room with all of you. I'll give you a sitrep when we get out."

Gabriel and Brevik entered the office, a decent-sized space considering the prefab construction limitations. It appeared to Gabriel that they had combined two standard LQ4 Living Quarters shells into one longer room, one half separated from the other with a knee wall. On the wall sat several holopics, rotating through various scenes from Earth and, what appeared to his quick glance, the famously doomed arkship *Caleuche*. The room beyond the knee wall was a sparsely furnished office area. A lone desk with a chair and small sofa opposite it, all made from local wood, shared the room with an overflowing wall of books and magazines. *Paper*, he thought with a start. *Must have cost a fortune to obtain, let alone transport.*

The other half of the area, the one they walked into, was more informal, yet quite luxurious. Yellowbole hardwood flooring was wall to wall, stained a deep ebony, with a large decorative rug in the center. Surrounding the rug were a large sofa with deep purple cushions, two matching chairs, and a wrought iron end table. In one chair was an olive-skinned man in his mid-forties, Gabriel guessed, and opposite him was Prime Minister Howarth. Gabriel did a slight double-take. Howarth was seated in a powered wheelchair. He ran a quick neuretic search, coming up blank on why or how the Prime Minister would be disabled or injured.

Howarth must have seen his look, as he smiled and waved the two men over. "Come," he said with a slight mumble. "I won't bite. Not with this mouth."

With his left hand that he waved with, Howarth picked up a tissue from his lap and wiped the right corner of his mouth. *Paralysis?* Gabriel thought, puzzled.

He walked over to the Prime Minister, Brevik a step behind him, and extended his hand. "Prime Minister Howarth, Commander Evan Gabriel, NAFN," he said.

The seated man set his tissue back in his lap and took Gabriel's extended right hand in his left, the backwards grip causing Gabriel to shake it lightly. "This is Lieutenant Harris Brevik."

Howarth released Gabriel's hand and motioned to the sofa and one empty chair. "Please, sit down gentlemen."

As the two soldiers sat, Gabriel in the chair and the much-larger Brevik taking up the bulk of the sofa space, Howarth continued. "This is Deputy Prime Minister Rasshid."

The other man nodded. "Pleasure to meet you." His low, raspy voice was like gravel tumbling down a mountain.

"I see you're confused, Commander," Howarth said as he dabbed his mouth again. "I'm sure you weren't aware of my condition."

"Wallace, please…" Rasshid started.

Howarth held up the hand with the tissue, cutting off his deputy. "No, they need to know." His hand dropped back into his lap heavily.

The wheelchair shifted slightly; not seeing any visible controls, Gabriel assumed it was neuretically-controlled.

"We've kept it in blackout for over a year, Wallace. What happens if the terrorists get a hold of this information? What if they are captured? What then?"

Brevik spoke up. "Sir, we have failsafes built in. If we're captured, any type of torture or electronic prying into our minds will result in an automatic mindwipe. Nothing can be used against you or any of us."

Howarth laughed out loud, which degenerated into a coughing fit. Rasshid started to rise but was waved off.

"I'm fine, Zahir," Howarth said, dabbing at his lips again. "I just didn't expect this conversation to go in *that* direction. Listen," he said, leaning forward slightly. His free hand pushed against the arm of the wheelchair to shift his weight. "I suffered a stroke early last year, something that has run in my family, and something I had been taking medication for to prevent most of my life. However, this planet," he said, slowly leaning his head towards the wide windows on one wall looking out over the jungle. "This planet works against humans, in nearly any way it can. The stroke hit me, and hit me hard, and came with an unexpected byproduct. I have been recently diagnosed with Nicolozakes-Korasajakovich Syndrome. Ever hear of it?"

Gabriel shook his head. "No sir, I have not," he said. He considered looking it up, but decided against it as Howarth continued right away.

"No one has. Hell, even our doctors here hadn't," he said. "Some damned mutation of some obscure blood disease, brought on by the stroke and the natural environment, they said. Only one case in history, killed a man on Ganymede a few years back. Two mining scientists discovered it and did some research." He smiled. "Just my luck they couldn't have been named Smith and Jones, right? Now I have to have a terminal disease with an entire alphabet as its name."

"Ah, terminal sir?" Brevik asked.

Howarth's smile faded a bit. "Yes, terminal. Hard to believe in 2176, isn't it? But, I showed those bastards. They gave me three months. That was eleven months ago."

Gabriel looked at the Prime Minister, now noticing the lack of movement on the right side of his body, the drooping eye and lip, the thinner right arm and immobile hand. He found it hard to believe that strokes were still even possible. Even cancer had been beaten by this point in time. An image floated across his mind, one of his mother driving a car, him seated in the passenger's seat, headed to hockey practice. *Most cancers*, he thought with a pang of sadness.

"No worries, Commander, I'm not going to drop dead today," Howarth said, apparently misunderstanding Gabriel's silence.

"No sir, I wasn't thinking that," he replied. "But the Deputy Prime Minister is correct. If you've been keeping this under wraps, what happens if the rebels…"

"Terrorists," Rasshid cut in.

Gabriel nodded in his direction. "Noted. What happens if the *terrorists* find out about this? Will this give them impetus to try for an all-out assault, a takeover?"

"That's a distinct possibility, Commander. Which is why we sent for you."

"Prime Minister," said Brevik. "We are here on a mission to retrieve a specific set of hostages."

"Yes," Howarth replied. "That you are. But it just so happens that your mission, and our objectives, look to dovetail nicely in this case."

"I'll just say this once more," Rasshid said. "And I know, Wallace, you don't agree with me on this, but I feel outside help is completely unnecessary in this case, and will only serve to undermine our government."

Howarth nodded to Rasshid. "Yes, yes, we've been over this. However our Eden Guard has so far been ineffective in stopping the raids, wouldn't you say? Even with a man inside. And now with this new information, and Commander Gabriel and his team, perhaps this is where we finish what you started many years ago."

Gabriel held up a hand. "Hold on," he said, taking a deep breath. "Back up. What objectives are you speaking of?"

"Governor Tarif told you that her son was taken prisoner by the terrorist leader himself, a man who fancies himself something of a visionary. Calls himself Prophet. Rasshid had some dealings with him several years ago when he was part of a smaller cell, and Rasshid was chief of the Eden Guard. I suppose if any of us knew he'd be who he is today, perhaps those dealings may have gone differently."

Rasshid grimaced and sat back in his chair. "I still don't think these men are necessary."

"What objectives?" Gabriel repeated. He felt his face getting warm as he wondered how much information was left out back on Mars. He hoped this wasn't a repeat of his original Eden mission.

"To destroy the terrorist organization, from the top down, Commander," Howarth said as he dabbed his lips again. "We need the leader eliminated so the hierarchy collapses, and you need the governor's son returned unharmed. With Prophet's reputation for brutality, I don't think those objectives are mutually exclusive."

CHAPTER SEVENTEEN

The team assembled before the sun rose in the Eden Guard's headquarters building, an unassuming blocky structure just outside the main street and government area. The briefing room barely held the eight of them and the equipment that had been dropped off by their driver earlier. It was arranged in a lecture hall layout with three staggered rows of four upright seats facing a small holotable and wide wallscreen display. Brevik had his customary seat in the front, two large gear bags taking up the seats on either side of him, and Jimenez in the fourth seat. The second row held Takahashi, Sowers, Sennett, and Olszewski, and in the third and back row sat Gabriel, Negassi, and the remaining gear bags and crates.

Overnight, Gabriel continued to dwell on the objectives the Prime Minister had laid out. Ostensibly, they had been sent to Eden to rescue a group of hostages; now, his mission had apparently turned into one of not only rescue, but also the crushing of an insurrection, and possible assassination of a terrorist leader. He glanced to his left at the crate marked "Chromosuits" and clenched his jaw. Not the right armor for a full-on battle, but nothing they could do about that now. Eden Guard simply didn't possess high-tech armor or weaponry, not this far out from Earth, and not for this small of a planetary population. He thought back to the feeling of invincibility the Otero battlesuits gave, especially during their Poliahu mission six months ago, and regretted not requesting them as a backup. *Well, near invincibility*, he thought, unconsciously rubbing his scarred shoulder. An image of Santander holding a railgun pistol creeped across his mind, but quickly dissolved as the door to the briefing room opened.

In the door strode a tall Eden Guard officer, a light bird if Gabriel saw his collar oak leaves correctly, followed by a much shorter young man, maybe mid-teens, in local clothing.

"Officer on deck!" said Brevik sharply, and rose from his seat. The other seven stood up, arms rigid at sides.

The captain waved them back down. "Thank you, but that's not necessary. Totally different services, eh?" He stepped behind the holotable and smiled. "And I believe your commander would outrank me anyway, if only by a few months." He touched a few icons on the holotable controls and the table came to life. An image of Eden rose from the surface.

"I am Lieutenant Colonel Ramon Pallante, commander of the Eden Guard, a police and self-defense force created in late 2171, just after the terrorist strike on our facilities. A strike I know Commander Gabriel is very familiar with," he said with a nod towards Gabriel in the back row, "and one we don't need to rehash, for any of our sakes."

The holoimage rotated halfway around, presenting an orbital view of Eden City towards the team. Several blinking dots were scattered throughout the image. Gabriel noticed the young man standing with Pallante nervously shifting from foot to foot, head down, and wondered who this civilian guest was. Pallante's next words answered his unspoken question.

"This is Willem," Pallante said. He placed his hand on the young man's shoulder. "He is an expert tracker and outdoorsman, and knows Eden City's surroundings, and the path you'll be taking, better than anyone on the planet. He will be joining you on your mission."

Several grumbles rose from the team, most notably Sowers, Gabriel noticed, who dropped his face into his hands and shook his head back and forth. "At ease, people," Gabriel said, trying to get the briefing back on track.

"I understand your reluctance on taking a civilian," Pallante said.

"Sir, with all due respect, he's just a kid," said Sowers. "He'll slow us down, or worse, get us into trouble by trying to watch out for him."

"You know, I noticed that whenever someone starts off a sentence 'with all due respect', they're about to say something disrespectful," said Pallante with a small smile. "But again, I understand. However, Willem will run circles around the best of you in this jungle. I think you'll find you'll have a hard time keeping up with him, and he'll be more invisible than your camos could ever be."

"I'm nineteen, actually, sir," said Willem. He stepped closer to the holotable and faced the team. "And I've got some ideas for your route."

"No more interruptions," Brevik said over his shoulder. "Let's get on with the briefing. We've got a long march ahead of us."

The holoimage zoomed in on the outskirts of the city, a region of heavy jungle bordered on the north by a mountain range. Pallante stepped from behind the image and reached into the 3D image, causing it to blur and fragment, then reform around his extended index finger.

"This is the only way in and out of the city, to the west. The Cherubim Mountains, one of the very few ranges Eden has, run along our northern borders, and are for all intents and purposes, impassible. The Gihon Sea River prevents any land movement to the south, and to the east, well, that's completely in the wrong direction of the terrorist camp and would add days to a trek. Actually encampment might not be the proper term. Small town is more like it, according to our latest intel."

The image panned to the west, across heavy jungle canopy several dozen miles, shifting into IR, until reaching a blotch of orange and red.

"The overhead canopy of the jungle, the yellowboles in particular, is completely opaque to visual sensors. Only infrared, and to some extent radar, is able to map out an idea of what their complex is like. But we know for sure, well mostly sure, according to tracking and eyewitnesses, that this is where the hostages are being held. However, as for the specific building, that's much more fuzzy."

"Fuzzy?" asked Jimenez from the front row.

"Fuzzy, yes. I know that's not a proper military term, but it's all we have. It's more optimistic than 'unknown', but, well, it's still fuzzy," Pallante replied with a shrug.

Gabriel felt the atmosphere of the room shifting towards... disgust? Resentment? No, more like... worry. A worry that they were being sent into a hostile situation, with very little intel, and being briefed by the head of the local military who didn't seem to have much confidence in his own information. The shrug and weak smile certainly weren't helping. An image of Renay Gesselli giving a precise, detailed, confident briefing crossed his mind. She could show this light bird a thing or two about commanding a room. *See you soon*, he thought to himself.

"Lieutenant Colonel," he said as he leaned forward in his seat. "Let's just jump to the route we're taking. We know our objectives, we just need a little heads-up on where we start." He hoped that would defuse the tension that was growing in the air.

"Of course," Pallante replied. "Obviously, as you know from the information provided to you prior to departing from Mars, you'll be humping over ground. No possibility of an air drop anywhere within forty miles or so from the complex, and the beach at the sea river is covered with heavy anti-aircraft batteries. Not to mention an air launch from here will most certainly be picked up by the terrorists. No sense in giving them a precise ETA for you."

"They know we're coming, sir. They must know about our arrival," said Takahashi.

"Yes, I'm sure they do," Pallante said, nodding his head. "But they won't know when, or which way you're coming. Which is where Willem comes in." With that, the lieutenant colonel stepped back and allowed the young man to come forward.

"I've hunted and fished in this area my entire life," said Willem. He pointed to the image. "Every one of these little lights the lieutenant colonel turned on is a hide that I or friends have used. If you'll notice, there is a distinct path that cuts through most of the heavy jungle between Eden City and the general area of the camp." A light yellow jagged line appeared on the image. "This is the easiest way from here to there, but it's not the way we'll be going. Unless you want to end up dead."

"Bravo, boy," Gabriel heard Negassi say under her breath next to him.

"By jumping from hide to hide, using small, undetectable paths between them that we use to avoid being seen by either the animals we're hunting, or worse, the terrorists who may be hunting us, your team will be able to stay out of sight from where the Eden Guard estimates they have sensors or sentries."

Gabriel looked at Willem with a newfound respect. The young man's confidence seemed to grow with every word, now that he was comfortable with the subject matter. It looked like he had the know-how to help out tremendously with the local terrain. Five years ago, Gabriel didn't have much time to learn the land, only the dangers inherent in it, so Willem may be a valuable addition to the team.

"Willem," Gabriel called out. "Have you seen any of the terrorists firsthand?"

The young man looked back at Gabriel with a fierce smile, almost a predator's grin. "Yes sir, we have. Dozens, maybe hundreds of times. But they've never seen us, sir."

"Willem has a nickname among his friends," said Pallante. "Isn't that right, son?"

"Yes," he answered. "They call me *Ghost*."

"Hey Galen, didn't that girl on Mars, Violeta or something, didn't she call you Ghost?" asked Jimenez, turning around in his seat.

Takahashi answered for him. "Yeah, because her husband said he'd kill him and burn his body before he'd ever let him near his wife again."

"Ha ha, very funny," said Sowers. "At least I got to…"

"Ladies," growled Brevik.

"Sorry, LT," said Takahashi. "Back on point, sir."

"Are you prepared to join a military mission, take orders, come under fire?" Gabriel asked.

Willem nodded vigorously, a little of his youth showing through his tough façade. "Yes sir, I can and I will. My mother was killed in a terrorist bombing last year," he said. "I have no problems giving a little payback. Sir."

Gabriel nodded. "Continue then."

He sat back in his seat, letting the briefing go on as Pallante and Willem went over the basics of the journey. His team asked several detailed questions throughout. He hated to have to run this op as a land march, but having seen the terrain and overhead cover, both land and air vehicles were out of the question. It looked to him to be a non-stop, full day, hot swampy and dangerous trip, but unavoidable.

Not for the first time, he wondered about the mindset of their opponents. What their preparation would be, what their armaments were, number of personnel, location of hostages, and so on. Intel the Eden Guard, or anyone on Eden save the terrorists themselves, didn't possess. Intel that could possibly affect the lives of his team. *Just like five years ago*, he thought.

He pinched the bridge of his nose tightly as the onset of a headache tickled at his brain. This was getting more and more complicated. He released his nose and ran his hand through the stubble of his blond hair, watching as Pallante wrapped up the briefing. He stood up from the chair and stretched his back. *Damn, I'm feeling older and older every day*, he thought. *Of course you are, dumb ass.* He smiled to himself. *Maybe this time, I'll let these kids run the show.*

"Thank you, Lieutenant Colonel, much appreciated," he said, bringing the briefing to a close. The rest of the team turned in their seats to look back at him. "We're going to grab some breakfast, and then we're heading right out. Can you have someone bring our equipment to the staging area?"

Pallante nodded and tapped a few icons on the holotable. The image of the camp and jungle dissolved into gray pixels, then faded from view. "Yes, Commander. Use the mess two doors down. I believe they have a full meal waiting for you and your team. The gear will be in the motor pool garage. Willem will meet you there."

"Thank you again," Gabriel replied. He started to turn to head for the door when Jimenez spoke up.

"Commander, I'm assuming these little boxes don't have eight sets of Oteros, am I correct? What's our kit for this mission?"

Gabriel smiled. "No, no Oteros, sorry to say. However, the NAFN boys shipped us some new toys to try out. Specially made for jungle warfare. I think you'll like 'em, Mister Jimenez."

The group filed out of the briefing room, Jimenez exchanging raised eyebrows with Sowers as they went. Brevik brought up the rear and gave the two a light shove out the door.

Steve Umstead

CHAPTER EIGHTEEN

"This, ladies and gentlemen, is the Paradigm Chromosuit, live and in person."

The disembodied voice came from near the wide double doors of the motor pool garage, where the team had assembled and were going through their personal weapons and equipment for the long march. Takahashi looked up from his Burton, his puzzled look matching the rest of the group.

"Commander?" he said to the doors.

A head appeared as if by magic, floating six feet from the floor. The others watched in amusement as one hand appeared, then another, then a chest with a NAFN T-shirt, then the entire upper torso of Gabriel finally revealed itself, now floating just three feet above the floor.

"Very nice, sir," said Brevik. "Gotta be some of the best active camo I've seen."

"Better than the Oteros, I'd say," Sowers chimed in. "But where'd they ship in from? I didn't see any battlesuit crates."

Gabriel pulled the pants off and dropped them, now completely visible in combat fatigue pants and T-shirt. He sent a neuretics command to the suit and it materialized on the floor, several pieces of light brown fabric piled in a heap with a minimalistic battle helmet next to it.

"Oh hell," said Sowers. "That ain't no battlesuit. How's that supposed to replace armor?"

"Get to that in a minute." Gabriel walked over to the rest of the team. He noticed each one had been prepping their personal weapons: Jimenez and Sowers with standard pulse rifles, Takahashi with a Burton sniper rifle (Gabriel remembered he had been training on the side to take the sniper position, the team having lost both snipers on Poliahu… for very different reasons). Sennett had a MDF-issued kinetic assault rifle, Olszewski a custom-made Dobranoc sniper rifle with an enormous powered scope, and Brevik with his usual Escobio Oso-11 heavy assault rifle. All of them carried standard Heckart sidearms, but he noticed Negassi didn't have any larger weapon.

"Specialist, are you in need of a primary firearm?" he asked. He walked up to her as she stood from the bag she had been rummaging through.

"No sir, not at all," she replied as she withdrew a long thin plastic tube.

"May I ask…?"

She pulled a cap off one end of the tube, stuck her hand inside, and slowly pulled out a pair of wicked-looking, shiny blades, each one close to three feet long, with handles made of carved ivory. He whistled in admiration.

"Sir, I'm not really a firearm kind of woman, if you catch my drift."

Gabriel watched as she took a cloth from her pocket and began wiping the blades down. "Are these katanas? I'm not really a sword person, if you catch my drift."

Negassi smiled and set the swords carefully on top of the bag she had taken them from. "Actually these are called *takobas*. They are a traditional weapon of the Tuareg people of northern Africa. My grandfather was given these by a Tuareg chieftain, and passed them down to me."

He slowly nodded in reply. "Beautiful. And remind me never to get within five feet of you if you're mad."

"Eleven feet, Commander. I can strike up to eleven feet in under half a second," she said proudly. "Been practicing for years. Never got to use them on Mars except for drills, but maybe here, right?"

Gabriel's smile faded a bit. "Let's hope we don't need to use them at all. Quick in and out, unseen. Which brings me to the suits," he said, stepping over to Sowers.

Sowers cocked his head to one side, almost as if he was expecting to be scolded. Gabriel lightly punched him in the chest. "No, they are not battlesuits, and certainly not Otero battlesuits at that. However, having been here myself, in combat, wearing armor, I can tell you. Armor is not practical by any stretch of the imagination."

He turned to the rest of the team. "Heavy armor is useless in a jungle march here. The moisture, the swamps, the low-hanging trees, the dangerous flora, all make standard ceramic or carbotanium armor a complete waste of baggage. Now," he said, holding up a hand, "I will say that I did not expect the full extent of this mission, this assault on a terrorist complex, to be on the table. But while I'd love full armor, it simply would slow us down, and possibly get us killed." He pointed back to the pile of clothing he had left by the doors. "This is the best option for our mission. And because of the bioterror threat, these have top of the line biofilters and active chemical resistance."

Sennett raised a hand. "But sir, I understand the light weight and all, and *mierda* that camo is awesome, but what about protection? I don't know about anyone else, but I'd like to have at least a quarter inch of plate between me and a projectile."

Gabriel walked back to the suit and picked up the jacket portion. He returned to Sennett, put the jacket on him and zipped the front, then sent the command to activate the camo. The upper half of Sennett's body disappeared.

"Lieutenant," Gabriel said, looking at Brevik. "Is your Heckart loaded?"

"Sir, I…" Sennett began.

Brevik set down the Oso-11 he had been assembling and pulled the handgun from his side holster. "Yes sir, powered up."

"Shoot the corporal, if you please."

"With pleasure, sir," Brevik said, raising the Heckart.

"Whoa, wait!" Sennett yelled as he backed away, two floating hands waving in the air.

Brevik fired, the 7mm German-made caseless slug making a barely-audible click as it exited the barrel. Sennett gasped and fell backwards onto the floor. Brevik safed the weapon and returned it to his side, resuming the assembly of his heavy assault rifle.

Sennett writhed on the floor, his head disconcertingly separated from his thrashing legs. Gabriel walked over to him and extended a hand. Sennett coughed and looked up at him.

"Sir, why? Why me?" he asked in a weak voice.

"Get up, Corporal. You're not dying. You're not even bruised," Gabriel replied.

Sennett stopping gulping for air and looked down at his invisible torso, then back at Gabriel. "Uh, I'm not, am I?"

"No, you're not." He reached down, and a floating hand grabbed his. He pulled the corporal up to a standing position.

"Kinetic fabric," Gabriel said. "Resists impacts up to and possibly including that Burton the ensign is carrying. You'll still get knocked on your ass, but the active fabric instantly spreads the impact of a projectile across the entire surface of the material. No penetration. Like the bulletproof vest of a hundred years ago, only much more effective, and much lighter weight. Also highly effective against beam weapons, as the fabric has built-in reflectors." He looked over at Negassi. "Resists blade strikes as well, but I can't speak to those oversized scalpels you're packing."

"Wait, why did Lieutenant Brevik just shoot me, no questions asked?" Sennett asked. He unzipped the jacket and becoming whole again.

"Orders, Corporal. Never question orders," answered Brevik. "Not to mention I was in on the development of the tech. I knew ahead of time we'd be bringing them along."

"So you've shot other people wearing it?" Sennett asked.

The corner of Brevik's mouth ticked upwards. "No, not a live person. Not until just now. Glad it worked."

"Damn," Sennett said as he handed the jacket back to Gabriel. "What did I get myself into?"

"You made the gold team, Karl," said Jimenez. "Welcome to the club. We always seem to get the best toys."

"Suits are in the crate near the door, each one separated into individual packets, labeled by name. Grab yours, make sure the helmet biofilters fit you properly, and get one last restroom break. We move out in ten," Gabriel said.

The device was innocuous enough. Innocent, unnoticed. To all outward appearances, it was just another small box of machine parts or engine supplies, one of dozens scattered around the motor pool garage. Cubic in shape, around eight inches per side, its dirty white plastic surface bore no markings, save for "*Gear Lube*" stamped on one side, along with a standard Eden scancode shipping label.

For the past hour, it had haphazardly rested on top of a crate marked "MDF", which had recently been brought in by a driver and set near one wall of the garage. Six minutes ago, Petty Officer Third Class Arturo Jimenez had picked it up from its perch and set it down next to the crate, then opened the crate itself and began removing equipment. That routine movement triggered the device's rudimentary brain, and a cascade of events began.

Inside the device, the motion sensor was tripped, and two tiny valves opened up. Each was mounted on the side of one-quart steel containers containing two very different, and very stable, colorless liquids. The liquids slowly came together in a larger, center-mounted cylindrical container, this one surrounded by thousands of tiny carbotanium flechettes in a half-inch thick layer around its perimeter. The container had two ounces of a bluish powder inside, which the two liquids quickly dissolved. The three substances mixed as one, and created a highly-unstable trinary combination.

The newly-created perflourocane nitrotoluene, or PFNT, gurgled softly as it poured into the center container. Once the PFNT reached the top of the cylinder, the valves closed silently, and another sensor was tripped, this one starting a countdown timer. The device sat quietly, with no electronic signals emitted, next to the now-empty crate as the team assembled their weapons and gear in the center of the garage. The device waited, if an inanimate object could be said to wait, until the timer reached its preset limit.

At the three minute mark, the device's brain sent an electronic signal to the final piece of the component, a detonator piezo. Sixteen microseconds later, the piezo sent a charge into a thin wire running inside the larger container, now completely full of the trinary explosive. Four microseconds after that, the PFNT exploded, and deadly flechettes scythed through the garage at four times the speed of sound.

CHAPTER NINETEEN

"Governor Tarif, I'm so pleased you could see us on such short notice."

Rafael extended his hand to Tarif, who let it hang in space, her glare boring into his eyes. Isidoro jostled past him through the doorway and entered the governor's office.

Rafael sighed. He had suspected the meeting wouldn't go over as cordially as the one they had the night before with Seidell. Then again, he also knew Seidell to be a spineless jellyfish of a man, while Tarif was a rock in every aspect. This meeting would present much more of a challenge. However, his ace in the hole, as the North Americans were fond of saying, was much more powerful than last night's.

"Yes, well," he said. He dropped his hand and followed Isidoro over to the two chairs in front of Tarif's desk. The coffee table in the center of the room had no chairs around it, and nothing on its surface. No other seating arrangements were apparent to Rafael, and he suspected he knew why. Tarif was not happy about this request, and Seidell had probably tipped her off about the true nature of their visit, so she planned to make them as uncomfortable as possible.

As he sat in the chair nearest the door, he realized it was shorter than standard height, so as Tarif sat in her chair behind her desk facing the two men, she sat several inches above them. *Childish*, he thought. But somewhat effective. He shifted in his seat, pushing back, trying to regain a few tenths of an inch. He noticed Isidoro next to him sitting perfectly still, staring back at the governor. He hoped another outburst wasn't on its way.

He cleared his throat as Tarif picked up a small espresso cup and sipped from it. "Governor, the reason we asked to meet with you…"

"Stop," she said in a stern tone. One of command and leadership, Rafael noticed. *Yes, this meeting will not be going as smoothly as the last.*

"I talked to Governor Seidell this morning," she continued in the same tone. "As I understand it, he is no longer the official governor of Eos Chasma? How did you and your South American Republic cronies pull that one off?"

"Governor," Rafael began. "I can assure you that…"

"Don't assure me of anything." She set her cup down with a loud clatter. "You and Buenos Aires have *zero* pull in Arsia. Do you understand that? I'm not sure what you had on Seidell, and honestly I don't care. He was a patsy for his council anyway. Who knows, maybe your little friend here," she indicated Isidoro with a casual wave of her hand, "will end up doing a better job."

Isidoro stirred in his seat, and Rafael held up a hand to forestall his reaction.

"Governor Seidell, or Vice-Governor as it is today, is a staunch ally of La Republica de Sudamérica. As such, he has seen fit to transfer authority of an important dome city to our leadership to ensure that Eos Chasma can grow and prosper under a more powerful government, one with many more resources than Mars can provide by herself. He does so without any official duress, I can assure you," Rafael said, hoping the inner smirk he felt wasn't showing on his face.

"Duress," Tarif repeated, shaking her head. "I'm sure word of his disgusting habits made its way back to Earth.

That will not be the case here, sorry to throw in a monkey wrench. Unless you are just here to discuss trading terms, which I highly doubt?"

"We don't need *terms*," spat Isidoro. He started to rise from his seat. Rafael put his hand on the other man's forearm and held him down with a light touch. Isidoro glanced over at him and calmed down, and smoothed his hair with his other hand. "Apologies, Governor."

Tarif said nothing, but continued to stare at Rafael, her dark eyes once again piercing his soul. He waited, but she showed no indication of looking away, or speaking.

He cleared his throat, not for the first time since entering her office. She was more intimidating than he expected. *No matter,* he thought. *We still have the upper hand.*

"No, we have not requested this meeting to discuss trading terms, nor do we have photos or documents that will implicate you in anything. Nothing so nefarious, I assure…"

"Stop trying to assure me, and get to the point," she said in a low tone, her eyes narrowed. "I've got several more meetings on the calendar for the day."

"You may want to cancel those, Governor," Isidoro said with a small smile.

Rafael continued. "We have come to discuss the orderly transition of Arsia Mons Dome to my leadership, under the authority of La Republica…"

"*Get. Out. Now,*" she growled and stood up. She leaned forward and placed her hands on her desk, fixing Rafael with a penetrating stare. "Before I have you thrown out an airlock."

"We have your son," Rafael simply said, returning her stare.

Her gaze faltered, and Rafael watched as emotion after emotion crossed her face. Shock, anger, distress, panic, helplessness. It settled back on distress, and she stood up straight and clutched her lapel with one hand.

"What… what are you," she began, then sat down heavily in her chair. She stared at her lap for several seconds, then looked up at Rafael. He saw a semblance of her steely gaze had returned. "You're lying," she said flatly. She cleared her throat and shook her head, apparently in an attempt to regain control of the situation. "He's on Eden, studying at the university. I just talked to him yesterday."

Rafael smiled. *He had her.* "Now you're lying, Mubina. Our people have contracted with some friends on Eden, and your son was taken hostage several days ago."

Her gaze faltered again, and Rafael noticed his use of her first name hadn't even registered. "No, it can't be," she said, the fire gone from her voice.

"I know you decided not to have neuretic implants, so I can't flash this to you, but I do have some important information to show you," Rafael said. He pulled a flexscreen tube from his jacket pocket, extended it, and tapped a few icons. He handed it to Tarif.

She slowly reached out and took it, looked at the image on the screen, and covered her mouth with her hand. The flexscreen dropped from her hand onto her desk. An image of a blindfolded young man was visible before the device automatically snapped shut.

"You bastards," she said, without much fire behind the words as she had earlier, Rafael heard.

"Well, that may be the case, Mubina, but we do have a transition plan I think you'll find quite reasonable." He pulled out an envelope from his jacket's other pocket and laid it on the desk in front of her, retrieving his flexscreen tube. "These papers will provide the necessary legal documentation…"

"Get out," Tarif said in a small voice. "Just… get out."

"Governor," Isidiro said, leaning forward in his chair. "You understand what's at stake here, do you not?"

"Tomorrow morning at nine local time," Rafael said. "We need this document signed by that time, or I cannot guarantee your son's safety. With the vagaries of interstellar communications, I would advise that you be prompt. It takes many hours for a message to reach Eden from here, and our friends have their own deadline."

Tarif rubbed her brow with one hand while picking up the envelope with the other. She didn't look up from the desk as she spoke. "You'll have my answer by nine. Now leave."

Rafael heard the defeated tone in her voice and smiled inwardly. He knew it was inevitable, and considered demanding the document be taken care of now, but thought the better of it. Better to let her stew over it so the transition would be more... what was the word? Efficient, maybe. Yes, an efficient, orderly transition first thing in the morning would be helpful. And the deadline was far too early for Gabriel and his team to even get close to their objective. Yes, Chimo, for all his annoyances, had planned this down to the minute, and very well.

He rose from his seat, Isidoro matching the action, and headed for the door, leaving a distraught soon-to-be ex-governor in their wake.

As the door closed behind the two men, Tarif threw the envelope down on her desk in disgust. *Jeromy*, she thought. *Damn them.*

She stood up and began pacing around the office. How could they? The SAR is behind the terrorists? Prophet? *Oh Jeromy.*

She walked over to her desk and sat back down. Opening up a drawer, she pulled out a thin, flat box and pressed her thumb to a small scanning pad on the top. It popped open, and she withdrew a paper notepad. She set the box down on her desk, opened the pad, and flipped past a few pages until she reached the one she was looking for. She ran her finger down a list of notes.

Too late, she thought. The plan they had put together for Gabriel and his team to travel to Eden, land, make their way to the camp, and free the hostages was too late. By a full day. Which cemented the fact that the Republic must have been behind the entire operation.

She tossed the notepad onto her desk, and it landed next to the envelope. The envelope that just stared back at her. Taunting her with its contents. She stared back. *I don't know if there is even a choice,* she thought. *I can't even get a message to them in time.*

She picked up her phone bug and slipped it in her ear, and tapped the call button for her assistant.

"Yes, Governor?" came the voice in her ear.

She paused, wheels spinning in her mind. Choice, no choice. Timing. Options. *Jeromy.*

"Governor?" the voice repeated.

Tarif took a deep breath and blew it out noisily. "Radja, please summon Major Andon to my office immediately."

"Ma'am, is everything okay?"

She closed her eyes, as if the darkness would shut out the pain. Understanding the absurdity of the thought, she popped them open again, only to realize somewhere in the back of her mind, a similarly-absurd thought waited, hoping that the nightmare would disappear when her eyes opened.

"Yes, Radja. Everything is fine. For now," she added. "Just please get a hold of him. I need him here right away."

"Of course, ma'am. Anything else?"

Choice. No choice. "Yes, actually." She took another deep breath. "Please get Vice-Governor Phillipe on the line for me. I have some… paperwork to discuss."

CHAPTER TWENTY

"I thought I might find you here, Chimo."

The man walked up behind his nephew, who was staring out through a thick pane of transparisteel. Chimo turned around, apparently startled at his uncle's silent approach.

"Oh, *lo siento*, uncle," the younger man said. "I didn't hear you approach. What brings you all the way out here?"

"Actually looking for you," he replied. He inclined his head in the direction of the window. "What are you watching?"

Chimo turned back and pointed with one hand. "Our new mining operation. The foreman called earlier, saying they had just run into a new, massive vein of rare earth elements. They just started the molecular drill, and any minute should be reporting their finds."

"Excellent," the man said. "I believe this operation was your call, was it not?"

Chimo turned back around to face him and leaned against the window. He gave a small smile and looked at the floor. "Yes, one of many. Many that didn't pan out, but perhaps this might save my reputation."

The man returned his smile. "Chin up, young man. Your reputation is in fine shape. Actually that's why I came down here to find you at this crazy hour of night."

"Oh?"

"I have received word from Isi and Rafa that their meetings have gone well," he said. "Eos Chasma is now officially and legally governed by us, with Isidoro installed as its governor, and they have presented your *offer*," he emphasized the word with a nod in Chimo's direction, "to Governor Tarif. They will know within eight hours the result of that offer, but I think we both know what that will be."

The man walked up to the transparisteel and looked down at the hustle and bustle below. Several white-suited figures were huddled over a monitor at one end of a large black tube assembly, while two more men were at the far end of the tube connecting hoses. There was a low thrum coming from below, and as the man watched, the two men at the far end stepped back and motioned to the men at the monitor. The thrum intensified and the tube assembly began vibrating.

The man knew from his past mining days that inside the tube was a series of molecular-level lasers that would now be firing in a precise sequence into the regolith below, boring out a helix-shaped hole into which a mechanical siphon would be fitted. The siphon would then use a magnetic coupler to extend and retract several hundred times per minute, forcing the minerals below into the inner column of the siphon, leaving the useless dust behind. The process was called differential retraction, and although the initial machinery cost was exorbitant, the resulting retrieval of the valuable minerals and elements was much more efficient. And immediate.

Chimo held up a hand, staring at the far wall, apparently receiving a neuretics transmission. A wide smile crossed his face after a few seconds. "They estimate it's a ninety-plus percent pure vein of terbium," he said. "A huge deposit, uncle."

The man patted his nephew on the back. "Your reputation is more than intact, young man."

"It's a financial windfall, it truly is. The Chinese have been begging for rare earths ever since the Shanghai event. This deposit... this deposit is worth countless millions in profit. This changes a lot," he said.

The man looked back out over the mining operation below, watching the white-suited men slapping each other on the back and scurrying from monitor to monitor. *Yes, perhaps it does. But maybe in a way that can benefit us even more than a simple cash transaction.* Wheels within wheels turned in his mind. Mars would work itself out. But something deep down in his brain kept nagging at him. *Gabriel.*

"Chimo," he said. "I want you to keep this discovery under wraps. We may have an even better use for the elements."

"I'm not sure I follow, uncle."

The man pursed his lips. *How far can I go with this?* he thought. "I have a concern," he said.

"What type of concern?"

The man placed his hands behind his back and turned from the window to face Chimo. "My concern is Commander Gabriel and his team. I don't trust the operation we have on Eden to take care of them."

"But uncle..."

"No no, I understand. The plan so far has been solid, and I'm proud of what you've put together. However, I have seen what Gabriel has been able to do to a solid plan before. I think we need to put together... contingencies."

Chimo looked at him with narrowed eyes. "Contingencies?" he repeated. "What types of contingencies?"

"I have some contacts still within the Chinese military, back from when I was a consultant. With their space forces in particular. Perhaps this new discovery can help grease the wheels for an agreement. Partnership, even."

He saw Chimo's eyes shift from curiosity to suspicion. "No worries, my nephew. I am not cutting you out of our plan. I am merely going to explore any and all options that will allow us to succeed. I just fear... no, suspect is more the term. I suspect that we have not heard the last of Gabriel, and we need to plan accordingly."

Chimo nodded, his look now shifted to thoughtful. "And what of Rafael and Isidoro? We need to contact them with this, *si*?"

The man turned back to the window, watching the operation proceed inside the massive tunneled-out cave the facility sat on top of. The terbium would soon be rising to the surface, filling their coffers with valuable trading assets. Payment for possible services to be rendered, if his contacts could come through as he hoped. But some things would need to remain compartmentalized. The fool Tevez didn't understand that, and it cost him his life.

"Not yet, Chimo," he said, continuing to look out the window. "Let me worry about the two of them. They have their plates full right now. We don't need to burden them with any additional work."

The thrum grew louder, and a secondary noise arose from the mining site. The man watched as two of the workers exchanged a high-five and knew that additional sound was the sound of the rare earth element flowing through the discharge conduit into the mining facility's hoppers. The sound of a contingency plan about to be created.

Rafael sat on his expansive balcony sipping a cup of coffee, overlooking the Chasman plain through the transparent fabric of the dome. He set the cup back on the saucer, then both down on the small table next to his chair. The coffee was excellent, obviously imported from South America, most likely for the express purpose of Seidell impressing his honored guests. Rafael wondered if the coffee selection would be changing soon, now that Seidell's graft and corruption were being swept out of Eos Chasma altogether. His inner smile faded a bit at the thought of losing some of the exquisite perks he and Isidoro had been able to take advantage of over the past couple of days. *No matter*, he thought. *Bigger plans afoot.*

He heard his inner door slam shut and the drapes inside his balcony door fluttered outwards, touching the back of his head. *Solace over*, he thought wryly.

"Yes, Isi, come to worry some more?" he called over his shoulder.

Clinking of glass came from his suite, then a muttered curse, then more cursing. After a few moments, Isidoro walked out on the balcony and joined him. He had a dripping coffee cup in one hand, embroidered hand towel in the other, and was dabbing at his shirt. A long brown stain ran from chest to waist on his white linen shirt.

"I will say it again, Rafa, I don't like this... this treatment." He sat down in the chair on the other side of the small table. "I'm going to clean house when I finally get full control here."

Rafael smiled at his friend's bluster. Clean house would be an appropriate term for fixing the mess Seidell had made of his government. The two men had spent most of the previous night after meeting with Tarif going over the books Seidell had left. As for the man himself, they hadn't seen a sign of him since that morning, when he had brought them into his office and handed them the keys to the city. Literally the keys, Rafael remembered. Seidell had given them a box full of code keys to every building under the dome, plus a ream of hardcopy printouts of access codes, passwords, and the like, to hundreds, if not thousands, of electronic accounts throughout Mars's economic system. They had only scratched the surface of the corruption he had left behind when they needed to call it a night. The ultrasonic tube system between Eos Chasma and Arsia Dome was high-speed, but still over a four hour ride down the length of Valles Marineris. This morning was an important step in the plan, and Rafael wanted to make sure they were both quite rested.

He did a quick neuretic check of the time: 8:46AM local. Any minute now. He glanced at the comm unit he had brought from the suite, the one coded to the private number he had given Tarif the night before. It sat silent.

Isidoro patted at the stain on his shirt, then finally threw the towel over the balcony in disgust. Rafael leaned slightly forward and watched through the railing as it floated slowly down ten stories in the calm dome air and light Mars gravity.

"Clean house, eh?" he said, looking at Isidoro with a grin. "Perhaps you can start with street sweeping tomorrow."

"No call yet?" Isidoro said, either ignorant or oblivious to Rafael's jibe. He picked up his cup and sipped the coffee. "Dishwater," he muttered, making a face.

"No, my friend, no call yet," he replied. He looked back out over the plain. The weak sunlight was just starting to creep over their building behind them, causing a glare off the fabric of the dome across the street. Rafael blinked. "But as I said after last night's meeting, this will work out exactly as planned."

"But what about Gabriel? What happens if we lose that leverage?"

"Not possible, Isi. We've already gone over the timetable. There is no physical way, and you know this, for the assault team to be anywhere near the rebels before this deadline, even with the Mars time zone difference. *Infierno*, they may not have even landed on Eden yet for all we know."

"I don't know, Rafa, I just don't know," Isidoro said as he rubbed his hands together.

Rafael chuckled. "So, you did come to worry, didn't you? Relax," he said as he reached for his coffee. "It is under control."

As he brought the cup to his lips, the comm unit trilled next to him. He sipped slowly, letting the unit ring a couple more times. He set the cup down, looked at Isidoro, and said, "Am I ever wrong, my friend?"

He picked up the comm unit. *"Hola?"*

Governor Mubina Tarif took a deep breath, trying to control her growing anger, which had long ago won over her frustration. She placed both hands flat on her desk, palms down. She glanced across the desk at Vice Governor Phillipe and Major Andon, both of whom sat with guarded looks on their faces. She had been up since before four in the morning, as did they, going over possible ways around the situation. Possible military action on Mars with Andon, possible political pressure with the SAR with Phillipe, and just a few minutes ago, the three had come to the crushing conclusion that all the cards were on the wrong side of the table.

She took another deep breath, this one to tamp down her annoyance at Rafael's cavalier tone and deliberate use of Spanish. She adjusted the phone bug in her ear, getting two confirming nods from the other men that their neuretics were linked in to listen in on the call, and answered.

"The SAR, and you two lapdogs, have won. This round," she said in a sharp tone. She saw the warning glance Andon gave her and grimaced. In a calmer voice, she continued, "I will transfer authority to you, Rafael, as of nine AM today, local Arsia time, three hours behind your time, so three hours from now."

"And the paperwork?" Rafael asked.

She sighed and dropped her head down to stare at the synthoak grain in her desk. *Oh, Jeromy,* she thought.

After a few seconds she picked her head back up and reached for a flexscreen. "Yes, the paperwork," she said.

With a look to Phillipe, who nodded back in reassurance, she opened the flexscreen and tapped a few icons. She brought up an electronic copy of the paper document Rafael had given her the night before, which both her and Phillip had signed.

"I have it ready to send to the code you gave," she said in a flat voice. "But this isn't over," she added, earning another warning look from Andon.

"Of course it is," the voice came back. "But no worries, we will take very good care of Arsia, and Mars."

"You know the others won't be as easily usurped," she said as she tapped in the code to send the document.

"Easy?" Rafael answered with a laugh. "Oh, I assure you, this wasn't easy at all. However, the rest of the governors will fall in line behind Arsia, as they always have. And your vaunted MDF take orders from the civilian governments, isn't that right Major Andon? You are there, correct?"

Tarif shook her head at the arrogance, the gall. But she couldn't shake the vision of a bound and gagged son. "The document has been sent. Call off your dogs on Eden, release the hostages."

"As soon as we receive it…oh, there it is now," Rafael answered. After a few moments, he said, "All looks in order. I will send our people the go ahead to release your son."

"And the others?" she asked, a growing feeling of dread inside her.

"Prophet is an… unusual man, you must understand. Our deal was Jeromy. It's up to him about the others."

The call ended in a click. Tarif took the phone bug out of her ear and flung it across the room. It bounced off the far wall and skittered across the floor. *Gabriel,* she thought. *Where are you?*

CHAPTER TWENTY-ONE

Gabriel struggled to open his eyes. The concussive shockwave of what he assumed was an explosion had slammed him into a set of vertical shelves holding wheels and tires, and now he was buried underneath a pile of metal and plastic. The ringing in his ears was like a dozen high-pitched air raid warning sirens, all stuck on the same tone. He pushed himself up on all fours. Tires fell off his back and bounced on the floor near him. The pungent smell of burned plastic and metal assaulted his nose, and memories of a burning school gymnasium flashed across his mind. He shook his head to clear them, but they only partially disappeared. *My team,* he thought, dismissing the images.

"Report," he croaked, then cleared his throat. "*REPORT!*" he boomed and stood upright to survey the garage.

The entire area was filled with a yellowish haze, thicker near the floor. Wisps of it blew out of the half-opened double doors to the outside jungle, adding to the pre-dawn gloom. Shelves, parts, boxes, and various tools and pieces of tools were scattered throughout the garage. He looked at the tire that remained leaning up against his right leg, and saw dozens of flechettes protruding from one side. *Anti-personnel bomb*, he thought with a mix of concern and anger.

He scanned the smoky room. Negassi was on all fours, coughing, with Brevik trying to help her up. Olszewski was leaning against the side wall, bleeding from both ears, and Sennett, sporting his own facial wound, was standing nose to nose with him, apparently trying to snap the private out of the stunned daze he was in. Takahashi was seated on the floor, picking flechettes from his chromosuit jacket. He looked up at Gabriel and gave a weak okay sign with his free hand. His eyes seemed glazed over in shock, but he otherwise appeared unharmed.

Gabriel felt a sense of relief begin to replace his earlier concern. Everyone had already suited up in the impact-resistant suits before the explosion. Only Brevik had had his helmet on, but with the exception of some minor facial cuts, everyone else seemed in good shape. Except...

"Commander!"

The panicked yell instantly cut through Gabriel's ringing ears. It came from the far side of the garage; judging by the blast pattern he saw, very near where the explosive must have been planted. The voice was Sowers's, and Gabriel didn't see any sign of Jimenez. He shoved aside the tire and ran towards the voice.

Turning the corner around a shattered equipment crate, he skidded to a halt. Sowers was bent on one knee, leaning over the battered, bloody body of Jimenez. Gabriel saw that Jimenez must have taken the full force of the explosion; his chromosuit was torn in several places, and blood poured from dozens of facial cuts. He must have been within feet of the explosion source. Gabriel ground his teeth together.

"Commander," Sowers said in a lower voice. "He's gone, sir. Ah, dammit, Arturo." He dropped down to both knees, setting Jimenez's head back down on the floor of the garage. Gabriel could feel the raw emotion pouring from Sowers, like an electric charge. He knew they were close; so much so that he had had to separate them on specific missions back on Mars so as not to have them drop their guard or be too relaxed. Sowers had asked Jimenez to be the best man at his wedding, even though he didn't even have a woman in mind. They were... *brothers*, he thought.

Sowers lowered his head, and Gabriel watched silently as he made the sign of the cross and touched Jimenez's forehead. After a long moment, he placed his other hand on the dead man's chest. "*Adios, mi hermano.*"

Gabriel took a few steps closer, and reached out, touching Sowers's shoulder. Behind him he heard someone else approach.

"Oh no, Arturo," Takahashi said. "No, no..."

Sowers stood up, still looking down at his friend. "Commander, I want the person who did this."

Gabriel squeezed his shoulder. "We'll find him, Galen."

"No sir," he replied, turning to face him. "I want him *personally.*"

Gabriel looked into the man's eyes, and saw fierce determination. Not anger, not recklessness, but a strong, powerful drive. The unblinking stare made it clear to Gabriel that Sowers wouldn't be dissuaded from this. He nodded. "You have my word."

"Thank you, sir." He turned back to Jimenez's lifeless body. "Sir, I understand we have a mission schedule, but..."

"Mister Sowers, Arturo will be taken care of properly in the matter befitting the soldier and man he was. I will see to it."

Sowers took a deep breath, staring at the body. He nodded, as if silently saying goodbye one last time, and turned to walk back into the main garage area. As he passed Takahashi, the other man patted him on the upper arm. Sowers tapped him back on the arm and continued walking. As he passed a mangled crate, he turned and gave it a powerful kick. The crate, already cracked and chipped from the explosion, splintered into several pieces and clattered across the floor.

"Commander," said Takahashi as he walked up to Gabriel, his eyes still cast towards Jimenez. "What the hell happened?"

The dazed look Gabriel had seen earlier in his eyes had only slightly diminished. He could feel the pain emanating from the ensign, pain he knew the entire team would be feeling. Jimenez had been with them since day one of the Poliahu mission, and before that for several of the team members, including Takahashi. Like the death of Teresita St. Laurent at the hands of a traitor, this loss would stay with them for a long time. It was up to Gabriel to keep them focused, keep them together, keep them strong. A lack of focus could get more of them killed.

He grabbed Takahashi by the shoulder. "Ensign, I need you. I need all of you, you understand?" He gave him a shake and pulled his upper body around, breaking the far-off stare Takahashi had. "This was a bomb intended to kill all of us. We need to pull ourselves together and get on with the mission."

Takahashi nodded slowly at first, then more vigorously as Gabriel stared into his eyes. "Aye aye, Commander." His voice was stronger now, Gabriel heard.

"Thank you Ensign," he replied. "We will mourn Arturo properly when the mission is complete. Right now, we need to saddle up and get on the road. Clear?"

"Clear, sir," he said, taking a deep breath. "What do you need from me?"

"Stay with Sowers, make sure he's okay. Work your checklists, get our gear ready to move out."

"You got it, sir." With that, Takahashi drew himself up to full height and snapped off a crisp salute.

Even without a proper lid, Gabriel returned the salute, and Takahashi turned to head back into the main area of the garage.

Gabriel took one last look at Jimenez and ground his teeth again. *We'll find you,* he thought. *And I'll put you and*

Sowers into a room together to have a chat. He turned on his heel and followed Takahashi.

Brevik was talking to Negassi, the big man's helmet now off, while Olszewski stood in the same spot as before, yawning and trying to pop his bloody ears. Sennett was talking in low tones to Sowers, whose face was a rigid mask of stone. Gabriel looked on as Takahashi walked up to the pair and stood in front of Sowers. The ensign said a few words he couldn't make out, then Sowers closed his eyes and dropped his head. As Gabriel watched, Sowers slowly nodded a few times, clenched both fists, and took a deep breath. He looked up at Takahashi, and mouthed the words, "Thank you." Takahashi lightly punched him in the chest, and the three men turned and began going through the debris to collect their equipment.

With a bang, the steel door from Eden Guard headquarters burst inwards. Two riot-gear suited Guards crashed in behind it, weapons drawn. Gabriel held his hands up.

"Under control," he said, making a downward motion with his hands to calm the troopers. "But we've got a casualty."

The Guards took a few steps into the garage, assault rifles scanning side to side. Gabriel watched as their eyes widened in unison at the sight of the destruction.

"Sir, we got here as quickly as we could," one Guard said as he lowered his weapon. "What happened?"

"Anti-personnel bomb," he replied. He motioned with his thumb over his shoulder. "We have a KIA and a few minor injuries. We need your medic here right away."

"Already on his way," the Guard replied. "KIA, sir?"

Gabriel grimaced. "Yes, KIA. Can you get a hold of Lieutenant…"

His request was interrupted by the sight of Lieutenant Colonel Pallante walking into the garage, a stunned look on his face. Behind him was Willem, and something in the back of Gabriel's mind noted that the young man had been conveniently late to the assembly point.

"*Jesu Cristo,*" Pallante mumbled, his jaw hanging slack. "Commander…"

"Bomb," Gabriel said flatly. "I'm afraid you have a mole in your midst, Lieutenant Colonel." He watched out of the corner of his eye as Willem shifted from foot to foot nervously. Guilt? Or just apprehension at joining a mission that had already suffered its first casualty?

"No," Pallante said, shaking his head slowly. "Not possible."

"Highly likely," Gabriel replied. "Someone knew we'd be in here, now, which is something that was not scheduled ahead of time. Matter of fact, our original assembly point was in the courtyard behind the building, but your staff had all of our gear in here."

"Who…"

"I don't know, and to be blunt, I don't have time to figure it out," Gabriel answered. "We need your medic to patch a few people up, and we have to get going. Our window is closing. I don't need these men humping through your damned jungle in the dark."

Pallante nodded. "Of course. Let me know what you need."

"A goddamned medic," Gabriel said in an exasperated tone. "And I need some of your corpsman to help with something else. One of my men was killed."

Pallante's eyes grew wide. "Commander, I am so sorry to hear…"

"Thank you," he said, cutting him off. "We'll handle the arrangements when we get back. Right now I need your people to take care of his body, and I need it done invisibly. I've already got some heavy hearts in here, I don't need them seeing their teammate carried out. Understand?"

"Yes, yes, of course," he said. "And Willem is ready to join you, we were just going over some last minute details."

Gabriel stared at the young man, who was still nervously looking around the destroyed garage.

"Is that so?" he asked.

Pallante cocked his head at Gabriel's tone. "Well, yes, what…"

"Never mind," he answered, turning back to the garage. "Let's go, kid," he said over his shoulder.

He walked back to where Brevik and Negassi were standing. She was still coughing and clearing her throat as Brevik was going over the checklist with her.

"Lieutenant," said Gabriel. "Where do we stand?"

Brevik looked back at him, and Gabriel detected the faintest hint of sadness in his eyes. He knew Brevik had been Jimenez's commanding officer for over two years, and although the big man rarely showed emotion, with the exception of Sowers and maybe Takahashi, he knew he'd be the hardest hit. And Renay. She had considered Jimenez a kid brother. *Ah hell, Renay. I'm sorry.*

"Sir, the specialist is fine, just inhaled some high-temperature air from the blast." He looked back at the explosion's origin, and the crate Jimenez's body rested behind. "Taking a quick look at the types of burns and the blast pattern, I'm going to say a small liquid explosive with anti-personnel darts. Sir, someone wanted us all dead, in a nasty way. Arturo was just…"

"I know, Harris. Wrong place at the wrong time. If it makes any difference, it doesn't appear he suffered."

"But someone else will."

Gabriel nodded. "I know," he repeated. "But right now I need you to rework our formations, down a man. And redistribute the gear. Use Sennett, he seems like he's in pretty good shape. And… keep an eye on Galen."

Brevik returned the nod. "Aye aye, sir."

Gabriel looked around the shattered garage, watching his team regroup mentally and throw themselves back into the mission prep. Taking one last glance at the blast site, he said a final silent goodbye to Jimenez and turned back to Brevik to assist with the gear.

CHAPTER TWENTY-TWO

Captain Jamar Chaud sat at his small makeshift desk, struggling to make sense of the data on the hardcopy in front of him. Spreadsheets were never his strong suit, he knew, but now because of the loss of Maybeck, he tried to fit personnel into slots by not only their specific skills and knowledge, but also by a grade given to them by Prophet himself. And they needed to fit just right, or he'd be redoing them through the night.

The plastic door to his tiny command headquarters office opened, allowing a weak stream of green-tinged sunlight to filter in to the shadowy room. With the light entered the faint calls of treemonkeys in the distance, along with a flat voice.

"Walk with me, Captain Chaud."

Chaud quickly stood up from his desk, setting down the pen he had been holding, and tugged at his tunic.

"Prophet, sir, what brings you here?" he asked.

"Come, walk with me," the voice replied, and a shadow moved away from the door entrance.

Chaud walked around from behind the desk, leaving the pile of hardcopy behind. He walked across the dirt floor of his office and stepped through the door. Prophet was standing a few feet away, facing out towards the jungle, shading one eye with his hand. Several soldiers were cleaning armor in the small courtyard in front of Chaud's office, a cleared area between six prefab buildings. Chaud walked up next to Prophet and followed his gaze.

"Synfox, do you see it?"

Chaud squinted in the direction Prophet was looking. Nothing caught his eye. He scanned back and forth, looking for something out of the ordinary, and was about to reply when a few small strands of creepervine rustled, perhaps a hundred yards away or so. As he looked on, a silvery flash leapt from the area and disappeared further into the jungle, leaving waving fronds in its wake.

"How did you…"

"Captain, it's my job to always be looking ahead, far ahead, many moves ahead. Wouldn't you agree?"

It was a rhetorical question, and Chaud knew it, so he simply waited, watching his leader stand motionless.

After a few more seconds staring into the jungle, Prophet nodded and turned to his right. "Come," he said, and walked between two buildings towards the coast of the Gihon Sea River to their southwest. Chaud immediately fell into step with him.

The men walked in silence for several minutes along a well-worn path to the sea river. Chaud noticed that one of the path's guide rails, multiple runs of a thick electrified wire on either side of the path installed to reduce the risk of predators from attacking a wandering soldier, showed signs of teeth marks. He patted his waist holster absently, just to reassure himself he was armed. He wondered which one of the dozens of Eden's carnivorous beasts had decided the enjoyment of chewing on wire trumped the pain of the electric shock.

As they reached the coast and crested a small dune, Chaud saw the Gihon Sea River laid out before them. Over a thousand miles across, the sea river was not much smaller than a typical ocean, but had a much more significant tidal current. Eden had four such massive sea rivers, the Gihon being the smallest of the four, and the one that had swept away the body of Chaud's brother many years ago. Every time he gazed upon the Gihon, he saw the image of the Eden Guard firing his weapon, and Hamal falling into the current.

"I've heard from our man," Prophet said as he came to a stop a few yards from the breaking surf.

Chaud shook his head to clear it. "Sorry, sir, pardon me?"

"Our man inside Government House." He kicked at a sand crab that was walking by, and it scuttled away into the water. "The bomb was a failure."

Chaud held his breath, waiting for the explosion, but it never came. After a few seconds, he asked, "So where do we go from here?"

Prophet gave a small laugh; to Chaud's ear it almost sounded like a snort. Scornful. "Chaud, did we ever fully trust our man?"

He cocked his head to one side, pondering his leader's question. Trust was something ingrained in all of them, in one another, but in an outsider? A bought man? "Probably not, sir. Not really one of us, is he?"

Prophet's lips twitched upwards in a semblance of a smile. "Absolutely correct, Captain. Not one of us. Which is why I never expected the bomb to work. And why I had you design the ambush plan for Gabriel's journey. However, I have learned something from our man that may be more useful than anything he has given us to date concerning Gabriel."

Chaud waited, watching as Prophet stared out over the sea river. The sun had just crested the horizon over his left shoulder and was lighting up the Gihon's whitecaps like miniature snow-covered mountains. The heat of the sun was only now starting to warm his back, and it felt like it was going to be another scorcher.

"Cat got your tongue, Captain?" Prophet asked without taking his eyes from the sea river.

"Ah, no sir, I just…"

"Don't worry, it's just you and I out here. Please speak your mind if you feel the need."

Chaud didn't doubt there wasn't one or two maser sniper scopes trained on him at this very moment. Maybe even the nearby anti-aircraft cannon. Prophet hadn't lived this long without taking precautions. Whether they'd be authorized to shoot him for using the wrong words, he wasn't so sure.

"Sir, I'm not sure what you learned, or if you're at liberty to fill me in on it, but I'm wondering. And don't take this the wrong way. But if we cannot trust this man, how are we now to trust this new information?"

"Excellent question, Chaud, very perceptive. We cannot. But we also cannot ignore it. So we are not changing our plans, we are merely adding a contingency. Or two," he said.

Chaud nodded. "Wise, sir." Almost as soon as the words came out of his mouth, he regretted the patronizing tone and words. He watched Prophet for any reaction, but he continued to simply stare out over the Gihon. "What is this information?"

"You're familiar with that group of young hunters we monitor, correct?"

"Yes, I believe we have a total of nine different subjects we're tracking off and on." Chaud had been out on recon with several of his own teams, usually a mix of experienced soldiers and fresh recruits, at various times over the past few months, and one of their most valuable tracking exercises was to try to get as close as possible to the youths without being spotted. Only once had a recruit been seen; that recruit was now handling laundry duties, Chaud remembered. They spent days on end, slowly following the youths as they went about hunting and fishing, stocking hidden caches of supplies, creating hides for themselves, building high archer perches in yellowboles, and generally clomping through the jungle unaware of the rebels' presence.

Not sure where Prophet was going with this, he asked, "Does one of them possess information we need?"

"No, Captain. Actually what I've come to find out is this. And again we're trusting intel we're receiving from a stressed-out, down on his luck mole, one who has already failed in a simple bomb mission. As an aside, Captain, are you sure your ordnance people sent him a proper setup?"

"Absolutely, sir. Zeno and I both supervised the assembly of the device. It was flawless. The only thing he needed to do was position it and set the timer according to Gabriel's schedule. Sir," he said, taking a deep breath. "If you don't mind me asking, and you don't mind me interrupting your train of thought, what went wrong?"

Prophet looked down and sent another sand crab scurrying away with a kick. "Timing. It all comes down to timing in most plans, doesn't it seem? Gabriel and his team were already suited up in some type of protective gear when the explosive detonated. They lost one man, or so we're told. But that's still seven on their way, and most likely they're on the road as we speak. Our man simply had the wrong timing. Or perhaps we had the wrong man to begin with."

He shook his head. "In any case, the intel we're receiving is that one of the hunters is joining Gabriel and his party for the march. So they will technically be back up to eight in the squad. Interesting, isn't it Captain?"

Prophet turned to look at Chaud, staring at his face, and Chaud shrank a bit. He knew Prophet expected him to know what that meant, but if having a bumbling kid along for the ride made any difference in the defense plan, he couldn't fathom how. He started to open his mouth to ask when Prophet continued.

"I believe this means they want to use a different route, a more indirect route, and take advantage of the hunters' trails and hides along the way. As opposed to the more direct, expected route, where you have emplaced the automatic sentries and sensors."

Chaud closed his mouth silently and looked back at Prophet. It made perfect sense. And it also meant that all of his planning might be getting tossed out the window. He had spent almost an entire 23-hour Eden day straight working on the logistics, the emplacements, the personnel, the communications. All for some kid to screw it up.

His face must have showed his emotions, as Prophet held up a hand. "Hold on, Captain, no need to panic. We are not changing anything in your original plan. As a matter of fact, my gut tells me that Gabriel and his team will still continue on the most likely path. I do believe he has some inner hubris we can exploit. I don't think he thinks very highly of our ragtag band, and will not be afraid to be obvious in his movements."

Prophet turned back to the Gihon. "However, I cannot ignore the presence of a scout, for lack of a better term, and we need to ensure Gabriel doesn't slip past our defenses, and suddenly end up drinking our beer and eating our pork in our own dining hall while our best forces are waiting for him miles away. Wouldn't you agree?"

Chaud pondered what Prophet had said for a moment, and thought back to a few minutes ago when Prophet had seen the synfox where no man should have been able to. *Yes, he does see many moves ahead,* he thought. *And we're both still alive because of it.*

"Sir, I agree, and I'd be happy to get to work on the contingency plan right away," he said.

"Excellent, I knew I could count on you," Prophet replied. "Take Harvin off of guard duty, I believe he's covering the northern passage. He's your best recon scout, is that correct?"

Chaud nodded. "Yes, no doubt about it. Thank you for noticing, sir."

"Yes, well, I can't be expected to lead without knowing who I'm leading," he said. "Take Harvin, and the two of you put together a plan using the intel you've gathered from tracking the hunters. Look for a path Gabriel might use. Look for hides along the way, for resupply caches they may wish to use. Have Harvin get inside this hunter's head. Think about what they'd do, from their perspective. It's the only way to defeat an enemy."

Prophet turned to leave. As he walked back over the dune, he said over his shoulder, "I trust you on this, Captain Chaud. Don't let us down."

Chaud remained on the beach for a few more moments after Prophet left, reflecting on the conversation. Trust. Perhaps the most important word spoken in the entire conversation.

He bent over and picked up a rock, smooth on one side and jagged on the other. He held it in his hand and stared out over the Gihon. With a flick of his wrist, he flung the rock, and it skipped across the surface several times before sinking into the depths. Like Hamal, never to be seen again. He turned and walked back towards camp.

Steve Umstead

CHAPTER TWENTY-THREE

The team traveled in silence. Only the electric troop transport's whining motor and the tires on the steelroot planking made any sounds. Gabriel sat in the front seat of the truck, the same one with the same driver that had dropped them off at Government House several hours before. But this ride had a much different atmosphere than the ride in. Much more somber, more serious. More determined.

Willem sat in the middle, his small frame easily able to fit between Gabriel and the driver, and stared out through the windscreen. Gabriel watched him out of the corner of his eye, still not sure what to make of him. He had a teenager's curiosity, having asked each one of the team members various questions on weapons, armor, and tactics. So much so that Gabriel had sent a team-net neuretics burst to make sure no one revealed anything out of the ordinary, as he still wasn't sure he could completely put his trust into the young man.

But seeing his calm demeanor, his casual eyes as they traveled towards the drop off point, he realized Willem had many years of outdoor experience. Eden must have been his home for most, if not all, of his life. *I've only been here one other time,* he thought. *And then, only for a day. May have to put more faith in the kid than I normally would.*

No chatter came from the open bed that carried the remaining six team members. *Remaining. That's a tough word to use in these cases,* he thought, grinding his teeth together. A good man lost, and others deeply affected. And to top it all off, an immediate embarkation on a mission against an unknown force, with the added responsibility of having to tear down an entire terrorist organization.

He closed his eyes to force the image away, but only succeeded in causing it to morph into a freeze frame shot of Brevik, head down, carrying the lifeless body of Teresita St. Laurent out of the Operations Center on Poliahu. Tee, shot to death by an out-of-control traitor. He shook his head. *Too much death.*

The truck slowed, and Willem pointed out the windscreen. "There," he said.

The driver squinted, cocking his head to one side as he turned in the direction of Willem's hand. "I don't see…"

"There," Willem repeated. "Just beyond that split yellowbole."

Gabriel followed the young man's hand and saw the tree, cracked down the middle by what must have been a lightning strike. A few feet past it was a break in the thick jungle wall, barely wide enough to fit a man. As the truck left the planked surface and jounced over the bumpy ground towards the opening, he wondered how Brevik would make out on this trek. He had enough trouble fitting through standard doorways, let alone trying to slip through the tightly-woven jungle foliage packing an Oso-11 on his back.

The driver expertly swung the vehicle around in the tight space between the roadway and the jungle's edge, turning the back of the bed to face the opening. Gabriel opened the door and hopped out, followed by Willem. He stepped around to the back of the truck where his team was starting to dismount from the vehicle.

The smells of the jungle, the dank stench of rotting vegetation and moisture, filled his nostrils. The air was heavy, as if a rainstorm had just gone through, but he remembered from his first visit that the air was always this thick. The combination of the massive plant growth and the dense overhead canopy made for a greenhouse-like environment across much of the habitable areas of Eden. Smells stirred up the deepest of memories in people, but Gabriel's thoughts were on his current situation. And his current team.

Brevik and Sennett had already jumped out and were helping the others. Gabriel watched as Takahashi and Olszewski handed equipment to the two on the ground, while Negassi and Sowers scanned their surroundings for threats. Again he thought they were traveling light, a lot lighter than he would have liked considering their new task. No longer simply a hostage rescue, their new mission was now encompassing an entirely different scope, one of retaliation and possible assassination.

Watching Sennett receive a small container of assault rifle ammunition, he frowned, thinking back to five years ago and his first trip to Eden. They had come in too light then also, and unprepared for their opponent. Light couldn't be helped at this point. Eden Guard didn't have much more firepower than hand weapons, and the caliber of ammunition, due to fractured bureaucracies and decades of intersystem trading and local needs, wasn't compatible with any of the NAF or MDF weapons the team carried. Which meant a limited supply. Which meant they were traveling light. They had filled their packs with as much ordnance as the Guard could provide, but Gabriel still wasn't comfortable. And now, on top of supply shortages, he was down a man. A good man.

He shook his head to clear it and walked over to the back of the truck to help. Grabbing the duffel of rations, he said, "How's it looking, Lieutenant?"

Brevik grunted and set the case containing his heavy assault rifle on the ground. "Good, sir. Not much to pack."

Gabriel nodded. "No kidding. How is Sowers?" he asked in a low voice.

Brevik paused, then took the pack of explosives from Takahashi, who then jumped out of the truck bed and joined them. "He's doing okay, sir, as best as can be expected I suppose."

Takahashi looked back at Sowers, who was facing the opposite direction watching the jungle across the roadway. "It hit him hard, sir," the ensign said. "Damn, I've never seen him so quiet."

"Understandable," Gabriel replied as he wiped sweat from his brow. "I know they were good friends. Lieutenant?"

"He's solid," Brevik replied instantly. "No doubts."

"I know, I know. No doubts with me either. Just..." He watched as Olszewski handed the last of the equipment to Brevik and jumped out of the truck bed. He looked at the small collection on the ground. *Just not comfortable. And now, a man down.*

"Willem," he called. The young man was nowhere to be seen. He looked at Sennett. "Go find the kid."

Sennett turned and started to head towards the jungle opening when Willem appeared on the other side of the roadway, zipping up his pants.

"Sorry, Commander," he said as he crossed the planking. "Nature called, and we can't very well piss where we walk if we want to do this quietly. Too many animals out here."

Gabriel expected a wise comment from Sowers, but none came. He was still standing in the bed of the truck facing outwards, watching. Gabriel knew he heard Willem, but chose to say nothing. He wasn't sure what to do about Sowers; he only hoped Brevik's assessment was accurate. He also hoped Willem was who he said he was, just a simple hunter, but the fact he was conveniently late to the garage before the explosion still gave him a creeping doubt.

"Okay, folks," he said as he motioned to Negassi and Sowers to join them. "Let's get this gear loaded up and covered. Use the chromosuit waist pouches for the small stuff. For your larger weapons, put them in the back pouch so they stay under the spoof cells. Lieutenant, do your best to get that cannon under wraps. I want us going in fully stealthed. Weapons only at a sign of a threat, and we're going short-range neuretics comm only. Understood?"

Three 'aye ayes' and three 'yes sirs' answered him, and he again reflected on his missing man. Low on firepower, and missing their weapons specialist.

He glanced at Willem, who was dressed in simple hunting gear. He hoped the young man wouldn't prove to be a liability without active camo or the ability to communicate silently with the rest of the team. He watched as Willem adjusted his belt and shifted a few pieces of cloth on his vest and pants, then slipped on a hat with a netting that hung over his face and neck. As the young man stepped towards the jungle's edge, Gabriel noticed that what he thought was a haphazard collection of fabric and netting blended nearly perfectly into the foliage, and he nearly disappeared as he approached the trees. *Ghost indeed*, he thought.

He slipped on his gloves and pulled on the helmet of his chromosuit. He sent the command to activate the suit, and watched as the others did the same and faded into hazy blurs.

"Let's move."

"There."

The one word sounded like a shout in the deathly quiet room. Three men sat around an old model holotable, the finish long having since cracked and peeled away in the humidity of Eden. The image projected above its surface was hazy and pixelated, and it shimmered in the smoky atmosphere of the room. The man who spoke pointed with his lit cigarette.

"Right there," he said. The dangling ember indicated a tiny flashing icon in one corner of the roughly cubic image.

Jamar Chaud leaned back in his chair and took a long drink of his now-cold coffee. He waited a few seconds before answering, his patience starting to wear thin after having been stuck in the ops tent for the past hour. Prophet had sent him in to monitor the sensor techs after having him redistribute the sensors themselves in accordance to what Harvin had come up with. The path between Eden City and their camp was well used, but as Prophet had told him, probably too obvious. And with the addition of a local hunter, the conclusion they had come to was the most likely one.

He set his coffee bottle on the edge of the holotable and blew his breath out noisily through his lips. "This is the third one, Ratner," he said, allowing a bit of exasperation to leak into his tone. The two techs had annoyed the hell out of him with their constant chatter and laughter. Only a stern command from him had shut them up, and he'd finally been able to gain a bit of traction on the massive headache that was on its way. At least for a few minutes.

"Yes, but this one is right where you said it would be, Captain," Ratner replied. "And the signs of a vehicle on the road."

The other tech, a weaselly little man Chaud thought of as more of a Ratner than the other, chimed in. "And it's the right size." He pointed to a readout on the edge of the image. "Showing a solid eight figures, then seven of them disappeared."

Chaud rubbed his eyes. The headache was returning with a vengeance. He decided to test the techs, maybe he could vent some of his pain on them. "Okay, Pietro, you tell me." He stabbed a finger in the second tech's direction. "What animal could be there, and then not, within seconds?"

"Uh, animal?" Pietro asked, looking at Ratner for support. Ratner just shook his head.

"Yes, animal," Chaud repeated. "I'm not sending my people out there on a wild goosehawk chase if this is another false alarm."

Pietro scratched his head. "Well, maybe a synfox because they're fast..."

"No," Chaud cut him off. "Sensors detect heat and movement."

"The spiderbats have cold bodies, they could..."

"Too small. Think faster, or I'll replace you," Chaud said as he picked up his coffee bottle. He already knew the answer, and fired off a quick neuretics message to Prophet.

"Fire lizards? They have a chameleon skin..."

"Closer. Think bigger."

Pietro stammered. "Uh, sir, I, uh, I'm really not..."

Ratner spoke up. "Only one animal, sir. Men in camo gear."

Chaud smiled. "Give the man a balloon," he said as he stood up from his chair. He leaned across the table and pointed at the blinking icon, which sat at the edge of the roadway from Eden City, miles from where the main path was. "It's them. Force of eight, seven in camo gear, one civilian. Exactly what our intel said."

He turned from the table and headed for the door flap. "Work on your false alarm filters, or Prophet will have you out there as the first to meet Gabriel."

Steve Umstead

CHAPTER TWENTY-FOUR

Jeromy rolled over on his side and opened his eyes, letting in the weak light of morning. The stickiness of the previous night's weather had combined with a lack of sleep to create a burning sensation in both eyes, and he rubbed them vigorously. He yawned and looked over at Magali, who was still asleep in the shadow of one of the housing unit's walls a few feet away. She had come a long way in the past few days, only to have her emotions wrecked by the sight of him being pummeled.

He sat up and winced as a spear of pain shot through his body. He coughed, resulting in several more spears being thrown. *Definitely a broken rib,* he thought. *Maybe two.* He drew his knees into his chest, which helped ease the ache. He pushed his tongue through the space where a canine was the day before. *Yep, still missing.*

He slowly stood up, clutching his side where Davitz had kicked him the night before. He looked over at the far wall where Mowab lay curled up in a fetal position and listened to the youth's ragged breathing. The terrorists had brought him back after several hours of what appeared to be regular beatings and threw him into the corner. Jeromy had checked him over, and although his body was in bad shape with several broken ribs, three broken fingers, a twisted knee, split lip, broken nose, and two rising shiners, his spirit remained intact. He had looked up at Jeromy with a smile as he was probing his wounds and began reciting Hebrew prayers.

Now in the growing morning light, Jeromy could see that the bruises were spreading on Mowab's arms and lower legs. He thought about waking him, but changed his mind. *Let the boy sleep it off*, he thought.

He turned back to Magali, who had opened her eyes and was watching him. "Well?" she asked with a questioning look.

"Well what?" he replied, walking over to where she lay.

"How are you feeling?"

He smiled, and she stifled a laugh. He was about to ask her why when he realized she was looking at the gap in the corner of his mouth where the tooth was knocked out. "Very funny."

"Sorry," she said, sitting up. "I can see you're feeling better. Otherwise I wouldn't have laughed, I promise."

He sat down next to her. He winced again as the broken rib or ribs pressed against nerve endings. "I know. The better question is how are you?"

She sat up and shrugged. "I don't know. Better. Maybe. It's just..." Her voice trailed off.

He reached out and touched the back of her hand, and her eyes lit up. "I know. Please," he said, squeezing her hand, "hang in there. I heard one of the guards last night when they brought Mowab back in. He was talking to one of the others about an assault force headed this way."

Her eyes grew wider. "Really? Why didn't you tell me?"

He shook his head. "You were having a rough night, I thought it better you slept."

She returned his squeeze and ran her other hand through her scraggly hair. "Sleep, sure. I don't think that's what anyone would call it."

He smiled as he saw her sense of humor, and hope, return. He was about to speak when the door to the unit flew open and banged into the wall, stirring the other hostages awake.

Through the door walked Davitz and two other guards. Davitz glared at Jeromy. "Hello kid," he said with a toothy grin.

Jeromy slitted his eyes but remained quiet. The beating from last night still resonated not only in his body, but in his mind, and he tried his best to tamp down his emotions to not run afoul of the guard again. *In due time*, he thought.

"What do you want?" said a student Jeromy knew only as Rip. He was standing against the back wall with several other fellow students. Jeromy watched as Davitz's eyes looked over the group and he started to walk in Rip's direction.

"Hold on, Davitz," said one of the other guards. "We've got instructions."

Davitz paused, staring at the group. After a few seconds he shook his head. "Right," he said. He turned and pointed to the guard who had spoken. "Go grab the military prisoners. Pick the four in the worst shape." He pointed to the other guard. "You, watch those assholes in the back. I need to have a little chat with our friend Tarif here."

Davitz walked over to where Jeromy and Magali sat and stood with his hands on his hips. "How's the ribcage, kid?"

"Just fine," Jeromy replied, meeting the larger man's gaze. "Looking forward to dinner with your boss."

Davitz threw his head back and laughed. "Are you now?" he said. "Don't get your hopes up. Around here, we don't exactly eat like you rich kids. And anyways, Prophet doesn't want you for company. He wants you for leverage. So don't expect wine and cheese." He laughed again, this time leering at Magali. "I'll take good care of your friend while you're gone."

"If you touch one hair…"

"Come on, Davitz, quit it!" said the other guard. "Gimme a hand."

Davitz turned around as the third guard emerged from the back room of the unit, dragging one of the badly injured military prisoners. The other guard walked over to help as another prisoner stumbled through the doorway, walking with a crudely fashioned crutch.

Davitz gave one last sneer to Jeromy. "I'll pick you up in a few hours, kid. Make sure to be presentable."

"Wait," Jeromy said as Davitz walked away. "Where are you taking them?"

"What do you care?" Davitz said over his shoulder.

"Because they're hurt!" Magali said. "You can't just move them around, they have serious injuries!"

The guards ignored her plea and continued to drag the prisoners out past the students. Jeromy watched in sadness as they passed, several of them having missing limbs, burned faces, and more; all four of them possessed lifeless, hopeless stares. He had been told many of them had been held by the terrorists for years. He had no idea how they survived even weeks considering the condition some of them were in.

"Don't worry about 'em," said Davitz as he pulled the last of the four through the main door. "You won't be seeing them again." He slammed the door closed behind him, and Jeromy heard the familiar sound of the lock being engaged.

"What are they going to do with them?" Magali whispered, gripping Jeromy's hand tighter.

He shook his head slowly, not wanting to upset her further. "I don't know."

Chaud knocked on Prophet's door and waited. Several minutes passed before he heard a voice.

"Come."

Chaud opened the door and walked into the darkened tent. Prophet had received many offers of a nicer, more spacious housing unit, but had always refused them, he remembered. It was about staying true to his troops, he had said, or something along those lines. Chaud paused inside the doorway and waited as his eyes adjusted to the gloom.

Another idiosyncrasy of their leader. He preferred darkness, and no one ever had the inclination to ask him why.

"Captain," said Prophet's disembodied voice. "Please, have a seat. Fill me in."

Chaud began to see shadows, slowly at first, then after a few moments was able to see the layout of the tent. Prophet sat in a canvas chair in front of a small table, another chair across from it. Chaud walked over, stumbling only once on some unseen object, and sat in the other chair.

"Thank you, sir," he said. "The second set of sensors Harvin and I emplaced picked up a slight trace of the assault team. It appears they are heading in the expected direction, towards one of the hunters' hides we marked. We have a few surprises waiting for them there. I did take the liberty of pulling a few men from the original route to cover this new approach. I hope that was not overstepping my bounds, sir."

"No, not at all, Captain. I expected that of you," Prophet said. "And the other?"

"The military prisoners have been brought out as you requested. Four of them, all in fairly serious medical condition. Davitz has them in the courtyard, awaiting your instructions." He shifted in his seat. "Sir, I understand the purpose, but these men…"

"Yes, Captain?"

Chaud paused, unsure whether to continue. His position within the organization was an enviable one, the commander of the military forces, but sometimes that position led him to agree to things he found… unsettling. Prophet was ruthless, as evidenced by the killing of Maybeck a few weeks back. But he was also calculating, methodical… and intelligent. This plan didn't fit with what he knew of their leader. *Hell*, he thought, *here goes*.

"These men are in pretty bad shape. I'm not entirely comfortable with using them as… well, bait. Sir," he added.

Prophet smiled, the white of his teeth showing slightly in the darkness. "Captain, I commend you for having the wherewithal to bring that up. Actually, more like having the balls to, I suppose. And I appreciate your candor."

Chaud let out a breath silently, a breath he hadn't even realized he was holding, and hoped the hammer wasn't about to drop.

"They are bait, yes. However I do not plan to strap them into a mousetrap and wait for them to be eaten. Not exactly sporting, wouldn't you say?"

Chaud waited, realizing this was another rhetorical question. He watched as Prophet picked up a glass from the table and drank from it. He caught a whiff of something: pricklefruit juice perhaps.

"Tell me, Captain. With a traveling force with a limited supply train, what could possibly be worse than killing some of them?"

The plan lit up in Chaud's mind like a beacon. It all made sense now. "Wounding them so they slow down the others," he said.

"Exactly. And since we cannot be guaranteed of clipping some of their wings before they arrive — Gabriel has shown himself to be very resourceful after all — we will simply *give* them some wounded to take care of. Little by little, we will slow them down to the point of a crawl. And then, Captain, you and your men can have your way with them."

Plans formed in Chaud's mind even before his leader spoke again.

"Take Davitz and two others and bring, or carry, whatever you need to do, the prisoners to the positions I have marked on the map." He slid a piece of paper across the table to Chaud. "One prisoner at each location. Save the most gravely wounded one for the last position, the one in close. I have something I'm working on."

Prophet stood up, and Chaud quickly mirrored the motion.

"One more thing, Captain," Prophet said as he picked up his glass again. "When you're done with the positioning, have Davitz bring Tarif to me. And please instruct him, in no uncertain terms, that he is not to touch the young man again. My orders."

Chaud caught the edge in his voice and chastised himself silently for not stopping the beating Davitz had given Tarif. Prophet was ruthless, but never without a reason or purpose. And he had no patience for others who showed unnecessary cruelty.

"Of course, sir," he replied. "Anything else?"

"No, Jamar. I appreciate your loyalty."

Chaud started at Prophet's use of his first name. Perhaps his position, while witness to some uncomfortable incidents, was growing less precarious.

"Thank you, sir," he said. He gave a small salute, knowing Prophet could see him quite clearly, and turned to leave.

As he closed the tent flap door behind him, he let out another breath. *Time.* He walked across the courtyard to where Davitz stood with the other guards and prisoners, leaving Prophet's tent behind.

CHAPTER TWENTY-FIVE

Gabriel swatted at another leafbee that tried to crawl inside the helmet flap of his chromosuit. *Half a dozen now in the past five minutes*, he thought. *Knew the easy part wouldn't last.*

The march through the jungle had started off well, with the team making strong progress through the more sparse areas. Their projected path, what Willem has laid out for them, took them along a small stream that meandered along their general route for over a mile. Where the stream took a dogleg left, the team turned right, and marched headlong into dense foliage.

Gabriel had placed Sennett on point with Sowers off his shoulder a few dozen feet. Sennett carried a molecular blade machete, which, without camo, looked very much out of place: a solitary, floating blade slicing through the thick jungle. However, there was no way around it. In order to penetrate the heavy undergrowth, they wouldn't be able to be completely invisible. For this reason, Gabriel had the team draw handguns for this part of the trek.

Gabriel followed Sennett and Sowers, Negassi off his shoulder. Behind him were Olszewski and Willem, then Takahashi and Brevik. He considered having Willem on point, but the fact that the teenager was unarmed and uncamouflaged made him uneasy. Instead he had Willem plot a general path for him at the stream turn, and would consult with him again at the next change in direction. *Which should be right about here*, he thought. He pulled up the map in his Mindseye, which had Willem's directions overlaid on it, and confirmed it.

[*Hold position*] he sent in a quick burst on the team net. He saw the machete stop in mid-arc ahead of him as Sennett came to a halt; the other dots superimposed on his vision did likewise. He walked forward to join up with Sennett and Sowers.

As he reached Sowers, he placed a hand on his shoulder and switched to a private neuretics channel.

[*You okay, Mister Sowers?*] he sent.

This close in, his combat helmet's heads-up display could see Sowers's head in a blurry outline. He saw it turn slightly towards him, then back to the jungle ahead.

[*Yes, sir.*] came the quick emotionless reply.

He considered pursuing it further with Sowers, as he needed a strong cohesive team on this mission, but put it aside. *Too much to do right now*, he thought. He'd just have to keep an eye on him. He gave his shoulder a quick squeeze, then moved up to Sennett.

[*We've got a fifteen degree turn to the west, Corporal,*] he sent.

[*Yes, sir.*] Sennett lifted the machete, which again seemed to Gabriel to float in midair like an object one might see at a magic show. The tip of the blade turned slightly to the left. [*Good?*]

[*Yes, let's move,*] he sent back. As he turned to take up his position, a rustle sounded from their right flank. He checked his Mindseye for positions and caught a faint infrared signal.

[*Ensign Takahashi, to your right,*] he sent on the team net.

Takahashi turned towards the sound, his handgun coming up at the ready. Suddenly in a burst of green leaves and brown fur, he was down, a huge screeching animal wrestling him to the ground.

"Shit!" yelled Olszewski, and jumped on the two figures. Gabriel saw a flash.

More loud sounds came from the scrum, the animal's high-pitched screeches now mixed with Takahashi's angry yells. Gabriel ran towards the pile, as did the others. As he approached, he picked up the outlines of his men and the animal, and more silvery flashes. His Heckart came up, tingling in his palm, but before he had a chance to aim, the fight was over.

Olszewski stood up, his invisible chromosuit dripping with a purplish blood. Takahashi rolled out from under the massive bulk on the now-dead animal, cursing softly.

[*Comm only,*] Gabriel reminded. [*Ensign, are you okay?*]

[*Dammit. Yes, sir, unharmed. Just... pissed off,*] Takahashi answered.

[*Negassi, do you have the medikit?*] Gabriel sent.

[*Sir, I'm fine...*] he began, only to be cut off by Gabriel with an override.

[*Not for you, for Olszewski's suit,*] Gabriel said. [*We need to get that blood off him, or the suit does him no good visually.*]

Negassi walked up and handed Gabriel a small pack. He opened it and withdrew a handful of sterilizing nanopads, which he handed to the corporal. Olszewski took them and began wiping away the blood from his chromosuit and his molyknife. The nanopads' properties broke down the molecular bonds of the blood and it wiped away almost instantly.

[*Commander, what the hell was that?*] It was Sennett.

Gabriel looked at the animal's body lying on the ground. It was close to five feet in length, had six legs ending in wicked-looking claws, a long snout reminiscent of an Earth aardvark, and was covered in long brownish-green fur. Several nasty knife wounds leaked purple ichor which dripped onto the dark soil, creating dirty black puddles.

[*Parweasel,*] he sent. [*Biggest one I've ever seen. Or heard of.*]

He heard the soft whine of a mag pistol powering up. [*Relax, they hunt alone,*] he sent. [*But stay alert, there's more out here than parweasels.*]

As the team regrouped to continue their march, he wondered just what else was actually waiting for them.

With the incessant leafbees, the ever-thickening jungle undergrowth, and the rising heat and humidity they were going through, Gabriel again felt they were traveling too light. *Maybe just one APC,* he thought. *We'd have been there already. Better yet, air drop.*

Olszewski had relieved Sennett on point and was using the machete. Takahashi had joined him with his own machete, and the two of them were hacking their way through the thick growth. Gabriel shook his head at the sound of the blades hitting branches. *So much for stealth.*

They had been marching for close to two hours, and had made decent progress according to Gabriel's original timetable. Even with the unexpected parweasel attack, and a subsequent treemonkey acid-throwing incident, they were on schedule. Fortunately, the chromosuits had been designed with the acid in mind, and no one took any damage.

He double-checked his Mindseye map again and called for a halt. They had reached the area where Willem said there was a hide built, and Gabriel wanted to rest up for a few minutes and collect some stashed water the youth said the hunters had collected.

They were about forty yards from the hide. He called Willem over with a low whistle.

"Commander?" the teenager said quietly, now standing next to Gabriel.

He was surprised how well the kid's outfit had blended into the jungle. One minute, he was a walking fashion disaster, a jumbled mass of fabric and net shreds, and the next he was invisible among the foliage. With the sun at certain angles through the trees, he was actually able to see his team's outlines better than Willem's.

"We're at the hide," he said in a low voice. "What's the best approach?"

Willem pointed towards a small footpath, barely visible between two massive yellowboles. "There. We'll have to go low, maybe even crawl for you and some of the others, as it's a passage only about four feet high."

Gabriel heard Brevik grumble behind him. He had seen the big man already had a tough time in some of the tighter spots along the way, and with the heavy assault rifle on his back, it wasn't going to get much easier.

He highlighted the entrance on his neuretics map and sent it to the team. Several low groans were heard as the others received the images.

[*I'll take point,*] he sent. [*Takahashi on me, Brevik take six. Stay low, and stay quiet.*]

He walked over to the break in the trees Willem had pointed out, and with a quick check to make sure all his team's icons were positioned properly, he bent over and stepped into the opening.

The height of the break in the foliage belied the true nature of the pathway. It seemed to Gabriel it was more of a tunnel than anything else. The low-hanging branches of the neopines interlocked overhead, completely blocking out the sun. Several sharp points protruded, giving it the feel of walking past an enormous animal's teeth, then down its throat. He had to bend at the waist, almost doubled over, to get through some of the lowest spots. He wondered how the hell Brevik was going to manage.

He stopped about thirty feet in and turned, beginning to rethink the approach because of the size issues, when a feeling came over him. The hairs on the back of his neck stood up. He checked his passive scans, all were clean. He debated an active scan but rejected the thought as too risky. He started to turn around to continue to the hide when he felt, under his chromosuit, all the hairs stand up on his arms.

Almost like the feeling he got when a ship's EM field generators spun up prior to…

"Down!" he yelled, dropping to the ground. His Mindseye showed all seven others matching his move, and none too soon. A bright turquoise bolt of energy sizzled overhead and blasted out of the entrance to the path, leaving smoking neopine branches in its wake.

"Army crawl out of here, double time!" he yelled, pushing at Takahashi's feet in front of him. Within seconds the team had exited the tunnel and positioned themselves away from the entrance, which was now crackling and sizzling from the particle beam.

"Holy shit," Sennett said, panting.

"Star formation, I want all approaches covered," Gabriel said and ran an active scan. *Damn the risk*, he thought. After a few seconds it came back clean, except for a hazy area near the end of the pathway, adjacent to the hide Willem had pointed out. Stealth field, he surmised. And a damned good one. Enough of a shield that he wasn't able to burn through. Didn't matter, though, as this approach was out. *Willem.*

He looked over at the hunter, who was standing near Sowers with a wide-eyed look on his face. He walked over and grabbed the youth by his tunic and shoved him up against the base of a young yellowbole.

"Tell me what you know, boy," he said, pushing his invisible hand up into Willem's chin. "How do they know we're coming this way?"

"Commander, I don't know anything," he said, gasping. "I just pissed my pants like the rest of you."

"You're telling me that somehow, some way, the terrorists pegged our approach with a lucky guess? That your secret hide, known only to you and a handful of other kids, coincidentally has a particle beam cannon set up to defend it?" He pushed harder, pressing Willem's head back against the bark of the tree. "Who did you tell?"

"No one!" he gurgled as he grabbed at Gabriel's hand.

"Commander," said Brevik quietly from his position nearby. "Perhaps he's telling the truth. Otherwise he probably wouldn't have gone in there with us."

Shit. His brain was so frazzled at the attack, he hadn't even considered that. He eased his grip ever so slightly, allowing Willem to gulp in some air. "Who else knows about this hide?"

"Six, maybe seven others, but none of them would tell the terrorists! Why would we?"

Gabriel released him, and the youth dropped to the ground rubbing his neck. He looked around the small clearing the team was in. Everyone's icon was in proper position, standard star defense formation, and he saw all had weapons drawn and armed. He looked back at Willem, who was staring up at him with a scared look. *Doesn't make any sense*, he thought.

He walked over to Brevik and spoke in low tones. "Lieutenant, we're going to make some changes in our route. Agreed?"

"Hell yes, sir. Are you asking or telling?"

"Both. I need you to plan the route with me. I want your input. I don't trust this kid. Didn't really to begin with, and not at all now."

He flashed Brevik his maps and data, and Brevik returned the receipt code. Gabriel linked the two neuretics systems together with a secure proximity pipe and began laying out the route. Brevik modified where he saw necessary as the two men began plotting the new course. After a few minutes, they had come up with an overall plan.

"Are we good?" asked Gabriel.

"Yes, sir, best I can see," Brevik answered.

Gabriel nodded and walked back over to Willem, who was now standing near Takahashi, still rubbing his neck. Willem's eyes widened at his approach.

"You stay with me, on my hip, where I can see you. Understood?" Gabriel asked.

"Uh, yes, Commander. Listen, I'm sorry…"

"Enough."

Willem closed his mouth with an audible click.

Gabriel turned back to the clearing, starting to put together the route packet to send to the rest of the team. [*Everyone set to move?*] he sent. Five affirmative bursts came back. One missing, he noted.

"Where the hell is Sennett?" he asked out loud.

"Confirmation of autosentry fire, sir," said the tech, who was wearing old-style VR goggles.

Chaud looked up from his book and set his coffee bottle down. Taking his feet off the edge of the holotable, he sat forward.

"Fire?" he asked.

"Yes, sir," the tech answered. "One burst, nothing on visual or IR sensors on the far end."

"Correct me if I'm wrong, but with a particle beam blast, IR sensors on the other end would be useless," Chaud said, shaking his head. *Kids*, he thought.

"Ah yes, sorry sir," the tech stammered. "Nothing on visual, no confirmation of targets hit or missed."

"Could be a misfire then?" Chaud asked.

"The timing for their arrival is right, so I'm assuming…"

"Assume nothing, Private. Who is in that area?"

The tech lifted his goggles and consulted the notepad he had in front of him. "Sweeney and Powers, sir. Another hundred yards down route."

Chaud nodded. He had already known who was stationed there; after all, he had placed them. He just wanted to make sure the kid was fully involved in the mission. They had a hard enough time paying attention in training, let alone a boring overwatch duty.

"Get Powers on the comm, have them move up to check the site," he said. "We need to know if the autosentry was successful, or if we still have company on the way."

"Yes, sir," the tech replied. He picked up a handset from the table and punched in a few codes.

As the tech spoke to Powers, Chaud picked up his coffee bottle again and took a sip. He didn't expect the initial package to be a hundred percent effective. He'd settle for picking off one or two of the approaching team. Anything to whittle the numbers down. He had read up on Commander Gabriel and his past actions on Poliahu, and couldn't escape the nagging feeling in the back of his mind that they were underprepared.

He stood up and headed for the door. "I have to hit the head," he called over his shoulder. "When I get back I expect Powers to have given you a full report."

Steve Umstead

CHAPTER TWENTY-SIX

Sowers pushed through the thick tangle of neopine branches, their sharp edges digging through his gloves and into his hands. They didn't penetrate; nothing short of a heavy assault rifle round could get through the kinetic fabric, but the pinpoints of pressure made his hands ache. More and more leafbees were buzzing at the flap below his combat helmet, as if they knew that was the only way in to bite at his skin. He slapped at his neck with one hand while bending a particularly thick branch out of the way with his other.

He still wasn't entirely sure why Commander Gabriel had sent him to find Sennett. He was the furthest away from Sennett's position, and had absolutely zero idea where he had gone. Or why. He only knew he had been given an assignment, and he'd follow through the best he could.

The ache was still there. Deep down, somewhere inside his chest, he ached. Arturo was gone, had died almost right in front of him. And from a cowardly bomb, not even a straight up firefight. He wasn't sure what was worse: the loss of a good friend, or the manner in which he died.

As he pushed another thick branch out of the way, he realized that was a stupid question. Losing his partner in crime, his training buddy, maybe the best friend he had known since his teen years, far outweighed any ridiculous thoughts of going out in a blaze of glory.

He'd find whoever had set that bomb. He'd find him, and then no one would ever find him again. Not even the smallest piece of him. He ground his teeth inside his helmet. *I'll find you*, he thought, the rage building up even more. But he set the vow aside, knowing he needed to support the rest of his team during this mission. Which, as he looked at the jungle in front of him, was turning out to be more of a pain in the ass than he had been led to believe.

He was about to change direction when he noticed several broken branches a few feet to his right, branches he hadn't gotten to yet, and well away from the rest of the team and their initial approach. *Must be Sennett.* He walked over to the site and saw footprints in the soil.

"*Sennett*," he called in a strong whisper, trying to project a soft voice into the trees. Sennett hadn't been answering neuretics calls, and his icon had dropped off the net. Not inactive, like no life signs, but more so that he had turned it off.

He took a few more steps, following the trail, and pushed aside a thicket of thorngrass. Behind it was a tiny clearing, and in the middle of it sat the blurry outline of Sennett. He was down on his knees, squatted on his haunches, and his combat helmet was off, exposing his head to full view. He was holding one ungloved hand in the air above his upturned face, creating an eerie scene of a floating head and hand. He was barely moving a muscle, and Sowers froze in his tracks. *Maybe a trap,* he thought.

He sent a passive neuretics scan out, checking the treeline around Sennett. The only return was Sennett himself. Again he hadn't moved, but was giving off healthy life signs. Sowers took one last glance around, drew his Heckart, and called out.

"*Corporal Sennett*," he said again in a low whisper.

Sennett's head snapped around in surprise, and he dropped a small item from his ungloved hand. It bounced off his shoulder and rolled into the grass near his feet. Sowers looked from Sennett's wide-eyed face down to the object. A microsyringe.

"Are you *shittin'* me?" Sowers roared. He burst through the rest of the thorngrass, oblivious to the drag caused by the grass catching on his legs. He took a half dozen quick strides over to Sennett and shoved his kneeling body over onto the ground. Standing over him, he looked down into his face.

"*Dew?* What the goddam hell are you doing with that?" he yelled, ignoring the stealth orders. "In the middle of a goddam mission? Are you trying to get us all killed?"

Sennett's face reddened as he gasped for air, his breath having been knocked out of him from Sowers's shove. Sowers saw tears beginning to form in the corners of his eyes, and wondered if they were real, or induced by the injection. He pushed the prone man with the bottom of his boot. "Well?" he asked as he took off his combat helmet.

"Ah, shit, Galen," Sennett said as he pushed himself up on one arm. "I'm sorry, man, it's just been a tough couple of hours, and..."

"Tough?" Sowers replied. "You have no idea how tough it's about to get for you."

He dropped his helmet on the ground and bent over, grabbing Sennett by one arm and pulling him upright. He moved in close, their noses almost touching. "How long you been doing it? How many doses?" he demanded.

Sennett shrank from Sowers's stare and looked down at the ground. "Just a couple, man. I've only done it a few times, just to get through rough patches. You know?"

"No, I don't know, asshole. And apparently, I don't know you as well as I thought."

Sowers released his arm and stepped back. Seeing the microsyringe on the ground, he raised his foot and stomped on it, shattering the thin glass. "Dammit, man. How am I, or anyone else, supposed to trust you? To have our backs?"

Sennett turned back, and Sowers saw a flash in his eye. "Trust? You're going to lecture me on trust? Someone who hasn't said word one since your buddy died, someone who barely acknowledges he's even on a team anymore?"

Sowers took a two quick steps and punched Sennett square in the jaw. The corporal dropped to the ground, a disembodied head amongst the grass and soil.

"Don't go there," Sowers spat. "I'm not hopped on dew."

"Yeah, but is your head right?" Sennett asked as he clambered to his feet. "Are you there for us if…"

Sowers held up a hand, cutting off his words. Something was registering in his passive neuretics scan, which he had left running in the background. Something, man or animal, was approaching from the east.

[*Shut up,*] he sent, pointing at the treeline. [*Company.*]

Sennett just stared back uncomprehendingly. Sowers realized the other man still had his neuretics shut down so the others wouldn't find him shooting dew. He tapped his temple. "Switch on," he whispered.

He sent a burst to his Heckart to arm it and motioned with the gun so Sennett would see where he was pointing. An icon popped up in his Mindseye as Sennett linked back into the team net. He sent him the data from his scan.

[*Helmets,*] Sennett reminded him. Sowers cursed under his breath and picked up his helmet, Sennett doing the same. He slipped it on over his head and adjusted the flaps, then relinked his neuretics to the combat sensors in the helmet. A heads-up display projected the threat onto his visor. Looked like a single person moving slowly from the east in their general direction. *Should have been a little quieter,* he chastised himself.

He sent an image to Sennett of where he wanted him stationed, then moved to his own defensive position. Both men had their Heckarts charged and armed. He had just crouched down to a firing position when a tiny sonic boom buffeted his helmet, and he rolled away from the near-miss.

[*Sniper, on our six!*] he sent in a frantic message to Sennett. His neuretics instantly computed the angle and direction the attack had come from. He turned to face the direction the sniper round had come from and his heads-up plotted a target. He raised his Heckart, squeezing off four shots towards the treeline. He didn't wait for a result; he pushed backwards in a crab walk further into the neopine branches.

His heads-up showed Sennett's icon doing the same a few dozen feet away, and the original target now just about upon them, but its approach had slowed to a standstill. He sent a burst on the team net to alert the others, tagging and including the images and data in his heads-up. Judging by how far he had walked to finally stumble across Sennett, this firefight would probably be over before anyone else arrived.

He checked his map overlays and saw the projected area where the sniper must be, approximately thirty feet up in one of two yellowboles just under a hundred yards away. Looking at Sennett's position, he saw that he had a much better angle at the perch.

[*Sennett,*] he sent. [*I've got the sniper pegged, I'll send you the data. See if you can take him out.*]

He watched as a thick rifle barrel appeared as if by magic in the shadow of a bush. As Sennett armed his MDF-issued kinetic assault rifle, Sowers pressed further back into the branches, towards the second target.

[*Ready,*] sent Sennett.

Sowers sent the burst of data to him, and received an acknowledgement. He shifted a bit to turn towards the other target, which had now started to move in their direction again. [*On my mark.*] Another acknowledgment.

Sowers counted to five in his head then simultaneously sent the firing command to Sennett and pushed himself fully through the neopine branches. As he fell forwards into a roll in a small break in the foliage, he heard the firing of the assault rifle behind him: three timed bursts, in rapid sequence.

A figure holding a pulse rifle stood in front of Sowers, frozen in place, apparently shocked at the sudden appearance of a floating mag pistol three feet above the jungle floor. The pause cost him his life. Two tiny red holes appeared, one below his left eye, and the other dead center of his forehead. The terrorist collapsed onto the ground, his weapon falling next to him. Sowers glanced down at the rifle; it wasn't even armed or charged. *Amateurs*, he thought.

[*Sennett, report,*] he sent.

[*Hold on,*] A minute or so went by, and Sowers began to worry. Then, [*Confirmed kill, one sniper.*]

He thought about checking the fallen man's pulse, but seeing the blood leaking out from under his head, changed his mind. He turned and pushed back into the area he had come from.

[*Sowers,*] came Gabriel's burst. [*What's going on over there?*]

As Sowers entered the clearing where he had initially found Sennett, he saw the cracked microsyringe. It was half-buried in the soil where his boot had pressed it down. He hesitated. Sennett was royally screwing the pooch and possibly putting the team at risk, especially if he had dosed enough to drop him into the typical coma-like crash afterwards. But maybe he had had a point. What use was Sowers himself to others if he wasn't fully in the game? What right was he to judge? By giving up Sennett to Gabriel and the others, the team would be down another man. He had no doubt Gabriel would boot the man's ass right out of the jungle, perhaps literally and not just figuratively. Sennett was a good man. Young, wet behind the ears, but a strong soldier. Someone he thought he could count on. Maybe he still could. Maybe they could count on each other.

[*Sowers!*] came Gabriel's burst again. [*We're on our way.*]

Sowers stared at the fractured glass tube. Dammit. [*Sennett,*] he sent on a private point-to-point frequency. [*Where are you?*]

[*Dragging the body back,*] came the answer.

Sowers checked the icons' positions on his heads-up. He saw Gabriel and Brevik headed his way; Sennett was closer, but dragging would slow him down. *Dammit*, he thought again. [*Double time it, I'm coming to meet you. We gotta talk.*]

[*Here, Commander. We're fine, Sennett had to take a leak and got ambushed,*] he sent to Gabriel. He reached over and picked up the remains of the microsyringe and walked off into the jungle towards Sennett, tossing the glass pieces far into the thick foliage.

Steve Umstead

CHAPTER TWENTY-SEVEN

"We've lost contact with Powers and Sweeney, sir."

The words hung in space like the haze filling the room. Chaud waited patiently for the explosion, adjusting his collar once again to allow his body heat to escape.

The afternoon had gotten downright steamy. Chaud had been sitting in the operations tent, overseeing the plans he had help put into action. He was seated in the same chair he was in previously when the techs had picked up the initial signs of the team. The same two techs were there, VR goggles on, but now the small tent was even more cramped, and humid, with the addition of Zeno and Harvin...and Prophet.

Chaud watched as Prophet stared at the tech who had spoken. The tech was unaware of the stare; the goggles covered his vision completely, and Chaud almost felt sorry for him. *What was the old saying, don't kill the messenger?*

The stare continued until the tech spoke again. "Did everyone get that?"

Zeno cleared his throat. "Yes, we got it. Is there any sign of them from the sensors in that area?"

The other tech answered, pushing his goggles up on his head. "No, they went out of range of the hide to check the autosentry status. I said that before…" His voice died as he saw Prophet's stare.

The room was dead silent. Chaud heard the creak of the tent's roof poles in a gust of wind, the laughter of a distant treemonkey. The haze in the room seemed to grow even more dense. Nearly a minute passed before Prophet spoke.

"I'm losing patience."

Chaud felt the tension in the tent ratchet higher. The second tech wiped his nose nervously and looked over at Chaud for support. Seeing none, he pushed his goggles back down over his eyes, mumbling about rechecking data.

"Captain Chaud."

Chaud stiffened at the mention of his name. Prophet hadn't turned in his direction, but both Zeno and Harvin had. He coughed into his hand. "Sir," he replied.

"Captain, this operation you have put together…does not seem to be progressing quite as expected, wouldn't you say?"

Chaud didn't miss the not-so-subtle emphasis on *you* when Prophet referred to the operation. He knew the success or failure of the encampment's defense rested squarely on his shoulders. He didn't fear the blame; he did, however, fear the consequences of failure. Not just with Prophet, but with the approaching force.

"No, sir, it is not. However, what we can do…"

Prophet raised his hand and Chaud closed his mouth. Another long minute passed, and Prophet lowered his hand back into his lap. "We aren't going to do anything, Captain. I am. Zeno," he said.

Zeno's eyes shot to the leader. "Sir?"

"Have the prisoners been positioned?"

"Ah, yes sir, as per Captain Chaud's orders."

Chaud winced inwardly at the attribution. He knew where Prophet was going with this, and it wasn't going to reflect well on him.

Prophet shifted his stare from the tech to Chaud. "We're changing it."

"Sir?" Zeno asked.

"Gabriel will change his route. Now that a poorly hidden trap was avoided, and two bumbling idiots were killed, he knows we have his route figured out," Prophet said in a near-monotone.

Chaud chewed on his inner cheek. He didn't dare speak up with any suggestions on new routes.

"I will tell you where to place them, along with additional fighters. You are in contact with them, I assume?"

Zeno nodded vigorously. "Real time. Just tell me where, and we can reposition them within minutes."

"Good," Prophet replied. "Harvin, I want you out with the final prisoner, awaiting Zeno's call. Ratner," he said, pointing towards the tech who had initially informed them of the loss of signal. The tech quickly removed his goggles. "Put up the holoimage on the table and give me admin control. I need to modify this... plan."

The tech nodded and began punching buttons on the table's edge. As the holo image began to rise from the table's surface, the tent flap door opened, allowing in a gust of hot, humid air. Standing in the doorway were two men's shadows: one quite large, one barely out of his teens. Chaud started to reprimand Davitz for his lack of subtlety when Prophet spoke again.

"Ah, Mr. Davitz has arrived with our special guest." He stood up and walked around the table, and to Chaud's surprise, walked up to the young man with Davitz and extended a hand.

"Good afternoon, Jeromy," he said. "You're just in time for the fireworks."

"Change of plans, folks," Gabriel said in a low voice.

The team was assembled in the clearing where Sowers had found Sennett. The two terrorists' bodies were lying off to one side, having been stripped of equipment and a handful of ration bars and water bottles. Gabriel had had

Sowers inspect their comm gear to see if they could possibly hack into communications, without much luck. Both radios were old-school, Sowers had said, nothing to track back; almost like two tin cans and a very long string.

"We're shifting our approach. They obviously know which way we're coming," he said, shooting a glance at Willem, "so we're going to have to start being unpredictable. Brevik and I have put together a new route. I'm sending it to you now."

He watched in his Mindseye as all six others received the route packet and acknowledged. "Good. Stealth is still on our side but not nearly as much as it was an hour ago. We stay in the chromosuits, and once we move out, stick with 'rets for comm. However, sneaking up on them may not be in the plans anymore. They're aware of our presence. We're now on a shoot-first, ask-questions-later program. Primary weapons drawn and charged. Got it?"

The other six all gave an affirmative, and Willem nodded. "You," said Gabriel, looking at Willem. "You and I will be on point. I need your eyes and ears out in front of us."

"Commander, do I get a weapon?" asked Willem.

Gabriel stared the young man in the eye. Still, he had questions. Too much wasn't fitting.

"No," he said. "Just me. Stay nearby."

Gabriel took one last look at the jungle behind them, then turned and stepped through a break in the foliage.

Another half hour of slogging through knee-deep swamp had gotten the team no more than a mile or so, if Gabriel's implant mapping was correct. He had everyone disable their GPS transceivers for fear of being picked up by overhead sensors, so they were all relying on 3-D neuretics maps. So far, everything on the map he and Brevik had seen was correct, except for the muck.

"Willem," he whispered to the youth off his right shoulder. "This swamp is unmarked, why?"

"It's not actually a swamp, Commander," he replied, his voice barely carrying to Gabriel. "Farmers dammed up a small tributary of the Gihon last month to flood the plain and create better planting areas. But they screwed up, and flooded dozens of acres, and the water hasn't receded yet."

"Fantastic," Gabriel replied. "When do we get out of it?" His boot came free of a particularly deep section with an audible slurp.

"Probably around a hundred yards or so, I think."

Gabriel shook his head. The leafbees were almost unbearable, the humidity was stifling (and damaging equipment; they already had to discard Sennett's personal handgun, as the kinetic action seized), and the sun was blazing directly overhead. He regretted the route the instant they stepped out from beneath the jungle canopy. The map showed a short plain area, not a swamp, and it would have been easily covered in a matter of minutes, not thirty-plus.

He slapped at another cluster of leafbees buzzing around the flap of his helmet, nearly dropping his pulse rifle. *Who knows what condition it would come out of this shit in?* he thought, gripping the rifle tighter.

He checked his heads-up for the team icons; all spread out in proper formation. The rear two were Sowers and Sennett. Something about the two of them, the way they were sticking together after the ambush, gave him the impression that he needed to keep them together. He actually saw a small smile from Sowers, the first he'd seen since before the garage explosion.

The explosion. It seemed like days ago, when in reality it had only been six or seven hours. *Time flies when you're having fun*, he thought.

His foot stepped on dry land, and he gave a small prayer of thanks. He hopped out of the swamp and walked over to a stand of pricklefruit trees, searching the area both visually and with passive scan. Willem stepped up next to him, seeming quite at home in the jungle, and with the mud dripping from the team's camo boots, maybe even more invisible.

[*On me,*] he sent, and the rest of the team joined him under the shade of the trees. Sennett walked up backwards, rifle trained behind him, panning back and forth.

[*Corporal, anything we should know about?*] Gabriel sent on the team net.

[*No sir, just paranoid. I'm from Mars, sir. Not a lot of swampland there.*]

[*Understood,*] Gabriel sent. [*Stay paranoid.*]

He lifted his helmet, allowing in not only fresh air (albeit heavy and humid), but also several gleeful leafbees. He swatted at them as he pulled a water bottle from a waist pouch. He took a deep drink of the now-warm water, then poured several ounces down the neck of his chromosuit.

"Okay, folks, hats and gloves off for a minute, let's cool down."

The others all did so and began pulling out their own water bottles.

"Halfway point," he continued. "From here on in, we can expect…"

"What the?" Takahashi said, looking down at his feet.

Gabriel looked over and saw a writhing green vine encircling the ensign's muddy boot outline. Before he could shout a warning, the vine tightened and pulled back into the bushes near the tree, knocking Takahashi over. He scrabbled at the soil as the vine dragged him across the ground towards the bushes.

"Razorvine!" Willem said. "Grab him!"

Brevik dropped his water bottle and fell to his knees, grabbing onto both of Takahashi's wrists. Sowers, who was closest to the bushes, also dropped to his knees and began clawing at the vines around the ensign's boots.

"No!" said Willem, running over to where Sowers was. "Don't touch the vine…"

Sowers cried out in pain, falling backwards from Takahashi's legs. He held his hands over his head. Blood was dripping from dozens of puncture wounds.

Sennett's assault rifle came up and Gabriel heard the soft whine of the charge. Before the corporal could even take aim, an incredibly quick silvery flash flew past him and chopped downwards at Takahashi's feet. A wet *chunkkk* sounded, and the vine slithered back into the bushes, leaving a gasping Takahashi with several feet of dead vine wrapped around his legs.

Specialist Negassi stood up from her combat sword crouch and pulled the blade of one of her takobas from the soil. She calmly pulled a black cloth from a waist pouch and wiped dirt and vine residue from the blade, then slid it back over her shoulder into the back pouch with the matching one.

"Eleven feet, Commander," she said with a nod. "Maybe twelve on that one."

Sennett whistled as he lowered his rifle. "Hot damn, woman."

Takahashi stood up, pulling the vine from his boots. "Thank you, Specialist," he said as he extended his hand.

Negassi took it and gave a small smile. "Anytime."

"Uh, a little help?"

Gabriel looked over to where the voice had come from. Sowers sat at the base of the pricklefruit tree, holding two bleeding hands over his head.

"Specialist, if you wouldn't mind?" he asked, indicating Sowers. "Also get extra wipes out, we need to get this mud off our camos."

Negassi pulled out the medikit and walked over to assist the injured man.

Brevik walked up to Gabriel. "Commander, we're going to need to keep moving. This place ain't conducive to standing still," he said as he pulled the tattered remnants of several swamp violets from his boots.

227

Gabriel nodded, looking back at the razorvine bush. "Agreed. Finish off the water and we'll…"

"Sir," Olszewski called. "Do you hear that?"

Gabriel looked over at the private, who was standing a few dozen feet from the treeline, looking out over the lower foliage, away from the team. He walked up to him. "What do you have?"

"Listen," he said. Gabriel waited. After a few moments he was about to speak when he heard it. A faint voice, barely audible above the buzzing of the jungle insects. Although he had read treemonkeys had been known to mimic voices, this seemed very… human.

"There," Olszewski said, pointing with his ungloved hand. Gabriel enhanced his audio implants in the direction he had pointed and tried to filter out the background noise. "It sounds like *help*, sir."

Gabriel heard it too. *Now what the hell was going on here?*

CHAPTER TWENTY-EIGHT

Mubina Tarif stood at the window of her new office, a tiny area that had formerly belonged to the Assistant Treasurer for Arsia Dome. Who along with most other cabinet staff, Tarif reflected, had been released from their positions within minutes of Rafael Molina taking the post of governor.

She still wasn't sure how he expected to govern a dome city of over a million inhabitants alone, or how the hot-tempered fool Isidoro expected to do the same with the almost-as-large Eos Chasma. They had been alone during their meetings, and she had not heard of any support they had outside of just the two of them.

The comm unit on her desk trilled, but she remained at the window, staring out at the corner of a rock face wall. *Not much of a view Karl had,* she thought with an inner smile. If she craned her neck a bit and pressed her face up to the plasteel window, she could just catch a glimpse of the edge of the street below and the tops of a few people's heads as they walked by. Otherwise, quite an unremarkable wall in front of her. She didn't like walls, never had. Even as a small child, she had an uneasy, claustrophobic feeling any time she was in a cramped space. Elevators were the worst, but the office she currently called home wasn't much better.

The comm unit trilled again, and she sighed and turned from the window. In two slow strides she was at her desk, and she picked up her ear bug, stuck it in her ear, and tapped the unit.

"This is Gov...this is Tarif," she said, frowning. *Ex-governor*, she thought. *For now, at least.*

"Governor, this is Major Andon in Intelligence," the voice replied.

She smiled. Andon had been a strong ally and good friend since she had taken power several years ago. Leave it to him to continue to use her former title, even though the transfer paperwork was made official just a few hours earlier by the Mars Central Governmental Council.

"Hello, Major," she said as she turned back to the window. "What can I do for you?"

"Mubina," he said, surprising her a bit with the informality, "I've just received some unusual reports from Orbital Defense."

She craned her neck at the window and saw the top of a woman's frilly lace hat, a small local bird perched on it. *The woman probably didn't even know it was there*, she though idly. *Looked like a finch, maybe one of the ones they had just imported in the last shipment from Earth...* She shook her head, annoyed at her recent mind wanderings. She was having a hard time concentrating on anything important since the meeting with the Republic lackeys.

"I'm sorry, Major, could you repeat that?" she asked as she walked back to her desk.

"Orbital Defense has picked up some odd readings from the high orbit satellites. Nothing specific, but I have a hunch, and I'd like to come up and discuss it with you."

She sat down in the small chair and crossed her arms on the desk, staring at a small globe of Mars Karl had left behind. *Orbital Defense? Now what?*

"Yes, Major, please do. I'll be here all afternoon," she said. *Nowhere else to go.*

"I'll be right up, I'm a floor below you."

She took the phone bug out of her ear and set it back on the desk. Orbital Defense, she pondered. The most that department had to do over the past decade was warn about space debris or chase the odd drug runner. What they could possibly have for her to worry about, she had no idea. Although now that she thought about it, and her earlier thoughts of Rafael and Isidoro being alone with no support, she began to get anxious. *And still no word from Eden,* she thought, an ache piercing her chest. *Jeromy...*

A knock at her door startled her, and she stood up to answer it. She opened the door to find Major Andon there, flexscreen in hand.

"Goodness, Major, you really meant right up." She stepped back to allow him to enter. "Please, come in, and try to find space."

He walked past her and stood on the opposite side of her desk, waiting. She closed the door and took her seat. "Sorry I don't have a coffee table, or even coffee, Major. Still getting adjusted to the new space, as you can see." She waved her hand around, indicating the office.

"Ma'am, if you ask me, the whole situation is a complete Charlie Foxtrot, if you catch my meaning," he said.

She smiled in return. "I agree. But for right now, it's all we can do."

"Right now?" he asked, arching an eyebrow.

She shook her head. "Don't get your hopes up. Might be a long process, but I have some ideas. Now," she said as she leaned back in her chair, "what is this unusual report you have?"

He extended the flexscreen to her, but she waved it off. "Just tell me, I'm not a big fan of technical readouts."

He pulled his hand back and snapped the screen shut, then tucked the tube into his breast pocket. "Orbital Defense is picking up what they believe are ships inbound from Earth. They're small, and apparently stealthed. They were originally identified as debris, but they're on a direct course. So they were then tagged as courier ships, but upon further analysis, and coupled with the fact that nothing is scheduled to arrive from Earth until at least tomorrow, my office is calling them fighters."

"Fighters?" she said, astonished. "Headed here?" She stood up from her desk and reached for her comm unit. "Who the hell is sending warships to an unarmed planet?"

"Wait," Andon said. He leaned over and placed his hand on top of hers, stopping her from dialing. "They don't know we're aware of their presence, at least we don't believe so. My recommendation is to let them approach while we analyze their origin. Then the Diplomatic Office can take it further."

Tarif pulled her hand out from under Andon's and crossed her arms in front of her. "So you, the military man, are telling me, the career diplomat, to avoid confrontation and negotiate?"

Andon smiled. "Well, when you put it that way, it does sound a bit strange. But yes. As you said, we are an unarmed planet, as per the original charter of Mars. We have no space defense save for low power particle beams for debris cleanup, and obviously no warships. I think the prudent plan of action is to try to identify them as soon as we can and go back-channel to find out why they are headed this way."

She stood for a moment, pondering what Andon had just said. Fighters, of an unknown origin, coming in undercover, unannounced, to an unarmed planet. Something was tickling the back of her mind.

"Does the SAR possess space fighters?" she asked.

Andon was taken aback for a second, then he nodded. "I see where you're going with this. Yes, they do, but not of this configuration. The ones we know of that they fly are much smaller. These are borderline frigate-sized, with what we are assuming is an active stealth system that allows them to…"

"Wait," she said, cutting him off with a raised hand. "That's all Greek to me. If you're telling me these can't be

SAR, then so be it. But I still have this odd feeling…" Her voice trailed off.

"Ma'am, if you want…"

"No, wait," she said. "I have an idea."

<<<<<>>>>>

Rafael slammed the comm unit's handset into its cradle with such force a small piece of plastic broke off its mouthpiece and bounced crazily across the desk.

"Fools!" he shouted. He looked around the office, trying to find someone to take his frustration out on, only to remember he was alone. He picked the handset up and slammed it down again.

He had only been in Tarif's office for a matter of hours before the assistant…*no*, he corrected himself, *HIS assistant*…had knocked and entered with a handful of documents that needed to be signed. Garbage collection days to be rescheduled, raises for miners, health benefit proposals for taxi drivers; the list went on. Not exactly what he had expected when initially presented with the plan to take over governance of a city.

The comm unit beeped almost incessantly, and he wondered again what use an assistant was if not to answer the damned phone. The last two calls had nearly put him over the edge. The first was from a citizen, a lone person, who had called with a request for lower fuel prices. Called the Governor's Office. Direct. To bitch at him. And he had been in office a grand total of three hours.

The second was a conference call, out of the blue, that somehow subverted the assistant. A group of coffee vendors had gotten together and created a foodservice union and needed his signature to ratify it. He looked down at the damaged comm unit. *That's what I thought of that idea.*

There was a knock at his door, and he rolled his eyes. "What?" he yelled.

The door opened and his assistant walked in, empty handed.

"No papers, Radja?" he asked with a sarcastic tone.

"No sir," he replied with a smile. *Dammit,* Rafael thought. *He's in on this.* After this all settled down, his first order of business, his first stamp on the city, would be the removal of Radja the assistant.

"Then?" Rafael asked, holding up both hands with palms up.

"Governor, er, sorry, Miss Tarif is calling, video. May I send it to your wall?"

Rafael frowned, wondering why she'd be calling. The transfer paperwork had gone through without a hitch, and she had packed up her things and left without a word earlier in the day. He really had no time for her now, but thought he may as well clear up any misconceptions she may have left. It would still be at least a day until anyone received word from Eden, so that wasn't even in the discussion at this point.

"Yes, please do," he replied.

Radja walked over to the flat wall adjacent to the governor's desk and tapped a few icons. The wallscreen lit up with the face of Mubina Tarif, over four feet in height. Radja turned and left the office, closing the door behind him.

Rafael stood up and walked to the bar across the room from the wallscreen. He poured himself three fingers of Irish whiskey from a crystal decanter, and without turning, said, "Hello, Mubina. What can I do for you?"

"Don't get too comfortable, Rafael," she said. He turned to face her image.

"What is that supposed to mean, Mubina?" He stressed her first name again, a dig at the loss of her title.

"You may not be aware of this, but it appears that your masters don't trust the two of you very much."

Rafael cocked his head, unsure of where she was going with this.

"We've detected a group of SAR fighters headed this way, and I'm going to hazard a guess you didn't know they were coming," she said.

Rafael tried to maintain a mask of composure, but he was rattled. He sipped from the glass while he collected his thoughts. *Fighters?* He tried in vain to wrap his head around the information. There was the possibility she was bluffing, but to what end?

"Mubina, La Republica de Sudamérica does not possess offensive warships."

"Don't try to bullshit me. We've known for years the SAR has fighters, just as you have offensive nuclear bombardment weapons, and genetically-engineered bioweapons. Hell, Rafael, everyone knows. So let's move on. Why would your people be sending fighters to Mars, a peaceful world, and a world where two Republic representatives now hold positions of power within the government?"

He was flabbergasted, and turned from the screen, ostensibly to refill his glass. As he picked up the decanter, he noticed his hand was shaking. *Fighters?* he thought again. Something wasn't right here. He needed to speak to Isidoro.

He turned back to Tarif's image. "It's nothing you need to worry about," he said, gritting his teeth. "It's routine for operations such as this."

"No, you didn't know, did you? Looks like you may not be the power here for much longer." She cut the connection before he could answer.

He tossed the whiskey off in one gulp and threw the glass across the room. It bounced lazily in the low gravity against the far wall. He walked over to the wallscreen and keyed in the private code for the Eos Chasma Governor's Office. After a few moments, Isidoro's image appeared.

"Isi, have you been in contact with Luna?" he asked.

Isidoro's image on the wallscreen flickered, then came back into focus. He looked puzzled.

"Luna? No, Rafa. I have not talked to them since we left," he replied. "Why do you ask?"

Rafael frowned. Something wasn't right with this situation. Tarif seemed sure that the RDS was behind the incoming ships. And honestly, when he thought about it, that would be the logical conclusion anyone, including himself, would come to.

They were on Mars, having just effected a peaceful transition of two dome cities' governments without a bullet being fired. They had come in alone, with no military support save for the loyal police force commanders they had bought ahead of time. And now, in what must be more than just a coincidence, unknown space fighters were headed their way. *If Tarif was telling the truth*, he thought. But she would have no reason to lie about this. She had no advantage to pick up, no leverage to use. It was only her gloating that was bothering him, and even that could be easily dismissed. *She had no, how do the North Americans say it? No dog in the fight? Why would she lie?*

"Rafa?" Isidoro asked.

He looked up at a blank wall, not realizing he had been pacing during his mind's wanderings. He turned back to the wallscreen to face Isidoro.

"Isi, my friend, I think we may have a problem."

CHAPTER TWENTY-NINE

It was a man, Gabriel saw. Eden Guard, if the tattered tunic was any indication. Sitting against a tree cradling a badly broken arm that was wrapped haphazardly. The angle of the arm was several degrees past what a healthy arm could do. Gabriel scanned the area, nothing more than small rodents and flying creatures coming back on the neuretics return. The man was alone, his legs covered in moorants, and he was softly moaning for help.

The team was spread out in the trees after having silently crept up on the sound Olszweski had detected. They all had weapons drawn and were waiting for Gabriel's orders.

Gabriel took a chance and sent a shielded active scan out. After a few seconds, it too came back clear of anything larger than a synfox, it being nearly a hundred yards away. He nudged Brevik next to him.

"Thoughts, Lieutenant?" he said in a low voice.

Several seconds went by before Brevik responded. "Three possibilities, sir. One, he escaped and this is as far as he got. Two, he's booby trapped. Three, he's a plant."

"I've got a fourth," Gabriel replied. "Cover me."

Standing up from the crouch he was in, he removed his helmet and stepped through the foliage into the open area in front of the man, who looked up in surprise.

"Holy shit," the man croaked as he tried to push himself up to a standing position. With his shattered arm, he struggled to use the tree behind him for leverage.

Gabriel held up a hand and put a finger to his lips. He walked over to the man, pulse rifle scanning left and right. The man held up his good arm.

"What the hell…" he began, but was cut off as Gabriel reached out and covered his mouth with an invisible hand. The man's eyes grew wide and he began clawing at Gabriel's hand.

"Stop it," Gabriel said. "We're here to help."

The man's struggles paused briefly as his eyes went back and forth between Gabriel's floating face and pulse rifle. "Mmmffff…"

"NAF Navy," he said, staring into the man's eyes. "Are you Guard?"

The man nodded, and Gabriel took his hand away from his mouth. "Baker," he said. "Sergeant. Been hostage for…" His voice trailed off and his eyes glazed over. "My God, almost a year," he whispered.

"What are you doing out here?"

"I… I honestly don't know, sir," he stammered. He was apparently still spooked by the sudden, and only partial, appearance of a solider in front of him. "They pulled four of us out of the camp. Just dragged me out here and dropped me. Every time I heard a noise, I tried calling for help. Thank God you found me, but…I don't know if I can walk very well." He glanced down, and Gabriel followed his gaze. He noticed the man was favoring one leg. "The bastard that put me here kicked me, broke my kneecap."

Gabriel looked back up into the man's face, then off into the jungle. He knew what the terrorists were up to, and at the point they were in the march, it just may work. No supply train to speak of, and they were already well past the halfway point. With no possibility of air or ground support. *So the fourth option it was*, he thought.

[*Brevik, on me,*] he sent, and walked a few feet away from Baker. Within seconds a floating Oso-11 appeared next to him.

He put his hand on Brevik's blurry shoulder and spoke under his breath to keep the Guard from hearing. "They're trying to bog us down with wounded," he said. "They'll slow our pace, then ambush us."

"Makes sense," he replied. He pulled off his helmet, exposing his head.

"Jesus, how many of you are there?" called Baker.

The two men ignored him. "So," said Brevik, looking out into the jungle, "how do we respond?"

Gabriel looked back at Baker, who was swatting at leafbees with his uninjured arm. He shook his head, knowing there really wasn't much in the way of good options. Take on wounded and slow down, or leave him here and move on. Now that he knew there were probably three other hostages out here didn't make the decision any easier.

"Mission first," he said to Brevik. "I'll talk to him." He walked back over to Baker, who watched with wide eyes, still apparently not used to the floating heads.

"Sergeant, this is going to be tough to hear, but we're going to have to leave you here." He watched as the man's eyes grew even larger. "For now," Gabriel said, holding up his hand, not realizing it was still in the chromosuit. "We'll give you some provisions and a weapon, but we're already falling behind and we have an objective."

Baker's shoulders slumped and he leaned back against the tree. "I figured that. As soon as you said Navy."

Gabriel cocked his head. "What do you mean?"

"The guards were talking about a Navy assault team headed their way. I'm guessing that's you. And I'm guessing now that they dropped me out here to get in your way." He sighed, scratching at several neck welts from leafbees. "I understand."

Gabriel pulled a water bottle from his waist pouch and handed it to Baker, who accepted it and drank heavily from it.

"What can you tell me about the camp?" Gabriel asked.

Baker polished off the water. "It's run by a bunch of bastards, I can tell you that much. But specifically, not much. They kept us tightly guarded and cut off from the rest of the camp. Handful of guards are all I really ever saw. And Prophet. The head bastard." He shook his head. "No mercy from that guy. When you run into him, don't give it a second thought. Kill him."

"How about the layout of the place where you were held?" he asked.

Baker nodded. "I can sketch that out for you." He tapped his temple. "They burned out our neuretics in the first hour after we were taken. But I can give you a general idea."

"Brevik," Gabriel said. The big man came over and joined them. "Get with Baker here and compile his info on top of what we have, and get it out on the team net. We've got to keep moving." Turning back to Baker, he said, "Sergeant, I'm sorry we need to leave you, but I'll send a message back to Eden City with your coordinates. They'll get some people out here."

Baker nodded in reply. "Again I understand. Just… kill them all." His face clouded with rage. "What they've done to some of the students, the kids…"

"Students?" Gabriel asked. "Was there a Jeromy Tarif among them?"

Baker nodded. "Yes, he's sort of the leader of their group. He's fine, but when they took us from where we were being held, I heard one of the guards saying that Tarif was being taken to Prophet personally."

Gabriel gritted his teeth and turned back to the jungle as Brevik and Baker got together. The sun had passed the halfway point in the sky; he could see through breaks in the overhead canopy. The heat would continue to rise for the next few hours. Their time was running short to get to the camp before night fell. A dusk assault would be preferred, but not a pitch black one. And he had no desire to still be slogging through Eden's godforsaken jungle at night. He hadn't even brought up the subject of the native nocturnal animals to his team.

[*Back on the road,*] he sent on the team net. Blurry shapes came out of the jungle foliage and assembled on Gabriel. Brevik finished his briefing with Baker and helped him conceal himself in a thicket. Gabriel saw that he had given him a couple of water bottles, a handful of rations, and a captured pistol from one of the killed terrorists. The lieutenant walked up to Gabriel, pulling his helmet back on. "All set, sir."

With one last look back at the clearing, satisfied Baker was out of sight, he turned and headed into the jungle once again.

They had come across another hostage just a mile or so further, this one a female Guard who had a shattered shin and held tightly to a crutch made of neopine branches. They had done the same as with Baker, leaving her with water, rations, and an extra handgun they had brought with them (Arturo's, Gabriel had noted with a grimace), and left her behind, much to her protestations. Gabriel had even considered restraining her to prevent unnecessary noise, but she relented and crawled into a break in the pricklefruit trees to hole up.

The third they came across presented a problem. Negassi was on point, Willem off her shoulder, when the young hunter had picked up what he called a 'wrong smell.' The team assembled in the lee of a clump of arwood bushes.

"What do you have, son?" asked Gabriel quietly.

Willem pointed towards a stand of yellowboles around sixty yards away. "That's one of our old hides, sir. Unused for a few years, wasn't any good to use as the game trail here ran dry. It's a perch about forty feet up, and it's got dense cover. We used steelroot for the walls, very thick."

Gabriel nodded in understanding. His passive scans weren't picking anything up except the life signs of what they presumed to be the third hostage just over a small rise they had been approaching. But steelroot, he knew from his briefings on his first Eden visit, not only made durable roadways, but also blocked a lot of electronic signals. The rise was fairly well exposed, and now that Willem explained the hide, he realized the rise was part of a well-worn game trail. They'd be exposed crossing the hill, and he had planned to call them to a halt to discuss the maneuvers anyway when Willem had stopped them.

"Go on," he said.

"Hard to explain, it's just..." He paused and looked around at the floating heads. The team had taken off their helmets to release some body heat. "Something smells wrong. There's someone here, and I'm guessing up there in the hide. From where you're saying the hostage is, it's a perfect lookdown from that hide."

Gabriel considered the young man's words while going over the site layout in Mindseye. Panning around the image, he found several useful spots nearby.

"Okay, folks. Looks like young Willem here may have spotted an ambush," he said. Willem beamed with pride. "Let's turn the tables."

He pointed to Olszewski. "Private, I want you up the yellowbole behind us." He sent the data over the team net. "Sowers, you here. Brevik, here. Negassi, here. Sennett with me here." Icons flashed on the site image everyone was now looking at. "On my mark, Olszewski you will put half a dozen shots into that hide. Steelroot won't block a Dobranoc round. Fire quickly, I'm not concerned about accuracy."

"Hey, Commander," protested Olszewski. "I am."

"I know, I know," Gabriel replied. "But it's secondary, I need fast and furious on this one. My guess is whoever is up there is not alone, and this'll draw his partner, or partners, out. Into the waiting arms of…"

"Me," said Sennett with a fierce grin. "Sorry, us," he said, looking around the circle.

"Right," said Gabriel. "Us. Now get moving, and keep it full stealth, including weapons. I don't want anything outside of the camo until the private fires. Clear?"

Everyone agreed, except Willem, who was raising his hand. "Uh, what about me?"

"Sorry, kid, you're sitting this one out. No suit, no combat," said Gabriel. He looked around at the faces, who one by one placed their helmets over their heads and disappeared from view. "Go."

[*In position,*] came Olszewski's burst.

Gabriel double checked the icons in his heads-up and verified everyone was set. He took a deep breath and reached over his shoulder to his concealed pulse rifle. His gloved hand closed around the stock, and he sent the confirmation.

[*Proceed when you have a shot.*]

Olszewski sighted down the scope and saw a minutely-detailed image of the hide. The steelroot was thick, but he saw some breaks in it, and the faintest hint of movement. Lining up the Dobranoc, he felt the tingle in his hand as he gripped the trigger pad. His neuretics removed the single-shot safety code, and he squeezed the pad.

Six depleted uranium rounds spat from the end of the long sniper rifle barrel at over nine thousand feet per second, only a few milliseconds between each round, and only a barely audible *clack* sounding at each one. The forty-eight caliber slugs tore into the steelroot, blowing huge chunks of wood in all directions. Olszewski watched the destruction through the scope the entire time, as the recoil on the

Dobranoc had been reduced to near zero by the finest Polish weapons techs the Olszewski family could afford.

Out of the carnage, a bloody body holding a long rifle dropped onto a flat part of the yellowbole branch the hide was built on, bounced, and tumbled to the jungle floor below. Olszewski quickly safed his rifle and tucked it over his shoulder into its back pouch, then scrambled down the tree trunk, on the side facing away from the hide.

On the ground, two terrorists, obviously shocked at the sudden turn of events forty feet over their heads, jumped from their concealed hideouts and started firing automatic kinetic rifles wildly in the direction of the tree Olszewski had fired from. Gabriel pulled his pulse rifle from its pouch and brought it to bear, but waited as the scene played out. He was a bit too far back from the two positions to make a difference at this point; Negassi and Sowers were nearly on top of them.

Sowers jumped up from his position, only fifteen feet from where the terrorist had popped up, and raised his assault rifle. The terrorist must have caught the movement, and he shifted his firing towards his new target. Gabriel saw Sowers get clipped by several rounds, the impacts staggering him back, but he managed to fire off a few rounds, and the terrorist went down in a spray of arterial blood.

Negassi's opponent was far closer, the icons in Gabriel's heads-up nearly blending into one. He was shocked she had been able to get in that close undetected, but not nearly as shocked as the gunman was as two takobas flashed in the green-filtered light. His right arm was severed at the elbow and the rifle immediately stopped firing. He screamed in agony and surprise as the second blade arced his way. The scream ended in a gurgle as the takoba slashed across his upper chest and throat. Gabriel didn't watch the end result, knowing it would be an image he wouldn't want to relive later on.

He stood up and grabbed Sennett by the upper arm. The corporal hopped up from his position, and the two men double-timed it to the scene of the carnage.

As Gabriel approached the fallen terrorist Sowers had taken out, he noticed Sowers had taken his helmet off and was breathing heavy. "You okay?" he asked.

Sowers nodded, trying to catch his breath. "Caught me off guard, sir, that's all. I'm fine." He looked down at the body, which had taken several rounds to the chest and face. "They're using steelroot as armor?"

Gabriel took his own helmet off, and looked down where Sowers was staring. He saw pieces of gray wood scattered around the body. "No, not as armor, but it looks like they've figured out it blocks our neuretics to a point. It appears he was lying underneath a pile of it."

"Same here," Negassi said. She was wiping her takobas clean, a blurry outline with two floating swords and a bloody towel making for a surreal image in Gabriel's visor.

"Sowers, tend to the hostage," Gabriel said, pointing towards where the unconscious man was tied to a tree. "If he's completely out cold, hide him somewhere." He paused and sent a shielded burst back to Eden City about the hostage, the third one he'd notified them of. *One more,* he thought.

A screech from above sounded, and Gabriel looked up to see a flutter of wings, followed by several dozen more as a large flock of spiderbats took flight from a nearby tree. He wondered what had set them off now after all the weapons fire, when suddenly a fat raindrop landed in his eye.

Shit, he thought. *This will make the last few miles a pain in the ass.*

The skies opened up.

CHAPTER THIRTY

"Are you telling me…"

Chaud watched as Prophet took a deep breath and slowly exhaled it. In the years he had been with the man, he had never seen him even bat an eye at any issue. Now, here, with Gabriel and his team so close, it looked as if he was starting to lose a little bit of his calm, cool, and collected exterior.

Several seconds passed before Prophet resumed. The rain thrumming on the tent roof punctuated each syllable. "Are you telling me that none of the ambushes have had any effect on Gabriel?"

He was addressing the group in the command tent: Chaud, Zeno, and the two techs. But Chaud could see the anger and frustration were directed at him. He shifted in his seat.

"None that we can detect, sir," he replied. He glanced at one of the techs, who shook his head. "According to the scant information we can pick up from the autosentries, the team is intact and approaching the outer perimeter."

He shrank a bit as Prophet's stare landed on him. He could feel the anger radiating from his leader. They had been successful, actually extremely successful, at just about every mission and plan Prophet had implemented over the years.

Very few things had gotten in his way, very few issues had blocked his goals. He was always so perceptive, almost like he knew what his opponent would do at every step of the way. But here, with Gabriel, the challenges they were running into looked like they were starting to rattle Prophet. Perhaps so much so that his judgment was being affected. As evidenced by the presence of the student hostage.

Chaud glanced at Tarif, who was seated with his hands bound in front of him in a chair next to Zeno. The kid had stayed quiet the entire time, a barely controlled rage on his young face. He wondered again why Prophet wanted to have him nearby as an assault team made its way towards them. He knew the kid was valuable as a hostage, but it almost appeared like Prophet was expecting to be defeated, and this was his insurance policy.

He looked over at Zeno, whose face was beginning to show signs of impending panic. He hoped the man could hold it together just a bit longer. Zeno was a true friend, and someone who didn't belong here. Someone who had... *morals*, he thought. *Morals I've probably pissed away over the past few years,* he thought. An image of Hamal's body floating away in the Gihon passed across his mind.

"Zeno," said Prophet, shifting his gaze. Zeno started, then cleared his throat.

"Sir?" he replied.

"Get a hold of our contact in Government House," he said. Chaud noticed several beads of sweat that had appeared on Prophet's forehead, something he didn't remember ever seeing. Even in the oppressive heat of late summer in the Eden jungle, he didn't recall ever having seen the man sweat.

"Ah, now sir?" Zeno asked, glancing over at Chaud as if for reassurance.

"Now!"

At that moment Chaud knew for a fact Prophet was losing it. He only hoped he could be far away when the shit really hit the fan. He started to rise from his seat as Zeno started punching keys on a small comm unit.

"Captain, something I'm keeping you from?"

Chaud looked at Prophet, who was fixing him with his usual stare. There was a glint in his eye, even in the dim light of the command tent, that Chaud recognized. Something that told him it wasn't yet time to trifle with him.

"I was going to recheck the guard emplacements outside," he said.

Prophet shook his head. "Zeno has already done so. Not necessary." He held out his hand to Zeno, who placed the comm unit in it. "Stick around, Jamar. It's just starting to get interesting."

He tapped a key on the comm unit and switched it to speakerphone. A small voice emanated from the speaker.

"Ah, yes?"

"It's me. I have a request," said Prophet, his gaze still fixing Chaud.

"Ah, not sure if I can…"

"Nonsense, it's what we are paying you for. And since you failed so miserably the first time, you have an extra incentive to get this one right."

A long moment passed before the voice sighed and said, "All right, yes. What is it?"

"Have Gabriel recalled. I don't care how you do it, or who you have to do it through. Have them cancel the mission."

"There's no way…"

"Yes," said Prophet, cutting him off. "There is a way, and you will find it. Or…" He glanced over at Tarif, who was nervously fingering his wrist restraints. "Or we will start killing hostages."

Tarif's eyes flew wide. "What?" he started before Prophet held up a hand to forestall his protests.

"Now you wait a minute," the voice said. Chaud detected both anger and panic in the tinny voice. "That was never part of the deal. You said hostages were leverage for people back on Earth, and they wouldn't be harmed!"

Prophet smiled, his lips stretched over his teeth in a death's head grin. "That was before you failed, and before Gabriel got so close. It's time for you to hold up your end of the bargain."

"No," the voice replied. "I won't do it. Gabriel's a matter of minutes away from killing you. I'm safe here, and I'll take care of myself. Where does that leave you?"

Prophet paused a few seconds, and Chaud wasn't sure what the looks that crossed his face meant, but none of them were pleasant. Finally, he said, "Then their blood is on your hands." As the voice started to protest again, he ended the call.

"Zeno," Prophet said. "Please activate the device."

Zeno's hands were shaking as he took the comm back from Prophet. "Sir, are you sure you want to…"

"Absolutely sure," came the flat reply.

Tarif was pushing at his chair, trying to stand up from the leg restraints that held him fast. "Please, don't do this," he pleaded.

Prophet stared at the young man. "Your mother's puppet leaves me no choice." He turned back to Zeno. "Well?"

Zeno had pulled out a separate comm unit, this one larger than the first. He tapped a few icons on the touchscreen, waited a few seconds, then nodded. "It's done, sir." Chaud looked at his old friend and saw the pain in his eyes, and a feeling of anger rose in him. *Killing hostages,* he thought with disgust. *It was one thing to be at war with armed men, quite another to resort to terrorism. It may be time to make a move.*

Prophet smiled at Tarif. "No worries, son. It's no one you know. Yet."

Gabriel called a halt to the march. [*Hold here,*] he sent. Willem was by his side in an instant, quiet and nearly invisible, and Gabriel was still surprised not only at his stealth, but the way he was able to pick out the blurred outlines of the team in their chromosuits, even to the point of knowing which outline was which person.

Rain rolled off his camo, outlining them as well as a bright light in a window would silhouette a person standing inside. He cursed the timing of the storm, shaking his head.

"Is this the stream?" he whispered to Willem.

The young man nodded and pointed with an outstretched arm. "Just past it is the grove of neopines I showed you on the map, and beyond that is the perimeter of the camp." He pushed back his netted hood and scratched the top of his head. "This is as far as I've been, sir. After this, you're on your own."

He sent a burst on the team net to form on him, and pulled up his map in his heads-up. Overlaid on the map was everything Willem had given him combined with what little the recon drones Eden City had been sending over the past year had gathered. *It wasn't much*, he thought, looking at fragments of lines and dots.

As the team assembled behind him, he sent out a passive scan. He was able to just reach it past the stream and into the thicket, seemed clear... *wait*. He narrowed his focus and picked up shallow breathing, a small heat source. He tweaked his neuretics a bit and pinned down the location to an area just before the neopine thicket broke clear.

He pondered the map for a few seconds. This was obviously the fourth hostage Baker had mentioned. They had expected to run across him or her several miles back, but he assumed they had taken a different route and passed by. But now here, surprisingly close to their target, it appeared they found the final one.

He turned back to his team and spoke in a low voice. "Looks like we have the last hostage, just on the other side of the stream. Sennett, you're with me. We're going to come up on the east side of the trees he's in. The rest, flanking positions, weapons at the ready. I don't want another ambush."

He checked his passive scan again, finding nothing but the hostage. He ground his teeth, contemplating an active scan, but deciding against it. It would be extremely risky this close in, and would pinpoint their location like a spotlight if the terrorists were looking. And judging by the noise they'd made at the last hostage site, they were most certainly looking.

"Pay attention to your heat sensors, the steelroot won't block that in close. I doubt they'll use the same tactics for an ambush here, but we need to stay alert. I'm sending you positioning."

He sent the data to his team, then turned to Sennett who was now crouched beside him. "Stay on my right shoulder, there's a break in the thicket a few dozen yards from where the hostage is. Full stealth."

"Yes sir," Sennett whispered back.

"Willem," Gabriel said. "Remain here, stay out of sight."

"But Commander, I can handle a weapon. I can..."

"I'm sure," Gabriel said, cutting him off. "You'll get your chance real soon. Just not now." He turned to the others. "Quick in, quick out, let's try to stay quiet."

With one last curse at the storm, he tapped Sennett on a blurry shoulder. He low-walked through a tuft of yellow-orange cytheria fronds, and stepped carefully into the shallow stream. He felt Sennett's presence behind him and continued across, their invisible boots making large ripples which thankfully blended with the smaller ones caused by the raindrops.

He reached the far side in under a minute, breathing a sigh of relief to be out of the exposed stream. No overhead canopy had covered them, and he felt almost naked, even with the chromosuit. He stepped into the neopine thicket and checked his heads-up. All icons were exactly where he wanted them, with Brevik and his heavy weapon set up on a small hillock overlooking the stream. Sennett moved up behind him.

[*Thirty feet,*] Gabriel sent to Sennett on a one-to-one frequency. He received a double click in response. He pushed aside the remaining branches and exposed the target area.

A man was secured to a young yellowbole tree, and his head was slumped over onto his chest. His left arm was missing, a tattered green shirtsleeve twisting in the low breeze. Even from this distance, Gabriel could see the man's face and scalp were badly burned, and his right leg was bent at an awkward angle. Rain streamed off his head. If his neuretics didn't confirm the breathing and body heat, he would have sworn the man was long dead. *Definitely not one we can leave behind with a bottle of water*, he thought with a frown.

He sent a packet to Sennett, showing him where each of them would go and how to approach. After he acknowledged it, the two men moved out, staying within the edge of the neopine thicket. Gabriel's senses were on full alert; even inside the helmet, he was picking up smells and sounds he shouldn't have been able to. After the last ambush, his entire nervous system was on edge. Every snap of a twig or whiff of rotting vegetation was causing him to think. He cursed his over-analysis, knowing it was slowing him down. *But it's keeping us alive.*

After a few minutes of careful approach, he was within a few feet of the hostage. He saw the man's chest slowly rising and falling, a ragged wheezing sounding on each exhale. Sennett was in position a few feet away, so Gabriel did one last neuretic check. Finding it clear, he stepped forward.

[*HOLD!*] sent Sennett. Gabriel froze, still ten feet from the hostage.

[*Report,*] he replied.

[*Steelroot,*] Sennett sent. [*He's wearing some on his torso.*]

Gabriel looked and saw a bulge at the man's stomach. He had assumed it was just a sign of the man being overweight, but Sennett's warning struck a chord. The terrorists had been using steelroot to block the basic scans, but they wouldn't block an active burn-through.

253

[*Going active,*] he sent.

[*Sir, hang on,*] Sennett replied. [*I worked a lot of IED disposal on Mars. Let me take a look.*]

Gabriel stepped back a few more feet, giving Sennett room. [*Clear,*] he sent.

Sennett's blurry outline approached the hostage and Gabriel saw him kneel in front of him. [*Yes sir, there's a device here. I think I can...*]

[*Wait,*] Gabriel began.

[*Sir, I got it. Child's play, done this a thousand...*]

His words were cut off by a blast of heat and light as the device strapped to the hostage's chest ignited. Gabriel was blown backwards by a wave of superheated air and landed a dozen feet away, flat on his back. His helmet's heads-up display beeped countless damage and air-quality warnings. He ignored them and tilted his head forward to find Sennett. He didn't need to see him to know what happened, as the screams pierced his already-heightened sense of hearing.

Sennett was stumbling around blindly, his entire body engulfed in a blue-white blaze of fire that dripped sizzling globules of flame wherever he stepped. He was screaming: a primal, agonizing scream, as the burning Geltex ate through his chromosuit and attacked his body. He fell to his knees, the screams fading into gasps, then a final gurgle as the liquefied explosive found his vital areas.

Gabriel pushed himself up on both elbows. "Sennett!" he yelled, but he knew the corporal was gone. He had seen it before.

A five-year old vision flashed across his mind: *The kid Tamander, pushing him out of the way of the flaming Geltex as the terrorists dumped it from above in the gymnasium as they fled. The screams, so like he had just heard. An incredibly painful death. And then of absolute silence aside from the crackling of the flames. The same crackling he heard in front of him now.*

"Oh God, Sennett," he said. "No..." *Burning Geltex, just like last time. It wasn't supposed to be like last time.*

The flames were just dying out in the heavy rain as the rest of the team burst into the small clearing.

"Commander!" yelled Takahashi as he ran over to where Gabriel lay.

The ensign began swatting at small fires that had ignited on the surface of his chromosuit, ones he hadn't even been aware were there. He started feeling himself slipping into shock, and ordered 10 CCs of saphedrine into his system. He shook his head and pushed himself up into a sitting position, feeling the stimulant coursing through his body. *Rest later*, he thought. *I have a team to lead.*

"Oh, Jesus Christ," he heard Sowers say.

He looked over and saw Sowers's exposed head standing over Sennett's body, the flames now self-extinguishing as they ran out of fuel. Gabriel stood up, pulled his own helmet off, and walked over to him. He grabbed him by both shoulders, turning his face towards him, and stared him directly in the eyes.

"Galen," he said. The lifeless eyes that stared back scared him. He shook his shoulders and said in a louder voice, "Galen!"

Sowers squeezed his eyes closed and kept them closed for several seconds. When he finally opened them, Gabriel saw the beginnings of tears forming in the corners, but also the fire in his eyes he had seen many times before. Not the spark of humor; he knew that would be a long time in returning. But he did see the fierce determination that led him to trust Sowers, implicitly.

"Galen, he saved my life," he said.

Sowers turned back to the blackened corpse on the ground, then back at Gabriel.

"How many more good men are we going to lose, Commander?" he asked in a low voice.

Gabriel gritted his teeth and squeezed Sowers's shoulder even harder. "No more, son."

He turned back to his team, who had all removed their helmets. Whether it was because he had taken his own off, or because of the heat, or most likely in respect to their lost comrade, he wasn't sure. Five faces stared back at him, four soldiers and a teenage hunter. Six other soldiers, including Sowers. All depending on him to get them out of this jungle alive. They had lost two men this day alone, and he was determined to make sure no one else was lost.

"Suit up, we're finishing this," he growled.

With a quick glance at the tree where only pieces of the hostage remained, and one last look back at Sennett's body, he jammed his combat helmet back onto his head and pulled his pulse rifle from his back pouch. Like a sign from above, the rain stopped.

"On me."

CHAPTER THIRTY-ONE

The team marched hard and fast. They had come across nine more terrorist guards, and taken out each and every one of them in an efficient, silent manner. Negassi's swords remained in their cases as the team used non-lethal methods; writhing personnel restraint bags littered their path like bread crumbs. With the terrorists not possessing neuretics or any type of defensive screens, they were sitting ducks, especially now that the steelroot deception had been seen through.

Willem had approached three of the terrorists completely undetected and knocked them out one-by-one with a firepipe branch. Gabriel had watched as the unsuspecting targets had dropped silently to the jungle floor as Willem, wearing a heavy glove he had pulled from his pocket, came up from behind and tapped their exposed necks with the branch. Willem explained after the first strike that the firepipe was a genetically-engineered tree Eden City's scientists had developed originally to plant around houses to prevent parweasels from entering. However, the firepipe's animal-resistant qualities had mutated uncontrollably, and now one touch of firepipe bark to exposed skin would knock a fully-grown man unconscious for hours. Gabriel looked on Willem with a newfound respect, and a bit more trust than he had before. He also made a mental note to avoid the thin orange branches he saw from time to time.

At last they arrived at the edge of a large meadow. In the distance Gabriel could see the glint of the Gihon Sea River as the sun set behind it. Darkness was falling, and the meadow was drifting into shadow. Dusk, when guards changed shifts, and looked forward to dinner, and rest and relaxation beyond that. When the long day wound to a close. *And when they would strike.*

He called the team to a halt, still in the treeline, and he ran a wide-band active scan. *The hell with it*, he thought. Instantly terabytes of data streamed back to his neuretics, and he called up several programs to sort through it.

He gathered them around him, helmets off, behind the cover of a wide five-trunked pricklefruit tree. "Okay, folks, here we go. I've got a full layout of the compound, inside and out. Thin-walled buildings are easy to scan."

He sent a packet to each person with highlighted locations. His battle programs had done a fast and efficient job of sorting and analyzing the scan data and had suggested several positions for his men to be in. He had only had to modify one or two just slightly for his preference.

"Let me just be clear on this. These are armed terrorists that have been killing civilians for many years, and they have over twenty hostages here. They also just killed one of them in an extraordinarily cruel manner, trying to take us all down. While I'd like to slip in and do this quietly like the last few guards we took out, that option is off the table because of the size of the compound. Anyone armed is a valid target. I'm not losing anyone else today. Clear?"

Everyone immediately acknowledged. He leaned in and began going over the plan.

"Private," he said to Olszewski. "Up a tree again, son. This one here." An icon flashed near the west side of the meadow. "Hightail it over there, you're overwatch. Anything that moves and is armed, even if it's a parweasel, I want taken out."

Olszewski gave a quick acknowledgement, fitted his helmet over his head, and took off through the trees, invisible.

"The rest of us. Three main targets. One, the main guard barracks here," he said, and everyone's heads-up displays flashed an icon. "Brevik and Willem, this is your responsibility. I'm showing a handful of guards inside, all armed, and that's what I'm seeing as their main weapons depot. I want the terrorists down and down for good. Lieutenant, when I give the go order, raze that building. Time to put that cannon to good use."

He turned to the young man. "Willem, you have straggler duty. Like Olszewski, any moving thing with a gun, drop the bastards. You did just fine with a stick. Are you okay with a rifle?"

The young man nodded. "Yes, sir, maybe better than some of your men."

Takahashi snorted. "Nice try, kid."

"Ensign," Gabriel said.

"Sir?" said Takahashi.

"Please issue the young man one of the captured assault rifles."

Takahashi pulled out a battered Chinese knock-off of an Army TK-20 from his camo carry bag, and a satchel of extra ammunition, and handed both to Willem. The young man strapped the satchel to his belt, then cleared the slide on the kinetic weapon, racked a round from the clip, and flipped the safety off and on, all in one smooth one-handed motion.

Takahashi pursed his lips. "Okay, okay. But don't forget, these aren't deer out here," he said.

Willem nodded silently, a more subdued look on his face. Brevik's blurry hand grabbed him on the shoulder and tugged him in the direction of their position.

"Two, the hostages." An icon lit up on a run-down two bedroom housing unit just inside the edge of the compound's perimeter. "Negassi, Takahashi. I want you in there, and fast. I'm counting nineteen people in the main room, my analysis calls them the students, and eleven in the second room, analysis says those are military. I'm flashing you the guard locations. They're not moving much, and I have a count of four, two in each room. Go in hot, take them down. Honestly," he said, pausing. "We have to take the risk of losing some hostages. The terrorists just killed one in an ambush attempt, so we have to assume they're ready to kill more." He sent the data to Negassi and Takahashi.

"Commander," said Takahashi after a few seconds. "Losing hostages?"

Gabriel nodded, momentarily forgetting they all still had helmets on. "Yes, I'm afraid so," he said after a few seconds. "I don't doubt they intend to kill every one of them. This is going to need to be a blitz. We've just seen firsthand what they're capable of. I don't think we have the luxury of waiting. Now get into positions."

"Aye aye, sir," said Takahashi, and he and Negassi slid through the treeline towards the housing unit.

"You and me boss?" said Sowers in a low voice.

"You and me, Mister Sowers. Command tent," Gabriel said, sending him the specific data. "Six people, one of whom I'm laying heavy money on is Prophet. You and I will be cutting off the head of the snake."

"With pleasure, sir," he replied. Gabriel could imagine the fierce glare Sowers would have beneath his helmet. *Yes, trust him with my life.*

He checked his neuretics for the positioning of his people and counted down silently. When all the icons were properly placed, and he reached zero, he sent the signal and stepped around the wide trunk of the tree, pulse rifle drawn and armed.

[*Go.*]

Prophet was pacing back and forth in the command tent, and was as animated as Chaud had ever seen him. Just a few moments earlier, he had shoved one of the techs out of the seat he was in and placed the VR goggles over his own head, demanding real-time information be streamed to him. When the other tech explained how the system worked, that only techs with the proper implant programming could interface with the visual data system, Prophet had almost come completely unglued. Only by Chaud taking the goggles from him and walking him to the opposite side of the room was the tech spared further wrath.

Chaud saw that Prophet was armed, perhaps the first time he had seen his leader with a weapon of any kind since the first few months he had known him. Since before he had taken command of their group, and began using his knowledge of tactics and strategies, and his persuasive tongue, in place of brute force. This afternoon, *no evening*, he corrected himself, Prophet had resorted back to that brute force. Chaud wasn't sure which Prophet he preferred anymore. *If either,* he thought. The small handgun flapped at his waist as he paced.

The kid was still restrained in the chair, and had grown more and more calm as the sea raged around him. Chaud noticed he had stopped trying to free himself and had just sat and watched Prophet stomp back and forth.

Zeno had changed in the preceding minutes as well. Chaud saw a new look, one of not just frustration, but determination. When Prophet had demanded Zeno kill the rest of the hostages, he had simply said no, and explained in careful terms why that would not gain them anything. When Prophet had demanded Zeno bring in the wives of the fighters who had failed in the jungle, he had also steadfastly refused.

As Chaud remained quiet, he saw around him a not-so-subtle shift in power, in influence. Even the techs were looking to him and Zeno now, as Prophet slowly but surely lost control.

The tech who had been knocked over had retaken his seat, and adjusted the goggles that Chaud had given him. "Sir, I'm picking up some readings from the autosentry just off the west ridge."

Prophet threw up his hands. "Gabriel! Who else?"

Chaud grimaced. The man was minutes away from falling apart. He had to take control of this situation, or they'd all be dead. He picked up his comm unit.

"Formento, Scarberry," he called on the wide net. "Check movement on west ridge, assume hostile." Switching to an individual frequency, he said, "Davitz, pull in extra guards. We know they want the hostages, so get 'em low and covered. No one in, clear?"

The comm crackled in reply. "No worries, Captain," Davitz replied. "I'm taking good care of our friends."

Chaud thought he heard a scream in the background. He squeezed the comm unit in frustration. *How the hell did I fall in with this bunch?* He set the comm unit down and pulled his sidearm out, checking the charge and ammunition levels.

Prophet gave a small laugh. "Handgun, Captain? Is that all we have for defense? Have your fighters all failed so miserably? Will we resort to throwing rocks when Gabriel gets here?"

Chaud sighed, glancing over at Zeno, who had an impassive look on his face. "Sir, please calm down. We've got plenty of firepower outside."

Prophet laughed again, and Chaud saw a bit of his old, more in control self reappear on his face. "I know Gabriel, I've studied him. We don't have enough firepower. He's coming for blood, Captain. Yours, mine, and everyone's." He waved his arm around the room. "We're just about finished here. But not me."

Chaud cocked his head slightly, unsure of what he meant by his last statement. Was he hanging them out to dry, leaving them to die here? Did he have an escape plan he didn't know about?

He was about to ask him when Prophet strode over to Tarif, who up until this time had remained quiet, watching and listening. A blade appeared in his hand and Chaud reflexively started to head in that direction when Prophet leaned over and cut the restraints holding the youth to the chair.

"Over there," Prophet said, motioning with the knife towards the back of the command tent, where a plotting table and flatscreen were.

Tarif stood up and rubbed his chafed wrists. "Why, you don't want to spill any blood on your furniture?" he said.

Chaud expected Prophet to snap, but he merely smiled, the same in-control look he had had up until a few minutes ago. "No, nothing like that, Jeromy. You're valuable, remember? Please, join me."

Tarif looked at Zeno, who gave a small palms-up who-knows gesture. He looked back at Prophet, then shrugged. "Fine."

Prophet allowed him to pass by him, then turned to Chaud. "Captain, I appreciate all you've done for me, but your services are no longer needed."

Chaud was surprised how fast Prophet was. Some corner of his mind had always pegged him as ex-military, now that same corner confirmed it as the handgun was suddenly in Prophet's hand and firing.

The slug tore into Chaud's stomach, and he felt the sharp pain of impact, followed by the burn of the supersonic projectile as it blasted through his body and exited his lower back. He staggered back, not from the force, but from the shock of being shot. His sidearm fell from his hand and he clutched at the spreading red stain on his shirt. He looked up just as Prophet shot the two techs, and a pair of shattered VR goggles fell to the floor of the tent.

He dropped to his knees, still grabbing at his stomach.

"Why?" he croaked, the pain starting to spread throughout his nervous system. He knew the wound was fatal; he had seen enough gut shots in his lifetime. He looked down at the gray soil as it rushed up to meet him, and his forehead impacted with the dirt in a cloud of dust. He could see the blood dripping from his ruined stomach, and he rolled onto his side.

A foot appeared in his line of vision, and he heard Prophet's voice, sounding like it was coming through a long tube. "Jamar, I never fully trusted your loyalties. You've served me well, but I can't help but thinking Gabriel's approach was too easy for him, and you're the only person I can trace that to. That, and the fact that only one of us could possibly get out of here alive. That has to be me. I'm sure you understand."

Chaud focused on his breathing, trying to get it under control and prolong what little life was left in his body. He heard faint arguing, seeming to come from the kid's mouth, but everything felt like it was under water. He pulled his hand to his face to clear his blurry eyes, only to see it was dripping with dark crimson blood. He closed his eyes and thought about Hamal. Lost to the currents of the Gihon at the hands of the Eden Guard. He had sworn vengeance, and allied himself with ruthless men. And now, he was paying the price.

He started to speak, to call to Zeno for help, when from outside the tent he heard the distinct rapid-fire sound of a pulse rifle. And one not belonging to the rebels. A higher-pitched whine, with heavier firing sounds, than anything his ragtag band possessed. He knew Gabriel had arrived. And they were all about to pay the ultimate price.

CHAPTER THIRTY-TWO

When Escobio Armory Ltd., a small company based in rural Mexico City, started producing weapons for the North American Federation military forces, they at first specialized in handguns, small caliber long range rifles, and man-portable light machine guns. They did not begin to manufacture pulse weapons until 2172, not long after the disastrous raid on Eden.

The NAF brass had asked Escobio's management to help create a larger, more powerful heavy assault weapon that a soldier could carry long distances, across and through difficult terrain, and that required little to no maintenance. They had deduced from the Eden mission that a small military force, far from home, with a limited supply train, still required heavy weapons to back them up, and ones that didn't need an ammo carrier to slow the soldier down, or vehicles to mount them on.

From this request came the *Oso*, or bear in Spanish. The newest incarnation of Escobio's creation, the Oso-11, was set atop a small hill on a bipod, and behind it squatted the blurry outline of Lieutenant Harris Brevik, NAFN.

Coherent light spat from Brevik's Oso-11, bright orange pulses of energy accelerated by shaped magnetic fields along the weapon's three-foot long, five-inch diameter carbotanium barrel. Brevik held the trigger pad down, feeling the heat wash over his visor as the energy pulses blasted from the end of the weapon, forty times per second.

The guard barracks, built from a standard extruded plastic housing unit reinforced with steelroot studs and neopine planking walls, stood no chance. The pulses tore the building to shreds, flashes of orange light mixing with flaming wood and melting plastic expanding in all directions. Brevik walked the pulses from side to side along the top of the building, and within seconds the entire top half of the structure was shattered beyond recognition.

Several terrorists ran from the burning building, the ones that survived the initial barrage, and began firing their rifles in the general direction of Brevik's pulses. The Oso immediately cut down two in flashes of energy, the bodies crumpling to the ground. One ran out with his hands in the air, then dropped to the ground prone. Brevik made sure the pulses skipped him.

One terrorist had made it to the cover of one of the nearby yellowboles, and was firing around the edge of it, only a glimpse of the rifle barrel visible. Brevik paused in his firing, surveying the area.

"Hey kid, can you see him?" he called.

The youth, who was squatted several yards away, rifle at the ready, nodded. "Yes, can you draw him out?"

Without a word, Brevik let loose several more pulses, blasting dirt and debris into the air on the opposite side of the yellowbole. The terrorist stepped away from the explosions, momentarily forgetting his cover. Three bullets stitched their way from his stomach to his neck, and he dropped.

"Nice shot, kid," Brevik said. He looked back at the guard shack, and saw several more armed men running from another building towards it, firing from the hip. He pressed the trigger pad, and the Oso roared to life again.

Gabriel's Return

A few moments before Brevik fired, Private Olszewski peered down the sight of his Dobranoc at the terrorist squatting in the treeline. He had been watching him for the past couple of minutes after having gotten into his tree perch. The terrorist was right in the path of Takahashi and Negassi, who were making their way towards the hostage area. Apparently the terrorist had snuck away to have a smoke of something, most likely contraband if he had to hide in the bush with an assault team on the way.

He almost felt sorry for the man and wondered if he might just leave him be, when the terrorist suddenly turned his head and raised his weapon, apparently having heard Takahashi and Negassi headed in his direction.

Sorry buddy, won't be finishing that smoke today, he thought as he squeezed the trigger pad. The .48 caliber depleted uranium slug caught the terrorist right under the chin and blew his lifeless body backwards into the foliage. The clack echoed in the trees, and Olszweski saw several spiderbats take flight. He raised his eye from the sight and surveyed the area below, but it didn't appear anyone else had heard it.

Takahashi obviously had, as Olszewski received a big thanks via neuretics comm. He watched as the icons in his heads-up for Takahashi and Negassi arrived at the back side of the housing unit. They split, one against the back wall of each section of the unit, and he saw the icons freeze in place.

As he was about to reply to Takahashi's thanks, he heard Brevik's cannon open up and watched as the guard barracks' roof erupted in flames. He pressed his eye back to the sight and began sweeping the rifle around the compound, tapping the trigger pad several times, reducing their armed opposition by one with each squeeze.

Takahashi had just finished placing the rope charge on the wall of the unit when he got Negassi's comm.

[*Placed and armed,*] she sent.

[*Done here also,*] he returned. [*Step back and get into position, and wait for the signal.*]

[*What's the signal?*] Negassi asked.

Takahashi paused for a second, thinking back to Gabriel's briefing. Was it on his go, or was it after the go? Was it someone else's go? *Shit, guess I should have cleared that one up.*

He was about to send Gabriel a query when the unmistakable whine of a heavy assault cannon came from the other side of the compound, followed immediately by large explosions.

[*That signal,*] he sent, and ordered the rope charges to detonate. Negassi did the same simultaneously.

The rope charges had been placed against the back wall of each half of the housing unit, Negassi's behind the area where Gabriel said the military prisoners were being held, and Takahashi's behind the student area. He had confirmed with passive scans the positions of the guards, all of whom were nearer the front walls and doors, expecting a frontal entry.

The charges burned white hot for a fraction of a second, flash-melting two six-foot high, three-foot wide holes through the thin extruded walls. In under two seconds, Negassi and Takahashi were inside their respective housing units, weapons drawn.

Negassi burst into the room, mag pistol held in both hands. The room was full of beds, each one occupied by all manner of injured men and women. All were turned in the direction of the explosion, but none realized she was there. A smell, a combination of rotting flesh and antiseptics, immediately assaulted her nose, even through the helmet filters.

Two guards stood with rifles drawn at the far end of the unit, both having just turned around in surprise. Before either of their rifles could swing up to meet her, she had fired two rounds into each of them. She rushed towards them, neuretics scanning the area, and reached them even before their bodies hit the floor. She looked down at the terrorists, both mortally wounded with perfectly-placed center-mass shots, and kicked away their rifles.

Turning back to the hostages, she momentarily switched off the active camo and said, "Who's well enough to fight?"

Several gasps were heard as she became visible. Slowly, but surely, eleven hands, some bandaged and oozing, raised into the air, one from every bed. She smiled behind her helmet.

Takahashi met with less initial success than his partner. Upon crashing through the opening the rope charge had created, he tripped over a student, who was holding his hands up to his ears and screaming. *Dammit*, he thought. *Missed him on the scan.*

After righting himself, he aimed his Heckart towards where the guards were positioned. He only found one who had started to head his way, but snapped off three quick shots, dropping the man in his tracks. He quickly scanned left and right, but found nothing but screaming, sobbing students. Two clusters of them had formed in the far corners, huddling for safety.

He stood up from the crouch he had reflexively dropped into after firing on the guard. He put his gun hand behind his back, hoping to completely blend in with the surroundings in the smoke-filled room. He stepped to the side wall, still passively scanning back and forth. His helmet heads-up showed multiple icons for targets.

As he reached the wall and stepped past a young girl covering her head, he sent out an active scan. Data streamed back into his neuretics, plotting the positions, size, and threat levels of all twenty targets. *Twenty*, he thought. *There were nineteen hostages.*

He filtered the data, and caught an electronic whiff of a kinetic weapon, being held by someone just slightly too large to be a typical college student. The man was behind the huddle of students in the corner at the end of the wall he was standing against. *Coward.*

He slowly walked towards the group, and was within twenty feet or so when a voice called out. "I know you're there, Navy puke. Turn off the camo or she dies."

His heads-up plotted the source of the voice and matched it up with the large icon. He focused in on the weapon, an old-school Colt .42 kinetic pistol. *Must have been thirty years old*, he thought. *But easy to conceal.* It was aimed at the side of one girl near the back of the group, with four other students between him and them.

He activated his helmet speaker. "Let the others go, we can chat."

The voice laughed. "No chatting, puke," he said. "But all I need is her, so here."

With that, he shoved the four other students forward, and they ran towards the other knot of hostages in the far corner. One bumped into Takahashi and looked back with a startled glance.

"Now, drop the camo," the voice said again.

Takahashi paused, debating the man's demand. At this point, there was no need for stealth. Between the racket outside and their explosive entry inside, there was probably little doubt in the terrorists' minds what was happening. He sent the command and the camo shut down.

"Ah, there you are," the man said, sneering.

Takahashi pulled his gun hand from behind his back slowly.

"Drop it," said the man as he pressed the Colt into the sobbing girl's ribs. "And lose the helmet."

He stretched his arm out from his side and released the Heckart, which thumped into the soil. He watched on his heads-up as Negassi creeped in from the other room, still in full stealth. He switched the visual feed from his heads-up to Mindseye, and removed his helmet.

"Where are you possibly going to go?" Takahashi asked.

The man laughed. "I'm sticking with the boss, puke. And this girl's my ticket out. Girls ain't good for but one thing, but in this case, I'll use her for something else."

He started to nudge the student forward, when without warning she pulled a small blade from inside her shirt and rammed it backwards into the man's upper thigh. He howled in pain as she pushed away from him and ran to Takahashi.

The wounded man roared in anger and pulled the paring knife from his leg with his free hand, a dribble of blood following it. He raised the Colt towards the two of them, and Takahashi grabbed the girl, pulling her behind him, counting on the chromosuit's kinetic fabric.

Before the man could squeeze off a shot, two long, wicked blades appeared out of thin air, and the man froze. He watched with wide eyes as one blade lopped off his hand at the wrist. The severed hand fired the Colt by reflex, the bullet embedding itself into the ground, and the bloody appendage and gun tumbled to the ground as one.

The man yelled again, this time a mixture of shock and anger. He raised the knife he had pulled from his leg, even as the stump of his other forearm spurted blood. The second takoba pierced his chest and pushed him back into the wall. He released the knife and clutched at the sword, now buried nearly up to its hilt in his body.

Negassi shut down her camo and became visible. She dropped the other takoba and pulled her helmet off, and the man's eyes grew even wider.

"This girl doesn't take too kindly to insults," she said in a flat voice. She pulled the takoba from his chest, and he slumped into a sitting position.

"Screw you," he gasped, then his eyes closed and he went silent.

Takahashi whistled. "Well, I'll be..."

He stopped when he heard sniffling behind him, and realized he was still holding the girl against his back with one arm. He released her and turned to face her.

"Miss, that was a very brave thing to do," he said. He looked into her tear-streaked eyes. "Are you okay?"

She nodded, casting her eyes over to where the man's hand lay. "He... he was a monster. What he did to Jeromy, oh God Jeromy..." Her voice trailed off.

Jeromy, Takahashi thought. *That's the governor's son.*

"What is your name?" he asked, trying to switch her focus.

"Magali," she said. "Magali Pearson. I'm a student at... was a student..." she said. After a few seconds, she gritted her teeth. "I'm a student, like the others. But Jeromy... they took him."

"Magali," said Negassi, walking up to them. Takahashi saw she had sheathed her blades and taken off her gloves. She took the girl's hands in hers and spoke quietly. "Magali, we're here to help. You're safe now, we'll get you out of here."

As if to reinforce her words, more pulse rifle blasts sounded outside. Magali started, and Negassi squeezed her hands tighter.

"Those are our people, our weapons. You're safe now."

"Magali, where is Jeromy?" Takahashi asked.

The girl looked from Negassi back to him and gave one last long sniff. "They took him. Prophet took him a few hours ago. I don't know where, they just said he was valuable. Is he going to be okay?"

Takahashi returned her gaze with what he hoped was a confident look. "Magali, don't you worry. Commander Gabriel is taking care of Prophet as we speak. And no one's better than him."

CHAPTER THIRTY-THREE

Gabriel and Sowers sprinted across the courtyard as the explosions from Brevik's assault created an overwhelming audio and visual chaos. Splinters of wood whizzed through the air from secondary detonations; Gabriel's neuretics noted that the terrorists' weapons cache had been destroyed under heavy fire from the pulse cannon.

The two men were visible only as blurs as they ran top-speed across the open ground. No one paid the floating weapons any attention as guards fired wildly in the general direction of Brevik's pulses. Sowers loosed a few bursts at two terrorists that were crouched behind a storage crate; his energy weapon cut them both down in an instant.

Within seconds they reached the west side of the command tent. There were two guards out front, both under cover of an overturned supply cart, staring in the opposite direction of the two soldiers. Gabriel sent a quick burst to Sowers, who acknowledged it.

Sowers pulled a small device from his waist pouch, something Jimenez had given him before the garage explosion, and sent the neuretics command to activate it. He leaned around the corner of the tent and rolled it towards the guards.

One guard looked down in surprise, the other one still firing bursts over the edge of the cart. Before he could react, the device went off, filling the air with electric pink sparks.

Both guards were hit by the pink lightning, their bodies stiffening as the charge overwhelmed their central nervous systems. The guard closest to the charge dropped instantly to the ground, unconscious, while the other was far enough away to maintain a semblance of control of his body. He tried to turn his rifle towards the source of the device, but the rifle had taken too much of the charge, and the ammunition clip exploded, showering the area with shards of carbotanium, incapacitating the guard.

[*Clear,*] sent Sowers.

The two men edged around the corner of the tent, stepping over the bodies of the two guards, and headed for the door.

Inside the tent, Zeno watched as Prophet tried to regain control of the situation. The two techs were dead, Chaud — Zeno's close friend — was dying on the floor. He struggled with his emotions. His fear had slowly given way to anger as Prophet raged and paced. Their leader, the ruthless man who had created their group from scraps of bickering factions, was coming apart at the seams. And he felt helpless to stop it.

Zeno listened to the rifle fire and explosions from outside the tent. He involuntarily cringed when shrapnel from a nearby blast peppered the front wall nearest where he sat.

"Sir, we've got to surrender, we've got no choice," he said in what he thought was a careful and respectful tone.

"Surrender?" Prophet said, waving his handgun towards the hostage. "Why, we have the golden ticket here, don't you see?"

Zeno shook his head. "No I don't, sorry to say. How will he..."

"We've been fighting with the government for years, and it's all been bullshit Zeno. You know this. Chaud knew this. This wasn't a crusade against oppression. It was about taking care of ourselves, and with Tarif, we can take care of ourselves in a far better manner than we ever could here."

Zeno stared at Prophet, the words coming out of his mouth ringing both true yet fanatical. Yes, he had realized long ago it wasn't a true rebellion. Chaud, having lost his brother to an overzealous Eden Guard, probably did too, but never wanted to admit it. But here, having the all-powerful Prophet say it out loud, just sounded... odd.

"He is our ticket off this planet, Zeno. You, me, him. Back to civilization, out of this hellhole." He waved the gun in the air, indicating the tent around them. "This, this is all over," he said. "Time to start a new life."

Zeno was about to reply when the door flap flew open behind him and he was shoved to the floor by an invisible hand.

<<<<<>>>>>

Gabriel pushed past Sowers, who was holding one man on the floor face down, and raised his pulse rifle towards the man in the back of the tent. The man was partly in the shadows, but he could see on his heads-up display that he was holding a weapon, and it was trained on the young man next to him. Jeromy Tarif, his neuretics confirmed.

"It's over, Prophet," he said through his helmet speaker.

The man snorted. "Over? Not quite. And would this mysterious voice with no body be the famous Commander Gabriel?"

"Enough," Gabriel growled. "This is over. Your forces are out of commission, and the hostages are safe. It's only you left."

[*Ensign,*] he sent to Takahashi. [*Send me the list of military personnel you recovered.*]

"Let me see you, Commander," Prophet said. "You owe me that."

Gabriel frowned inside his helmet. With his location on the back of the tent, he suspected Prophet may not know of Sowers's presence, so going visible may distract him enough.

He sent a burst to Sowers, who had just secured the other man in restraints, to come around one side and cover him. He switched off the active camo, and slowly pulled off his helmet, keeping his pulse rifle trained one-handed on the other man.

Prophet smiled. "It is you, isn't it?"

Gabriel wondered what he meant by that, but his thoughts were interrupted by a stream of neuretic data from Takahashi. He flicked through the names. The one he was looking for was missing.

"Where's Katoa? Is he the one you strapped to a tree and killed?" he asked. He took a step forward. "Was he a message to me?"

Prophet threw his head back and laughed, a maniacal laugh that echoed even in the soft-sided tent. Gun still aimed at Tarif, he took a step forward, into the weak dusk light that was streaming in from the open doors.

"You forget so soon?"

Gabriel saw that his eye was missing, replaced by a mechanical device with scanner, and his left arm was prosthetic, ending in a crude three-fingered claw. Something about his set jaw...

"You're looking for Katoa?" Prophet screeched. "*I'm Katoa, you bastard!*"

Gabriel rocked back on his heels, dropping the helmet to the floor. Thoughts, memories, images flooded through his mind. Images of Katoa on the *Damocles*, laughing with Kasey as he hit on her. Sitting with Renaldo in the mess. Fighting alongside his other men in the gymnasium. Losing sight of him behind a wall of flame. And here... yes, the jaw, the eye, the slight tinge of a Spanish accent. It was Katoa.

"Why..." he began.

"Why? You *left* me here, *Commander*," he said, spitting out the last word as if it was poison. "You survived, while no one else did. You left me. They rescued you, the commander, but didn't bother to search the area for survivors. You led us into that trap, and left me to die. And now here you are, the hero once again."

"But the message..." Gabriel stammered, trying to regain control. The rifle fire and explosions from outside the tent had nearly ceased, and his neuretics were receiving reports from his team of secured areas, but he dismissed those. It had shocked him to the core that the man he had known, fought alongside, was leading the terrorists. "You were never a hostage, were you," he said. "And there are no bioweapons."

Prophet/Katoa sneered. "No, Commander. They *saved* me. Their medical techs repaired my wounds. They took me in, treated me like one of theirs. And in time, I was. I've never felt more a part of a team than I had then, nor more of a leader than I am now." He laughed, waving the pistol around. "And the irony of all of this is, you trained me. The same training I've used for nearly five years now to create a force to be reckoned with. One that, in the ultimate irony, they sent you to destroy. Hell, Commander, that mission taught me that Geltex could be modified."

Gabriel gritted his teeth, still trying to slow the spinning in his head. *Geltex. Sennett.*

"And bioweapons?" Katoa continued. "Just a little added incentive to get you and your merry band here."

Gabriel started to speak, then saw Sowers's icon in Mindseye creeping around one of the bodies on the floor towards Katoa. He sent a quick '*back off*' signal to him, and the icon stopped. This was once a man he could trust, not a madman. Maybe there was still a chance.

"Tomas, hold on," he said. He saw Katoa start at the use of his first name, and went for the opening. "Please, let me take you back to the NAF..."

"NAF?" he yelled, waving the pistol again. "Not a chance, Commander. If anything, I'll be joining my friends in the SAR. They've got larger plans than this little backwater hellhole, and I believe I'll fit in a lot better with them."

Gabriel shook his head at the mention of the South American Republic. *Again, it comes back to them?* He had had enough of political dealings, especially with them, since the Poliahu mission. *What hand did they have in all of this? Larger plans?*

"Tomas, please." He let his pulse rifle fall to his side. "I know this has been hard..."

"Stop, Commander." His voice was ice, and Gabriel knew he had struck a nerve. Maybe not the right one, but it was progress. "You have no idea how hard it's been."

"Tell me," Gabriel said. He held out a hand, palm up, and took a step forward. He thought he saw a flicker in his good eye, a sign of understanding, but that quickly it was extinguished, replaced by fire.

"Conversation over, Commander," he said in a cold voice. "It's time for me to leave."

With that, he raised his pistol, and Gabriel knew there was only one option. Before he could reach for the pulse rifle he had left purposely within inches of his lowered hand, three shots rang out. Gabriel instantly knew the weapon was not NAF, and not Sowers.

Two bullets hit Katoa in the upper chest, and the third struck his right eye, snapping his head backward in a spray of blood. The pistol fell from his grip, and his lifeless body fell back, leaving a stunned Jeromy Tarif standing there, trembling.

Gabriel's Mindseye located the source of the shots as he saw a blurry outline pounce on one of the bodies on the floor, Sowers apparently also having tracked the shots. He strode over to the downed man and saw that he had a pistol in his hand. He was curled into a fetal position, blood soaking the soil under his body, and was spitting blood from his lips. Sowers, kneeling on the man's thigh, pulled the pistol from his grip and tossed it aside.

"Gabriel," the man gasped.

He sent a burst to Sowers to step back and he bent down on one knee in front of the man's face.

"No saving Prophet," the man said through ragged breaths. "Sick, twisted..." He coughed, bright red blood dripping onto the ground. "No choice."

"Hang in there," Gabriel said. "We'll get medical attention..."

"Too late for me," the man said. "Screwed up... paid for it." More coughs, more blood. "Trust Zeno, he'll try to do the right thing here."

Gabriel looked over to the restrained man Sowers had left a few feet away.

"Yes, Zeno," the man said. "Tell him I'm sorry..." He gave one last gasp and closed his eyes. Gabriel's neuretics confirmed the life signs winking out.

A final report came in through his neuretics from Brevik, giving the all-clear for the compound. Sowers switched off his camo and walked over to the man he had restrained.

"Zeno?" he asked. The man nodded, and Sowers released the restraints and helped him stand. He brought him over to where Gabriel knelt next to the dead man.

"He's clean, Commander," said Sowers as he stepped back a few feet.

"Ah hell, Jamar," Zeno said. He squatted on his haunches in front of the downed man. "We should be fixing this together."

"You're Zeno?" asked Gabriel.

"Yes, and this is... was... Jamar Chaud, our military commander," he replied in a sad voice. "None of this was his fault, you have to understand that. All of this," he waved his hand in the air, "was Prophet. He brought us together, gave us purpose, but then... twisted it. Somehow, some way, and we all got caught up in it. He found the most ruthless men to turn into his fighters, and put Jamar in charge of them. Jamar wasn't an angel, none of us were. But I don't think he knew what he was getting himself into."

Gabriel looked down at Chaud's body. Something the Prime Minister had alluded to in their meeting popped into the front of his mind. Something about a man inside. "Are you…"

Zeno must have sensed his thoughts. "Yes, Commander, I've been in contact with the Prime Minister. I've been trying to slow things down on this end to help your team out, but I never had an opportunity to bring Jamar in on it. He didn't know. And Prophet killed him for failing. Which…" His voice cracked a bit, and he paused to gather himself. "Which is ultimately my fault." He dropped his head and reached out, touching Chaud's shoulder. "I'm the one who's sorry, my old friend."

Gabriel stood up to let Zeno have a few minutes. He motioned Sowers to join him at the back of the tent.

"This is over now," Gabriel said. He pointed to the tech's station. "I need you to go through their database, see what information you can pull out about whatever the hell Katoa was going on about with the SAR. We're done here, but there's apparently more going on than we thought."

"We're not done yet," said Sowers through gritted teeth. "There's someone I need to find back in Eden City."

Gabriel nodded. "Understood, Mister Sowers. But let's get this wrapped up first."

He turned from Sowers to let him get to work and waved Jeromy over. He knew the students had a hell of a time over the past few weeks, and it would take a long time to forget it all. *Maybe they never would*, he thought, an image of the burning gymnasium flashing across his mind.

"Let's get you back with your friends, kid."

He took one last look at Katoa's body. Sadness, anger, frustration, all ran through his head. If only he had… no, he couldn't look at it that way. Not now. This wasn't the Tomas

Katoa he had shipped out with, commanded, all those years ago. But there was a nagging guilt in the back of his mind, that who he had become, the terrorist leader, the brutal monster, had been his fault.

"Uh, sir?"

He looked up to see Jeromy's plaintive face staring at him.

"Sorry, just… thinking," he said. He turned from Katoa's body, patted the student on the upper arm, and walked out into the shadowed courtyard.

Steve Umstead

CHAPTER THIRTY-FOUR

They had rounded up almost a dozen live terrorists, and while it would be a while before they had an exact figure on dead and missing, due in no small part to Brevik's pounding of the barracks, Gabriel was satisfied the terrorist camp would be causing no further problems for Eden City. The surviving terrorists were grouped together near what appeared to be a mess tent, with Brevik and Willem standing guard. Olszewski was walking among them, snapping on wrist restraints, his Dobranoc slung over one shoulder.

Gabriel walked with Jeromy over to the housing unit that had held the hostages. The youth walked with a stunned look on his face as they passed through the carnage left over from the firefight.

Jeromy stepped over a smoldering piece of steelroot that had been blown off the barracks. Gabriel noticed out of the corner of his eye that tears had started to form on his face.

"It's over, kid," he said, trying to reassure him.

"Do you ever get used to it? I mean, is it over for you?" he asked.

Gabriel remained silent for several moments as they continued towards the housing unit. Most of his adult life had been spent in this type of environment. Battles, destruction, death. Or at the very least, training for it. As the stench of burning flesh assaulted his nostrils, he remembered that smells were the worst. Those never went away.

"No, you never get used to it. You can only file it away somewhere, try not to look at it again," he replied. "I wish I had better advice, but I'm still working on some of that myself."

Jeromy simply nodded and continued on. He wiped his face with a dirty sleeve. "Is everyone okay?"

"As far as our information can tell, all the students are fine," he said. "Looks like a few of the military hostages didn't..." He paused. "One was killed, and another couple are unaccounted for. Eden City will send a team... listen, don't worry about that. You're fine, as are your friends, and we're getting you out of here."

After a moment, Jeromy asked, "How is my mother?"

Gabriel gave a small laugh. "Stronger than you or I, son. I'll get word to her as soon as we get back to the city."

They had just reached the housing unit when the door burst open and a young female student ran out, jumping into Jeromy's arms.

"Oh God, Jeromy, I'm so glad you're okay!" she squealed, kissing him all over his face. His eyes got wide and his skin flushed, and Gabriel turned away with a smile.

"Everyone okay, boss?" asked Takahashi. He had just come out of the housing unit, followed by Negassi.

"Yeah, so far so good. We're all intact, that's always nice," he said. He saw Negassi had just put a bloody towel in her waist pouch. "More sword play, Specialist?"

She grinned. "Just keeping in practice, sir. I think I've got it up to about thirteen feet now."

"What's the plan, sir?" Takahashi asked.

Gabriel looked over the smoky courtyard. *Plan?* he thought. *Get back home and find out what's really behind all of this.* But he simply said, "Clean up and get out of here."

He turned back to Takahashi. "Sowers is going through their systems to pull out any data we or Eden City might find useful. I'm going to call for an evac. Take Olszewski and head down to the beach, disable the triple-A and clear landing spot for the hopper. Negassi, stay here with the hostages, er, personnel," he said.

He looked back towards the command tent and watched as Zeno talked to a handful of women who had come out of their homes after the firing ceased. Several of them were holding small children, and he felt a pang of sadness as he thought back to the young boy in the Mars skyhook station. The boy who said bad soldiers killed his father. Here, some of these children had bad soldiers for fathers. How would the mothers explain that? How would these kids grow up? *Too much death*, he thought.

A signal came from Takahashi, who had apparently run down to the beach, giving an all-clear for a landing area. Gabriel pulled his gaze away from the sad scene and sent a message on the private frequency the Prime Minister had given him.

Within an hour, and without threat of anti-aircraft weapons for the first time in years, an Eden Guard transport hopper settled on the beach. Twin turbofans kicked up a hailstorm of sand and pebbles. Gabriel shielded his eyes, regretting having left his helmet off.

Once the engines slowed and the dust storm ceased, he waved Brevik and Willem up with the prisoners. They had eleven alive and relatively intact (just one with a grave injury), all of whom would be facing serious charges back in Eden City. Zeno, he had left behind. After a long talk with him, Gabriel took the chance that Chaud had suggested. The compound was no longer a terrorist base, but it still held dozens of people. People with lives, people who needed a leader. He hoped the chance wouldn't come back to bite.

Gabriel stopped Willem as Brevik escorted the prisoners across the sand. "Hang on, kid."

Willem stopped short, looked up at Gabriel, and nodded. He handed the rifle to him.

Gabriel accepted the weapon, but shook his head. "Thanks, but that's not why I stopped you. Listen, I just want to apologize for doubting you, giving you a hard time. Everything pointed to…"

"I understand, Commander," Willem cut him off. Gabriel's eyes widened a fraction at the interruption. *Confident indeed,* he thought.

"I'm sorry about your man," Willem continued. "Sorry I couldn't have helped more."

Gabriel put his hand on the young man's shoulder. "You helped tremendously, and my team… I… appreciate it." He looked past Willem to the hopper. "What's next for you?"

Willem smiled slightly. "Back to the jungle, I suppose. My friends and I have a few hides that need repair, and looks like we won't have to sneak around so much now."

Gabriel gave his shoulder a squeeze. "Good luck, Ghost. And thanks again."

Willem turned and walked off with a casual wave, not seeing Gabriel's smile.

Olszewski brought up the rear of the prisoner group and helped secure them in the cargo hold of the hopper, then the students and military personnel came forward. The rush of bodies flowed past him, and he felt a mixture of emotions. Raw, unadulterated joy from the students, and simple relief from the military.

The last soldier, an older man in his sixties with a heavy white beard, dressed in the tattered remnants of an Eden Guard uniform, stopped as he passed Gabriel. He turned towards him, and slowly raised his hand to his forehead in a perfect, crisp military salute. Gabriel returned the salute just as slowly.

"Commander," the man said. "My eternal gratitude. You've saved many lives here."

Gabriel nodded as the turbofans spun up behind him. "Just doing my job, Sergeant Major."

The man smiled at Gabriel's recognition of his rank, which barely showed on the sleeve of his stained shirt. "Listen," he said, his low voice just barely audible above the turbofans. "Rasshid, former commander of mine. Watch him. Don't trust him." He walked past Gabriel and turned, shouting over his shoulder. "Don't trust him!"

Gabriel pondered his remark as the rest of his team clambered aboard and the hopper's engines reached takeoff speed. *Maybe...* he filed that way as he ran across the beach and jumped into the open door, leaving the camp behind.

The Prime Minster's office felt slightly less cramped than Gabriel's first visit, and he wasn't yet sure why. Casting a glance at Takahashi next to him, he realized Brevik had joined him the first time. Much less body mass.

Prime Minister Howarth had rolled his powered wheelchair into the library area of his office, and Deputy Prime Minister Rasshid was seated on the small sofa next to him. Howarth had offered the two of them tea, but Gabriel had politely declined. It had been a long, restless night's sleep after the harrowing events of the previous day.

The hopper had landed near midnight at the spaceport, and Gabriel had been shocked at the number of people that had shown up to greet it. And shocked at the poor security that had allowed the information to leak. As the former hostages were led from the hopper, dozens of crying faces had rushed to meet them, causing quite a scene on the small landing platform. On the flight back, he had spoken with Jeromy, who had expressed his strong desire to stay on Eden and continue his education. As Gabriel had started to protest, he had cut him off with a stare, one very reminiscent of the governor's, and told him to just tell his mother he was fine.

Gabriel and his team had quietly escorted the prisoners to the waiting groundtruck, accepted the government's offer of a ride and a hotel stay, and after a hot meal, the entire group had crashed. All but Gabriel, who still hadn't wound down from the combat high.

"I cannot thank you enough, Commander," said Howarth as he sipped from his tea. "And I'm sorry again for your losses."

Gabriel simply nodded.

"Our military, and civilians, owe you a great deal of thanks," he continued. "This changes everything on our planet. I know we've had some… unpopular decisions and policies, and perhaps we should take a closer look at them." He shook his head, the paralysis making it more of a twitch. "I don't know how much time I have left here, but in the time I have, the time you've given me, I'll do my best."

Gabriel noticed Rasshid, who had been silent during their visit so far, was grinding his teeth. His neuretics even picked up the low frequency from it. The sergeant major's warning came back to him. [*Sowers,*] he sent. [*Location.*]

Within a few seconds, Sowers replied, [*Military Ops with Pallante, sir, just dropping off the intel.*]

[*I've got something different for you.*]

Gabriel sent him a packet of data while listening to the Prime Minister continue to thank them.

Sowers stood up straight as the data came in. Lieutenant Colonel Pallante stopped entering the data on his flexscreen.

"Is there a problem, Mister Sowers?" he asked.

Sowers held up a hand. "Hang on."

As Gabriel's plan finished transferring, he whistled. "Do you have a main network terminal?"

"Well, yes, in the control room. Do you need full or limited access?"

"Full, thanks, just to run a few checks on our flight status."

"Right this way," Pallante said, and led him into the next room.

Gabriel did finally take Howarth's offer of tea, just to be polite, as it seemed the man was planning to prattle on and on until their flight was scheduled to depart.

"And the students," he was saying. "Oh my, are they excited to be back. I don't know if they'll be able to run classes for weeks, it was such a difficult experience for them."

Takahashi nodded, biting at what Gabriel thought must have been his fourth cookie. "They certainly were talkative on the flight back. If you don't mind me asking, sir, how long…"

He was cut off as the door to Howarth's office banged open and Sowers flew in, his face contorted with rage.

"YOU!" he screamed as he strode towards Howarth and Rasshid.

Rasshid quickly reached behind Howarth's powered wheelchair and pulled out a mag pistol. Gabriel reached for his Heckart, only to grab at an empty waist. Neither he nor Takahashi had been permitted to bring weapons in to see the Prime Minister. He began to stand to stop Sowers, but Rasshid stopped him with a shout.

"Sit down!" he yelled, waving the mag pistol. He stood up and walked behind Howarth's wheelchair, placing the barrel of the pistol against the back of the Prime Minister's head.

Sowers skidded to a halt at the half wall separating the two halves of the office. "It was him, Commander. Just as you thought."

Howarth was sputtering. "What the hell is going on here, Zahir? Where did that gun come from?"

Rasshid pushed the barrel into the back of his head harder. Howarth took the hint and closed his mouth.

"I found the communications between Prophet and Rasshid," Sowers continued. "And the order to plant the goddamn bomb that killed Arturo."

Gabriel saw the fire in Sowers's eyes, and the spittle that was flying from his lips in anger. He regretted sending Sowers to do the investigating for this exact reason. If the search turned up that Rasshid was the mole, Sowers wouldn't be stopped. However, Sowers was probably the only one systems-savvy enough on his team that could have uncovered it.

"Is this true?" roared Howarth, trying in vain to turn his head to see the Deputy Prime Minister.

"I've been waiting for months for you to just *die*, Wallace. I had a deal with Prophet, a very lucrative one, but you just wouldn't die."

"How could you?" Howarth said, his voice cracking.

"I've known Prophet from way back when, since I was a Guard. Back when we were both nobodies, when he was just Katoa. So when he contacted me last year, we made a pact. He runs his side, I'd run mine. But then he decided to snatch a political prisoner, and you had to accept these... these mercenaries."

He lifted the gun from the back of Howarth's head and pointed it at Gabriel and Takahashi, who were still seated. "And now it's all gone to hell. And so will you."

He raised the pistol and Gabriel heard the soft whine of the charge as it armed, but also a smaller, fainter whine. He glanced over at Sowers, who had one hand in his pocket and a look of death on his face.

Rasshid looked down at the pistol with wide eyes. "What the..." he began, taking a few steps back, still staring at the gun.

Gabriel heard the unmistakable sound of a battery on overload, and he lunged out of his seat. He grabbed the wheelchair and tipped Howarth out of it, putting the wheelchair between him and Rasshid.

Takahashi dove to the floor, and Sowers crouched behind the half wall. Rasshid still gripped the pistol, almost as if he clung to it for survival. He stumbled backwards into a shelf full of books, and the pistol went critical. It made a popping sound and ignited, causing Rasshid's entire arm to be engulfed in flames. Books crashed over his head as he tried to push away from the pistol, which was still stuck in his hand. The intense heat from the overloaded battery ignited books in muffled *whoomps,* and more and more fell onto him. Within seconds, he was buried in a funeral pyre, his screams fading into nothingness.

The sprinkler system kicked in, spraying liquid fire retardant across the room. The fire slowly went out, and Sowers walked up to it, liquid dripping from his face.

"That's for Arturo, you bastard." He kicked at the smoldering pile, and Rasshid's lifeless cinder of an arm bent backwards. The melted pistol finally fell from its grip.

Pallante burst in through the open door to the office. "What happened here?"

Gabriel ignored him and helped Howarth back into his wheelchair, which had avoided any fire damage. The air was thick with smoke and chemicals, and Howarth was having a tough time breathing.

"Commander," he coughed. "I... I don't know what to say. I knew Zahir for years..."

"Only thing I can say, Prime Minister, is you never know who your true friends are until it's too late," Gabriel said. "Choose wisely."

A fire crew ran into the office carrying portable extinguishing systems. Gabriel put his hand on Sowers's shoulder and led him to the far side of the room.

"Are you okay, Galen?"

Sowers nodded slowly, taking one last look at the pile of charred papers and flesh. "I'm better now, sir."

"Sir," Takahashi cut in. "Can we get the hell off this planet?"

CHAPTER THIRTY-FIVE

They arrived at the spaceport just before dusk, Gabriel having turned down the Prime Minister's offer of another night's stay to recover. He had also told Howarth he didn't want him traveling with them to the spaceport to see them off, as he had certainly had a rough enough afternoon with the assassination attempt. And the loss of what he thought was a friend. He didn't envy Howarth's job going forward. Changing policies, opening up relations with the so-called rebels, trying to unite a city, all with the specter of impending mortality hovering over him. *Sometimes my simple life has its benefits*, he thought.

Pallante had gone with them in the transport and helped them load their cargo onto the shuttle on the platform. "Sorry to see your team go, Commander. We could use a few more men like you."

Negassi cleared her throat next to him as she tossed another duffel bag into the hold.

"Ah, sorry," said Pallante. "Women too."

Gabriel looked around the platform, seeing the beauty of the jungle in the fading light. The sun was just setting over the western horizon, and the oranges and reds it cast over the green of the foliage was spectacular. But that jungle held more danger than any one planet should have. And he had no regrets about leaving. He sniffed the air. *Rain's on its way,* he thought. *Don't need any more of that.*

"No thank you, Lieutenant Colonel," he said as he hefted his own duffel. "The sooner I get home, the better." He smiled. "I've got someone waiting for me, and she's not the patient type."

"Understood. Sorry again about the communication issue."

"What communication issue?"

Pallante cocked his head. "Didn't the driver tell you? Sorry about that. We lost contact with the T-Gate station earlier today, we were not able to forward your mission message back to Mars. Happens sometimes. We don't tend to get routine maintenance trips way out here. Shouldn't be an issue, you'll be at the gate in a matter of hours and can send from the other side."

Alarm bells went off in Gabriel's mind. Everything that had happened to them over the past several days seemed to be for a reason. Nothing just 'happened,' he had seen. And he didn't assume the communication problem was routine, as Pallante did. The bigger problem was the *Lady Cydonia* wasn't built for offensive, or even defensive, operations. Looking around the barren spaceport, he didn't see as he had any option.

"Thanks again for the ride," he said, and Pallante saluted. Gabriel returned the salute, then climbed the stairs to the shuttle. As he reached the top, he looked back at the two body bags being loaded into the cargo hold and clenched his jaw. Jimenez and Sennett, two more good men lost on Eden. *It's time to tell Renay the whole story of the first mission,* he thought. *Too much death for one man to hold inside any more.*

<<<<<>>>>>

The acceleration phase of the journey had gone smoothly, as did the coasting, but it also went very quietly,

Gabriel noticed. The good-natured ribbing and conversations were noticeably absent, as were Sowers's jokes. Sowers had... changed. And understandably. He had seen two friends die within hours of each other. *Changes anyone*, he thought. And more than once, Gabriel had caught himself wondering where Jimenez's guitar pluckings were.

As the *Lady Cydonia* flipped for deceleration, the captain contacted Gabriel.

"Commander, we still cannot raise the T-Gate station," he said. "We've only got commercial sensors, so we're still too far out to see anything out of the ordinary. We can see the station, doesn't appear to be anything amiss, so it's probably just a comm breakdown."

Gabriel thanked him and cut the connection. *We'll see*, he thought. He felt the rumble of the engines kick in, and he settled down in his couch to ride out the 1.2G journey.

"Commander Gabriel to the bridge."

The call made Gabriel look up from the book he had been reading. The decel phase had just ended and the *Lady Cydonia* had flipped end over end to approach the T-Gate. He unclasped his lap belt and set the book down, then stood up.

"Anything wrong, Commander?" asked Negassi behind him. She had joined him in the lounge, the others choosing to spend the flight in their own quarters.

"I'm not sure yet," he answered. "Probably nothing."

He left the lounge and the artificial gravity of the rotating ring, then sent a quick burst to Brevik to have him join him on the bridge.

When he floated into the small command bridge, he saw there were only two flight officers manning two small workstations, and the captain strapped in a chair overlooking the bridge. A large wallscreen dominated the front wall with several other, smaller screens down each side. *Not bad for a commercial vessel*, he thought, not having visited the bridge on the outbound journey.

"Hello, Commander," said the captain, extending his hand. Gabriel shook it, then said, "This is Lieutenant Brevik, my second-in-command."

The captain took Brevik's outstretched hand. "Pleasure, Lieutenant. I'm Captain Meltzer."

Gabriel looked at the main screen, seeing an image of the T-Gate station. "What's the issue, Captain?"

"Sorry, Commander. It appears the T-Gate has had a meteoroid strike on its main antenna array."

The image zoomed in to the top part of the station, where a blackened husk of metal spikes was.

"That's as close as we can see it, but looks like they'll be down for a while, at least until a maintenance crew can get here."

Gabriel frowned at the image. It looked like the spikes were torn off, but... something about them. Too perfect maybe? No...

"Captain, I'm not familiar with the stations. Do those antennas have major power going to them?" Brevik asked.

Meltzer cocked his head. "No, not really. Just microbursts of radio waves, I believe. Why?"

Brevik pointed to the image. "They look burned off. A meteoroid strike would have just broken them off, not caused any type of burn, correct?"

Gabriel looked closely. Definitely signs of burns, perhaps an explosion, but that...

His thoughts were cut off by a shout from one of the bridge officers.

"Captain, I've got a ship! No, two ships! Small ones, coming out from behind the station!"

Gabriel's alarm bells were now ringing like the Cathedral at Notre Dame.

"Put it on the screen," said Meltzer.

The image blurred a bit, then focused. Two dots had appeared, one from either side of the station, and were growing larger.

"Can you enhance?" asked Meltzer. The officer tapped at his workstation, and the image zoomed in on one of the dots.

"Fighters," said Brevik. "Gunboats probably."

Dammit, thought Gabriel. *We're sitting, unarmed ducks.* He turned to Meltzer.

"Can you make the gate?" he asked.

Meltzer shook his head. "No chance, we've already powered down. We'd need close to five minutes to spool the engines back up."

"Captain!" the other officer yelled. "I'm picking up two weapons locks, sir. They're going to fire!"

Mubina Tarif sat on a park bench at the edge of Canali Park. She watched people walk by, giving her the occasional wave. People who were oblivious to the governmental change that had just happened. People who, in her opinion, probably didn't even care.

She watched as a young girl splashed in the fountain nearby, throwing water into the air and squealing as the droplets fell in slow motion. It was all so... *normal.* She glanced down at the folder in her hand. *Yet it was so far from it.*

"May I sit, Mubina?"

She looked up to see Major Andon, in civilian clothes, holding a small bag of popcorn. *Normal,* she thought again.

"Of course," she said. She slid over a bit to give Andon room and he sat next to her.

After a few moments, he said, "Your message reached the proper parties."

She turned to him with a look of surprise. "But you said the fighters had blocked all communications, in and out?"

He gave a small smile. "Not all. I still have a few… friends in the right places."

She grabbed his forearm, jostling the popcorn in the bag. "Have you heard from Gabriel? Or Jeromy?"

He shook his head. "No, it's an outbound channel only. But your warning was passed. If it's not too late, then they'll be fine."

She looked down at the folder again. Her letter of resignation from Mars government, her will, and her memoirs. "How long?" she asked.

He stared out over the park. "I don't know. We just have to be patient. And hope."

She took the folder off her lap and set it next to her. *Patient.* In light of the shocking information she had received from her police force commander a couple of hours ago, she wasn't sure if Gabriel would be feeling very patient when he received her message. *If he does.* She took a deep breath and let it out slowly. "Yes, hope."

"Captain, did you hear me? They've got weapons lock!" yelled the officer.

Gabriel turned to Meltzer, who had apparently frozen. He knew a civilian cargo ship captain wasn't prepared for combat operations, but even so, the most green of newbies had some type of fight or flight reaction. But not Meltzer.

"Captain, flip the ship and burn the engines," he said. "It'll shield you from fire, at least initially."

Meltzer sat open-mouthed until Gabriel grabbed his arm. He snapped his mouth closed and blinked. "What?"

"Flip the damned ship, Captain," Gabriel repeated, pointing at the image.

"Ah, no, we, uh, can't… it's too late, we'd, uh, have to…" he stammered, punching at keys on his armrest.

Gabriel was about to shout an order to the navigator when the other officer on the deck called out. "Captain, we've got emergence at the gate!"

Gabriel and Brevik turned to the wallscreen and saw the typical blue-flecked blurring of space behind the station that signaled a gate transit. A black mass was silhouetted in front of the glow, then disappeared.

"Sir, was that…" Brevik began.

"I'm not sure, but it may have been," Gabriel replied.

"Contact, I'm showing multiple missiles inbound. No, correction, they're from the ship that just transited… ah hell, I don't know Captain." The officer gave up trying to verbally describe the scene and threw the computer's representation up on the wallscreen.

The two incoming fighters were about halfway between the station and the *Lady Cydonia*, but behind them were six hypersonic missiles, three targeted on each. Within seconds, the weapons locks the fighters had on the cargo ship had broken off, and the fighters wheeled over, trying to escape the missiles while turning back towards the unknown threat.

It was over in a heartbeat. Even fast gunboats were no match for missiles of that speed, and they had been fired from such a close range, the closing time was measured in seconds. Both fighters erupted into static in the image. The officer switched to visual, showing the remains of two small explosions thousands of miles in front of them.

"What the hell just happened?" asked Meltzer.

No one spoke for a few moments, then the officer who was manning the communication systems said, "Sir, we have an incoming audio transmission."

Meltzer's eyes widened and he looked at Gabriel and Brevik, as if for advice. Gabriel just looked back, letting the captain command his ship. He already suspected who'd be on the other end of that transmission.

"Ah, go ahead, Jackson. Put it on the overhead."

After a few seconds, static crackled in the worn bridge speakers, then a voice came through.

"*Lady Cydonia*, this is Captain McTiernan of the NAFS *Richard Marcinko*, here to render assistance."

EPILOGUE

The team had transferred to the *Marcinko* after having said their goodbyes to the *Lady Cydonia* crew. Gabriel had spent a few extra minutes with Meltzer, both to help him understand what had just happened and to reassure him that none of his actions, or inactions, would be reported.

The team's gear had also made its way across, and the two ships slowly separated. Meltzer had said the crew was tired of drifting during their forced R&R while the team was on Eden, and his bridge staff was still shaking from the fighter encounter, so they were headed for the Calypso system where they would be freelancing for a bit.

After the transit, Gabriel and his team sat in stunned silence in the acceleration lounge as Captain McTiernan and his first officer Lieutenant Commander Vaillancourt explained the situation on Mars. More than one mouth was hanging wide open as they finished.

"Wait," said Olszewski, who Gabriel knew was from Eos Chasma. "Are you saying the two domes have seceded from Mars Central?"

"No, what I'm saying is they are now run by the SAR," McTiernan answered. "And legally, apparently."

"If it's legal, what are the fighters doing blockading the planet?" asked Takahashi.

"We don't know, exactly," replied Vaillancourt. She looked at McTiernan, who nodded. "From the information we received, it appears they may be Chinese in origin."

Gabriel shook his head. "Doesn't fit," he said. "China wouldn't stick its nose into Mars's affairs."

"We only received a secure data packet from Governor Tarif," said McTiernan. "Our analysts went through it with a fine-toothed comb, and that's what they came up with."

"So where did you come from?" asked Takahashi. Gabriel saw the signs of dozens more questions bubbling at the surface, but allowed the team just the one more.

"We were on patrol around the Canaan system, testing new weapons packages, when we got the packet," replied Vaillancourt. "We hightailed it here as soon as we could."

"And we thank you for that, Captain," said Gabriel. "Now if you can, please get us back to Mars as quickly as possible."

"But the…" McTiernan began.

"Tarif wouldn't have sent that data unless she needed us. We have to go back," said Gabriel.

McTiernan nodded. "Understood." He stood and waved a hand around the lounge. "You have our full hospitality and support."

The team rose to leave when McTiernan laid a hand on Gabriel's shoulder, stopping him from walking out of the hatch. "There's one more thing, Commander. Governor Tarif sent a private packet for you. It's encoded, the header says you'll have the codes."

Gabriel looked back at McTiernan. *Always something else*, he thought. "Where is it?"

"I will have it sent to your stateroom."

Gabriel nodded. "Thank you again, Captain. We keep running into each other, don't we?" he said as he walked out of the room.

McTiernan chuckled as he followed. "If only it could be under more enjoyable circumstances."

In his stateroom, Gabriel closed the door behind him and activated the small wallscreen. He silently thanked McTiernan for obtaining a single room for him.

The wallscreen came to life, and strings of data appeared. He had his neuretics seek out the proper string, decode it, and play the message.

It was Governor Tarif, apparently speaking into a video pickup in a tiny office. Her face was drawn, and he felt a pang of concern for her. *She's gone through a lot*, he thought. *Fortunately we come bringing some good news for her.*

"Commander, I hope you receive this message. And I hope…" She paused, looking off-camera to compose herself. "I hope Jeromy is safe."

She took a deep breath and continued. "There has been a lot that has gone on while you were away. If you are in receipt of this message, then the *Marcinko* has found you and you've been briefed. However, what was not in that briefing is something of a personal nature."

She paused again, looking down, then looked back up with pain in her eyes. "Evan, they've taken Renay. The Republic bastards took her, probably as insurance in case you survived Eden. There was apparently a struggle in your apartment, and there was…" She took another deep breath. "Blood, hers. I… I honestly don't know if she's alive. Oh Evan, I'm so sorry to have gotten you involved in this."

Gabriel felt a punch in the gut, a twisting of his fragile emotions. Pain, then sorrow, then anger. He squeezed his eyes shut as Tarif continued.

"We don't know where she is, but she hasn't left Mars. The SAR, they are behind all of this. The Eden hostages, the blockade, and now Renay. Evan, please hurry back. I'm… I'm so sorry."

The transmission ended in a hiss of static. Gabriel waited, his heart pounding in his ears. *Renay.*

He stood up, fists clenching and unclenching. Everyone close to him got hurt. Friends, family, soldiers. His parents.

He turned and picked up the bunk in a rage and slammed it against the wall. The metal frame clanged off the carbotanium wall. He picked it up and threw it again, again, again. The pain, the anger, radiated from him like heat.

Images flashed across his mind. Images of enemies: Santander, MacFarland, Katoa. Images of friends: St. Laurent. Arturo. *Renay.* He slammed the bunk one last time, then collapsed on it, gasping for air.

He would find them. He would find all of them. And they would pay.

<<<<< END >>>>>

PREVIEW OF BOOK 3:
GABRIEL'S REVENGE

A missile has no conscience. It is an inanimate steel object: cold, emotionless. But once ignited, it burns white hot inside, and cannot be shut off. Fired in combat, it has but one objective: the total destruction of its intended target. And it will only stop when its objective has been achieved, or it runs out of fuel.

Not all missiles are made of steel.

The warship glided through the inky blackness of the Canaan system. To an outside observer, the ship appeared lifeless, dead: no navigation lights, no active sensors, no starlight reflecting from its surface. The NAFS *Richard Marcinko*, CAS-408, drifted between the white dwarf secondary Jacob and the gas giant Rebekah, the outermost planet orbiting the primary star Esau. Background radiation from Jacob was the only noise that an outside observer would have been able to detect. The *Marcinko* ran silent... as did its personnel.

The bridge crew went through their routine navigation tasks as the ship prepared for flipover. The engines would be fired in under twenty minutes for deceleration into the Arkangel Gate, the wormhole that led back to the Nu Ophiuchi system, one transition from Earth... and Mars. The crew had maintained near-complete silence for the entire five hour max-accel flight from the Hodgson wormhole, due in no small part to the man who occupied a normally-vacant medical officer station. A man who had only left the bridge twice since the battle at the Eden T-Gate station twenty-two hours prior. A man whose clenched jaw invited no questions, nor allowed for any debate as to whether or not he belonged on the bridge during operations.

North American Federation Navy Commander Evan Gabriel sat stone-faced in the acceleration couch, hands clasped on the workstation's surface in front of him. A unsecured half-empty coffee bulb floated in the zero-G nearby. A day's worth of stubble covered his usually-clean shaven face, and his tired eyes were rimmed in red. He hadn't said a word since arriving on the bridge, after a long conversation with the *Marcinko's* captain. A captain who appeared almost as exhausted as Gabriel.

"Commander," said the captain quietly. He was seated at the rearmost section of the small bridge, in a command chair that overlooked the rest of the crew stations.

Gabriel didn't move a muscle, just continued to stare straight ahead at the wallscreen display showing the surrounding starfield and the edge of Jacob.

"Commander."

Gabriel cracked his knuckles. He reached up and plucked the coffee bulb from the air and set it down on the workstation, securing it in the cupholder. "No, Captain McTiernan, I'm staying."

McTiernan frowned and glanced over at the *Marcinko's* communications officer, Ensign Davis Giroux. Giroux simply shrugged and returned the frown, mixed with a look of concern.

McTiernan unbuckled his lap belt and pushed up from the command chair. He floated over to where Gabriel sat and pulled himself down using the armrest of the couch.

"Listen, Commander, I understand..."

"No, you don't," Gabriel interrupted. "With all due respect, sir, this is your ship, and as such you are my commanding officer. But I am not leaving this bridge until we get to Mars." He scratched at his facial hair. "I need to be here."

McTiernan shook his head slightly. "You'll be no good to anyone when we get there, Commander. Not with two straight days of max flight with no sleep." He reached over and took the coffee bulb out of the cupholder. "And you've switched to regular coffee. From what Mister Sowers tells me, that's very out of character. You can't keep this up. And your team..." He paused. "Your team is worried about you."

Gabriel's jaw clenched, his temple pulsing. "My team will be fine, Captain. I appreciate your concern. I'll be fine."

"I have my doubts," McTiernan replied.

"Noted."

McTiernan blew noisily through his lips. "Commander, I don't want to make this an order..."

"Then don't. Sir."

"But you need to get some rest. We have another system to travel before the Ryokou gate. Fourteen hours. Take that time, and..."

"No. I need to see this through, start to finish."

McTiernan stood upright, still holding onto the armrest of the acceleration couch to steady himself in the zero-G. "Commander, as I explained to you in our meeting, my ship and its crew are at your disposal for this mission. We are with you every step of the way, and will support you in any way we can. But you need to do what's best for your team, and yourself, right now."

"Captain, as I told you, I'm fine."

The bridge crew, five other naval personnel, had been casting surreptitious glances in the direction of the conversation, but at Gabriel's sharp tone they turned almost as one.

McTiernan shook his head. "Then you leave me no choice, Commander." He turned to the man seated at the communications station and snapped his fingers. "Ensign Giroux, escort the Commander to his quarters, immediately. He is to remain there until we arrive at the initial Ryokou approach marker. If he leaves his quarters, you have my permission to shoot him."

Giroux's eyes widened, and he looked from McTiernan's stern face to Gabriel's reddening one. "Sir?"

"You heard me, Ensign."

"Captain," Gabriel said as he unbuckled his lap belt. "Don't do this. I need to be here, I need…"

"Bullshit, Commander. Are you saying you'll step in if my navigator suddenly passes out at her station? Or will repair our radar if it fails? I don't need you here, and you don't need to be here. You need to sleep. And now it's an order. Don't push me any further."

The two men's eyes met, locked for several seconds, until finally Gabriel pushed up from his seat. McTiernan edged back a bit as the larger man stood fully upright, but Gabriel merely looked him in the eyes.

"I get it. I'm going, Captain. But if anything…"

"Nothing will," McTiernan replied. "Stay in your quarters, get some rack time before things heat up. You heard the reports. Nu Ophiuchi is clear. But Mars isn't. That's when we'll need you. When your team will need you. At full strength."

Gabriel cast his gaze around the bridge, and the crew again as one turned back to their stations. With one last look at McTiernan, he turned to Giroux.

"Let's go, Ensign. Escort me."

Giroux led Gabriel through the corridor from the bridge. The two men pushed off the walls and handholds expertly in the weightless environment.

"Sorry about this, Commander," said Giroux when they reached the hatch to the rotating torus that provided the staterooms with artificial gravity. He pushed open the steel hatch and held out his arm.

Gabriel pushed off the ceiling and placed his boots on the decking, grabbing the edge of the hatch in the process. "Not your fault, son."

Giroux allowed him to pass through the hatch. "Ah, sir, do I need to walk you to…"

Gabriel held up a hand as he stepped into the vertical shaft. "No, Ensign, I know where I'm going. And I respect the captain's order."

"Okay, sir, sure," said Giroux. He hovered nervously at the entrance to the transfer shaft. "Sir, I just want to say, what happened to you guys on Eden, and whatever you're heading off to now… well, we're with you. As much as we can be, I guess."

Gabriel paused before descending and looked back at Giroux. With one foot down a rung on the ladder, and Giroux hovering a few inches above the decking, his eyes were level with the smaller man's.

"I appreciate that, Davis," Gabriel said, earning a surprised look at the use of the man's first name. "You and the rest of the crew have been a great help to us, to me, on more than one occasion. This time…" His voice trailed off and his eyes went to the far wall. "I don't know. This isn't a typical mission."

"It never is, sir," Giroux replied. "Not for this ship."

With that he waved and turned to head back to the bridge, leaving Gabriel alone with his thoughts as he made his way down the shaft.

The stateroom door closed with a muffled thunk, and Gabriel engaged the lock. His neuretics sent a command to the room's systems, lowering the light to half level. Without the glare from the wall-mounted lightstrip, the gouges in the bulkhead steel were more apparent. Gouges caused by him repeatedly slamming his bunk against it the previous day after hearing the news of Renay's disappearance. *Renay. Dammit.*

The bunk itself had been replaced sometime while he was on the bridge. He didn't doubt the rest of his team had heard his rage and anger being taken out on the unfortunate object. The wall he had bashed it into, turning it into a twisted mass of steel beams and springs, was the separating wall between his stateroom and the first of his team's.

He saw that the new bunk was not only spot welded to the bulkhead, but also bolted to the deck. He walked over to it, gave a tug on the edge of its frame, and heard a creak from one of the bolts. His enhanced combat muscles gave a little extra pull, and the bolt popped free. He shook his head and flopped down on the bed, face up. *If only everything was that easy to accomplish.*

He stared at the slate gray ceiling and images flooded his mind, almost as clear as a Mindseye visual data stream. Poliahu, six months ago. The ice planet where he lost three team members, two having been revealed as traitors, and one killed by one of those traitors. Then Mars, six months of long work cleaning up the mess Santander had left in Arsia Mons, six months of learning his new team, six months of getting closer to Renay.

Lieutenant Renay Gesselli. The woman partially responsible for sending him to Poliahu, and who he had left behind for this damned Eden mission. It had only been two days since they returned to Eden City after the takedown of the terrorist organization. And less than three days since Jimenez had died in the explosion. *My God,* he thought. *How much more of this was there?* He squeezed his eyes shut, trying to push aside the memories of those close to him who had died. All he saw was Renay.

Renay. The woman he loved. The woman now missing, taken by those South American Republic bastards. He felt the anger building inside him again, and ordered a small dose of comtranq sent to his spinal column. His internal systems complied and he took a deep breath, trying to relax his racing heartbeat.

The SAR had taken over two of Mars's most populated domes, one of which he had called home for the past six months, Arsia Mons. Where ex-Governor Mubina Tarif had sent the message from, the message that said Renay was missing, presumed taken by the SAR. And where the *Marcinko* was headed now.

Back to Mars. Back to find Renay. Back to finish this, once and for all.

GABRIEL'S REVENGE, THE FINALE, AVAILABLE IN E-BOOK AND PRINT FORMATS!

ABOUT THE AUTHOR

Steve Umstead has been the owner of a Caribbean & Mexico travel company for the past ten years, but never forgot his lifelong dream of becoming an author. After a successful stab at National Novel Writing Month, he decided to pursue his dream more vigorously...but hasn't given up the traveling.

Steve lives in New Jersey with his wife, two kids, and several bookshelves full of other authors' science fiction novels. Gabriel's Redemption was released in February 2011, Gabriel's Return in August 2011, and Gabriel's Revenge, the finale, in December 2011.

You can find Steve either at a swim-up bar in Mexico, or online at www.SteveUmstead.com.

Follow & chat:
Twitter: @SteveUmstead
Facebook: facebook.com/steveumsteadwrites